HOSTAGE

A nerve in his stubbled jaw was twitching as he stared out the window. His breathing was tight and raspy and as she stared at him, she saw the tip of his tongue moistening his sensual lips. He rubbed a hand across his young face and swallowed heavily. "I think they're down there in the street. I can't see them but I think they're down there."

"Who?" she asked, nervous and afraid.

He turned and looked at her, his eyes haggard and haunted. "The police. They're after me. I killed a cop."

Peg trembled and backed away from him.

He jumped forward, clamping a heavy hand over her mouth, stifling the scream that came to her throat. "I didn't want this to happen, but it has," he whispered. "I didn't mean to mix you up in this thing but that's the way it worked out. I need a place to hide, a place to stay. I've got to stay here with you and your family, you understand? You hear what I'm saying?"

Peg nodded numbly, terror flooding her.

"I'm going to take my hand away from your mouth," he continued. "When I do, don't yell or scream or nothing. Be very quiet. If you want to live, be very quiet. I've got a gun in my pocket and I'm already nervous as hell. If you scream, I'll start shooting up the joint. Think about your old man and your mother and your kid brother."

Peg nodded again and the hand fell away. "Don't hurt us, please."

He looked tormented. "I don't want to hurt nobody."

HE RAN
ALL THE WAY

by

SAM ROSS

A Novel

Published in 1987 by
Academy Chicago Publishers
425 North Michigan Avenue
Chicago, Illinois 60611

Library of Congress Cataloging-in-Publication Data

Ross, Sam, 1912–
  He ran all the way.

  Reprint. Originally published: New York: Farrar,
Straus, 1947.
  I. Title.
PS3535.07493H4   1987   813'.54   86-32234
ISBN 0-89733-256-3 (pbk.)

Chapter I

NICK ROBEY sat up in bed with a start, holding his head in his hands while his mind still retreated and cringed from the dream that had awakened him, and he cried inwardly: "No. Oh, Jesus, no!"

The dream had started with himself staring at an image of a maze of streets, when suddenly a huge rat scurried across the picture, and he found himself running—running like crazy—from one dead-end street into another, until he almost collapsed. But he found an alley dense with shadows. He squeezed in among the shadows. When his breath came back he heard a strange sound: the click and roll of dice. Then he caught sight of the white dice rolling out of unseen hands. He stooped over to grab them; but they were whisked away into the shadows about him. He heard them click and saw them roll out again and then he said:

"It's my dice."

"Who the hell are you?" The voice came from the shadows huddled over the game, but it sounded like his own voice.

"I am—" he said, but he was suddenly not able to name himself. He knew who he was, all right. He was Nick Robey. But he could not name what he was called. Still, the shadow with his voice knew who he was.

"Oh, you are, hey."

"I am, hey, and it's my dice."

He scooped up the dice and began to shake them.

5

"A thousand bucks," he said.

"You're covered."

The bet was called by the shadow with his voice. He looked up and wanted to throw the dice away. He felt that he was playing against himself and that he would lose. But he couldn't back out. He had to go ahead. He humped over as he shook the dice. His thighs became strained; his throat ached with prayer; and his lips muttered: "Seven. Oh, you seven. Oh, come on seven." Then his throat choked, and his hopes and prayers became stifled. And though he tried to keep the dice from rolling out of his hand while he had no control over them, the shadow with his voice said, "Crap out." And when the dice rolled out two black dots shone from the smooth white surfaces.

"Yah, that's it," grunted the shadow with his voice. "Crap."

"You shouldn't of said that," he said.

"Who said what?"

"You did. You said: crap out. You said it with my voice. You're making me play against myself."

"You're nuts. Roll them or get off the pot."

"I'll roll them, all right. A thousand bucks."

"You're covered."

He whipped a pistol out of his back pocket.

"You're covered, too," he said.

"What do you mean, I'm covered?"

The pistol gleamed in his hand. But the shadow with his voice wasn't scared. He just stared at the gun in black silence, mocking the blackness within him.

"I said: you're covered," he said. "If you say crap out again, you'll never say anything again. You're going to say like I say. You're going to say: seven, seven, seven. You're going to play *with* me, not against me. You're going to say: seven, seven, seven!"

He glowered as he began to shake the dice again. And when he stooped over, his eyeballs faded out of his head, leaving white holes in his face, and they flitted before the shadow with his voice. Then just as he was about to shoot the dice he found himself saying: "Don't. Don't. Don't." And as he tried to hold the dice back he heard his voice in

6

the shadow say, "Crap out." The words unlocked his hand. The dice rolled up and settled into two black dots on the white surfaces. He stood up slowly from his hunched position. His eyeballs jiggled back into his sockets. And then he pulled the trigger of his gun. But he didn't shoot the shadow. He shot himself. The explosion of the gunfire and a searing pain woke him up. And now, awake, his back teeth ached and his head felt as though barbed wire were being pulled through it and his heart pounded against his whole body.

He lay back on the bed still holding his head in his hands and still muttering, "No. Oh, no. Oh, Jesus, no!" He lay there a long while without being able to move. Then he became limp as the ache of his head and teeth and the pounding of his heart subsided. He felt as though he had watched himself die. When he tried to gather himself together he found he could not move. He was afraid to move. Any motion he might make would propel him into the rest of the day. He did not want to face the day. His luck had run out. This time he was going to get it. He knew it. This time something was going to happen to him. So he could not move. He would not move.

Then, slowly growing alive, he stared at the green walls and the white splotches where the paint had peeled off. He saw the dusty bedspread crumpled on the floor like an old drunk. He felt a waft of warm air from the open window and saw it stir the stiff, dirty curtains and window shade. He had no desire to move toward his clothes, which were bunched on the dresser, and he saw his life again taking shape in the lusterless mirror.

He did not know how long he lay there before his mother opened the door to his bedroom.

"Nick," she said timidly. "Nicky? You sleeping?"

"Yah."

"How long you going to lay there? It's late. It's eleven o'clock. It's practically the end of the day. So get up, will you?"

"Beat it."

"You ought to get up, Nicky. You ought to get up and

7

look for a job. You ought to find yourself a job. It ain't right for a man not to be working."

"Blow, will you."

"If you don't find a job soon—if you don't bring in any money soon—"

"I know. You'll go back on the streets."

"Shut up, you. Shut up and get out of here and let me straighten out the room."

He sat up and faced her. She had a thick mass of black hair, scrawled with gray. Her forehead tensed over her deep-set eyes, but the rest of her face was sallow and flaccid. Her arms were fleshy and bare and her apron constrained her loose, heavy breasts, sagging belly, and broad thick hips.

"You going to get out of here?" she asked.

"Why? So you can have the rest of the day to whore around? Beat it."

"I don't want you to talk like that to me, Nick. I'll kill you if you talk like that."

"What do you want me to say, you're peaches and cream?"

"Don't say nothing. Just don't say nothing."

"Okay, then let me alone and I won't say a word."

"Get up and get out."

"Okay. Maybe today I'll get up and go out and never come back."

"I hope so. My sweet mother of Christ, I hope so."

"I should of died in your belly and you with me."

"That would of been the greatest pleasure I could of ever enjoyed."

"Okay, then get the hell out of here and let me get dressed."

"Why? You scared I'll steal something?"

"Yah. You'd steal anything if it's got what makes a man. Even what I got, if I'd let you. Beat it."

She stepped over to him and before he could lift his arms he felt the full impact and sting of her hand striking his face. She stepped back and glared at him, then walked out of the room and slammed the door. He saw himself quiver in the shaking mirror on the dresser.

He reached over for his pants and thrust his legs through them and went to the washroom. He hated the sight of himself when he glanced in the mirror. He felt like the scum on his teeth as he slid his tongue over them. He tried to smile, but it didn't look like a smile. Somehow, he could never get a smile or a laugh past the frown on his forehead. His neck was tense and he looked like a man carrying a heavy weight on his head. His head jutted forward slightly from the strain, but without knowing it he was protecting himself from a sudden blow that always threatened to strike his neck. He looked at his shock of curly black hair, his dark restless eyes, his olive skin, and hard bony face. The only thing he felt good about was his body. It was strong and tall and well packed, with long muscular arms and legs and broad shoulders. He could feel his body: its firmness, its flow, its rippling grace. But his face felt oppressed. There was nothing in his face but the lingering pain of his back teeth, his head, and his heart.

When he got out of the washroom his mother was gone. He went into the kitchen, cut himself a piece of bread, buttered it, then poured himself a cup of stale coffee. He rubbed his feet nervously into the worn-out linoleum on the floor as he thought of the dice game in his dream and as he saw himself burst into a million fragments of orange-red from the gunshot. He jumped up and got a deck of cards out of his dresser. He cleared the kitchen table and began to play solitaire.

If he could beat the game once, he told himself, it would mean the dream was a phony; it would mean his luck had not run out. But he couldn't even turn up an ace the first four games. Then he began to cheat. And still he could not win. The cards were against him. Everything was against him. And in a rage he tore up the cards. He looked at them scattered on the floor and he thought: I couldn't even beat the game once, though I gave myself every break; I lost, just like in my dream, but there I killed a man and the man was myself.

He knew now that he had better not see Al Molin today. He had to avoid Al Molin somehow. He could never go through what he had planned for this day with Al. He went into his room and put on his shirt, socks, and shoes. But when he stepped out of the house he saw Al Molin coming up the stairs.

"Hey, what do you say, Nick?"

"Hi, Al."

"What's the matter? Ain't you glad to see your pal, Al?"

"Yah, Al. Sure."

Al was beside him now. He did not like Al, who was thin and wiry and much smaller than himself. Al was always sniffing and rubbing the tip of his nose nervously. His shoulders were rounded and his nose hawked out of his face. And today he was well dressed in a tan summer tropical suit and a Panama hat. Nick didn't trust him. Al, he felt, was the kind of guy who was always making use of someone. Now, he knew, Al was going to make use of him.

"Why the hell didn't you show up this morning at Lombardi's?" asked Al. "For Christ sake, I wait and wait and wait, and no Nick."

"I don't know. I couldn't get up, Al."

"What! A day like today and you couldn't get up? Do you know what day this is for us, Nick? It's independence day. Every day after this one's going to be a holiday for us."

"Al," Nick said slowly. "Not today."

"Today's the day! What do you mean, not today?"

"I had a dream."

"So did I."

"Yah?" said Nick eagerly. "What kind? How was it?"

"It was the garbage can for the way we live now. It was us on the beach at Miami. And who do you think was in our arms?"

"Who?"

"Hedy Lamarr was in mine."

"Sure, you always go for the big, slick dolls."

"And you, Nick. You had Rita Hayworth. Plenty big doll, too. And her legs, you know how long they are, they was wrapped all around your back."

10

"But in my dream, Al, I killed a guy."

"Just a dream. Smoke it away."

"So's Hedy and Rita."

"Okay. But with dough you get two more like them."

"But the guy I killed in my dream, Al, he was me."

"Ah, you're talking like a Jonah."

"Then I played solitaire. I never won once. For a solid hour I never won once."

"You was playing with a marked deck."

"So let's make it some other time, Al."

Al grabbed his shirt.

"No other time," he said. "Another time and you'll get just as scared and you'll get the dream again. You're just scared."

"The hell I'm scared."

"Then take the dandruff out of your blood. I'll carry you on my luck."

"But I ain't scared."

"Okay, show me. But first get back into the house and put on some decent clothes. When you're traveling with Al Molin you got to look right, you got to look like you belong."

Al let go Nick's shirt and slapped his broad back and they went back into the house. Al looked into the clothes closet and picked out Nick's gray pin-striped tropical suit and threw it at him.

"The first thing you got to look like is an all right guy," said Al. "The rest is easy."

Nick got into the suit. Al beamed looking at him.

"You look good, kid," he said. "You're sharp as a tack. Now don't forget the gat and take some extra rounds of ammunition."

Nick went through all the motions, but he still did not know whether he was going through with the holdup. There were still four hours ahead of him. Anything could happen in those four hours. So he walked with Al down the hot dusty street to Lombardi's poolroom. Nick felt peculiar, as though he were seeing the neighborhood for the first time after a long absence. He was in that part of Chicago, just northwest of the Loop, where the river scummed its way like a dark snake, where the railroad sidings and the roaring trains were sight and sound to him, where the vibrations of factories throbbed through his body, where the houses were old and gutted and heat-dry with garbage-heaped alleys behind them and with rubbled lots that looked as though bombs had hit them. From the broad window of the poolroom Nick could see the street-cars and the people going by and the glare of the sun shimmer over the asphalt. Nick took off his jacket and pulled his shirt away from his wet skin. Al jabbed a hole in a punchboard and won two dollars in trade. That made Nick feel better. Maybe Al *was* just lousy with luck. He had never got into trouble before when he was with Al. He had got into trouble with other guys and when he was alone, but never when he was with Al. So maybe he was just scared. That was nothing new. He was always scared just before. And then something would happen to him that would turn his fear into a hard strength. He never knew how it came about. First he was so scared he quivered until he thought he'd fall off his feet. Then the quivering stopped and he'd feel a cool sweat bubble over his skin and he'd feel helpless and doomed but ready to face what was coming to him. And then, suddenly, his insides would recoil against his helplessness and they would spring at it, wrestle with it, choke the life out of it; and then, he would become crazed by the sense of power he felt and he would become like another self who had lifted him from his sense of doom. And after that everything turned out all right.

But now, still doubtful, he thought that any time some-body dreamed of dying and killing it came true. It always came true. A guy couldn't ignore that kind of a dream. But who really did the dying? And who really did the killing? He did the killing. Sure, he did. But he also did the dying. Yet he didn't die in his own body. He died in his voice. That's what made it so hard to figure out. That's why he didn't know exactly where he stood. And he knew, without thinking about it, that he would have to find out. He knew that as well as he knew that his fate was sealed; he couldn't struggle against it, until at a certain moment

12

something snapped within him that gave him a sense of mastery over himself for which he knew he would die if he had to.

"Al," he said. "Supposing something happens?"

"What's going to happen?"

"Nothing, Al. But suppose something does?"

"Hey, you talk like that and something will happen. You're wishing for it, like."

"I mean, suppose he don't hand over the bag with the payroll?"

"So suppose he don't. We just take it, then."

"I mean, suppose he's got a gun, too, and he starts shooting?"

"Suppose, suppose, suppose. And what do we do all the time? Just stand there with empty hands?"

"I mean, we got to plan careful, Al. We don't want any trouble. Like, after we get the money, we don't want to kill the guy. We just konk him on the head and knock him out good so we can get away."

"Okay, that's the plan. You think I'm crazy to kill a guy? Sure, we'll just knock him out."

"Let's talk about it some more, Al."

"No. There's nothing more to talk about. We're through talking. All we got to do now is pull off the job."

"But there's a lot of things we didn't talk about, Al."

"Listen, you're always this way just before. You're scared crapless. Did anything ever happen when you was with me before?"

"No."

"Then shut up. For Christ sake, if you didn't know about this deal, and if I wasn't such a little guy so's everybody thinks they can haul off at me and then make me shoot at them, I'd tell you to go to hell. What are you trying to do, give me the creeps? I tell you everything's going to be all right. I got everything worked out in my head. So long as you're with me, I'm telling you, things is going to work out right. So shut up."

"But supposing something happens to you and I'm left alone?"

13

"Listen, you bastard—"

Al had his hand inside his coat pocket where his gun was.

"Okay, okay, Al. I was just talking."

"Talk is crap."

They stood still, their eyes glued to each other. Then Al lowered his eyes and said:

"Let's shoot a game of pool, Nick, and relax. We'll shoot a fast one."

But Nick couldn't relax over the game of pocket billiards. He couldn't even figure out the right angles, the position for the next shots, nor any combinations. Nothing seemed to work for him as he sweated through the game, and Al beat him. Al had never beaten him before. But this time Al beat him bad. This time he knew that he would have to ride on Al's luck. And if Al didn't have it, well, there was nothing he could do about it—not until something happened to him.

Chapter II

NICK and Al got off the streetcar at the main entrance to Navy Pier. They walked inside a moment and meandered in and out of the tables, brushing against the people eating and wandering about. They avoided the few policemen stationed there. It was a hot day and the Pier was crowded and people were boarding an excursion boat and the lake was very calm. Al bought a bag of peanuts. Nick bit into a couple, but they became like wads of paper in his mouth and he had to spit them out. Then they walked back out of the main entrance of the Pier to where the streetcar had dropped them off. They moved casually within the shadows of the two long buildings, which came together in a long V before they ended a mile away. Then they came to an empty warehouse about two blocks down. They stepped into it, saw the ship's upper decks through the high windows, and began to wait.

Nick had told Al about the set-up. He had known about it when he had worked as a lifeguard at the Pier. That was early in the summer, before he was fired. This big boat came in every couple of weeks. It tied up alongside the Pier, away from the crowds at the main section, and discharged its passengers. He used to go aboard for a free meal. One day, while he was eating, he saw the crew gang up outside the saloon. He hung around and saw a fat guy walk in with a briefcase. The fat guy opened the briefcase and pulled out a payroll and so much money that he could hardly see straight. Then the members of the crew stepped up one at a time, signed the payroll, got paid, and walked away. He looked around for a cop. There was nobody there, no police, nothing, just the paymaster and the captain and the purser of the ship, paying off. Every two weeks this happened. He told Al about it in a casual conversation. But Al saw how it worked. He followed the paymaster from the steamship offices to the bank. From the bank the paymaster got into a cab and rode out to the Pier. The paymaster walked through the warehouse out on the dock where the ship was moored. And that was the last Al saw of him. The whole business was so simple when they talked it over and thought about it that they looked at each other in amazement. Nothing had ever seemed so easy before. The only thing Nick worried about later was that the police patrolled the Pier regularly. He knew about that and Al didn't. But Al talked him out of that fear. Al was always talking him out of something. Sometimes he felt like he wanted to kill Al, because of the way he was leashed to him. But he needed Al, the way Al needed him, and that kept him from feeling completely shut out of the world.

But now, Nick did not know how long he could keep waiting for the paymaster to show up. He leaned hard against the building to stop his trembling. His throat was so dry he could hardly swallow.

"Relax, Nick," said Al hoarsely. "Just a few more minutes."

"What if he shows this time with a cop?"

"Then we'll walk away like we just finished taking a leak."

"Okay." Then after a pause, Nick said, "Supposing he's got another guy with him?"

"Listen, Nick. We got guns. They kill people. You're a big guy, too. Nobody monkeys with a big guy."

"But you're sticking with me, Al, all the way through, no matter what."

"Now shut up and relax."

They heard a car pull up outside the warehouse. They pulled out their guns and braced themselves against the building. Nick glanced at Al and looked away. He couldn't stand the rigid stare of Al's eyes. They heard the door of the car slam shut, the sound of footsteps, only one man's footsteps, and then it began to happen to Nick: the wild terror, himself turning into a shrill whistle packed with breath, his wanting to scream and scream and scream until he spiraled out into space; then came the jar, the sense of having conquered himself, the excited sense of power in overwhelming the doom within himself. The paymaster walked into his pistol, and he said, "Just hand it over, Mac."

The paymaster handed over the briefcase and Nick grabbed it. He knocked off the paymaster's hat and hit him over the head with the butt of his revolver. When they started to walk out of the warehouse, Al said, "Put that gat away. Put it away." But it was too late. A cop had walked in.

Then the shooting and running started. And when Nick turned about in his wild flight to see what had happened, he saw the cop lying on the ground and Al was also doubled up on the ground yelling, "Nick. Nick. Nick."

Al's voice struck him from all directions.

"Nick. Nick. Nick."

Then he thought he heard:

"You did it, Nick. You did it, Nick. You did it, Nick."

The voice surrounded him and he found himself hurling against it in every direction. He stopped suddenly, whirled about, and fired at Al. The sound of the gunshot in the great warehouse deafened him. And for awhile, as he continued running, he lost the sound of Al's voice. Then it beat at him again.

"Nick, don't leave me. Nick. Nick. Nick."

He whirled about and fired again, and in the deafening sound of the gunshot he escaped out of the warehouse and hopped on a passing truck. Breathing hard, but unmoving, his nerves and blood still raced on and he began to pray: "Oh, Jesus, please let Al die. Don't let Al get caught alive. Don't let the sound of my name be heard. Let Al die good and easy and nice, like going to sleep, and don't let him be caught alive to burn. Oh, Jesus, please, do Al a favor and make him dead and make him unable to talk. Oh, Mary, mother of Christ, don't let Al talk and don't keep him alive to burn."

17

The truck stopped and jolted him into action. He began running again. Then, growing tired, he began to feel the weight of the briefcase. He had to get rid of it. He was out in the open now, with the lake on one side, the cindered empty lots that led to the freight yards and the Chicago River on the other, and ahead of him loomed the tall structures of the city. He scooped up a paper bag and ran to a little shed off the lake. It was an outhouse. He emptied all the bills into the paper bag and threw the briefcase jangling with change into the outhouse hole. He did not know how much money he had but it didn't seem like much if it could fit into a paper bag. Finally he stepped out. He had to stay in the open, stay where there were crowds of people; then if anything happened he would have a better chance of getting away. He walked on to the breakwater. His legs were stiff, still quivery from the long run and from what had happened. The sun was hot overhead and moving toward the city. He wanted to take off his jacket, but his shirt was wet and stuck to his body. Even his pants felt like gum against his legs as he moved along. He combed his fingers through his shiny wet hair, then tried to rub the sweat off his face, and kept walking quickly alongside the lake and past the staring people sitting in the sun. There weren't enough people on the breakwater. He skirted the bend and saw Oak Street beach farther down, mobbed with people and colors and looped by the tall buildings facing the lake; sounds of yelling and screaming came to him in a steady wave. He quickened his pace toward the sandy beach. He felt himself being tugged by the sight of the crowds. He could get lost there, he told himself. He could really get lost there.

But as he got closer to the beach and had to step in and out of the denser crowds he began to feel that people were staring at him. A jumble of eyes began to move in front of him. He brushed them away with his hands. They darted to the sides, wincing in the sunlight, peering in the shade, poking through flesh and shooting up beside him. He began trotting, scuffing the granite breakwater, and winding in and out of the sitting and standing and lying people. He wondered if he looked queer. He was around water and he was not in trunks and he was sweating like a steamroom wall. He felt that he looked very suspicious. He would look even more suspicious on the beach: a guy in a suit of clothes sitting on the sand instead of on the grass off the boulevard. He began to jog toward the city, away from the beach. Suddenly, he stopped and stood very still and felt his thick blood pound through his body. He was running home. He must be going crazy, he thought, running home. And then he realized he had nowhere to go. He became overwhelmed with the thought. He knew suddenly why he had never run away from his mother before: he had nowhere to go. He felt stunned, rooted to the ground. He could never go home.

He began moving again, straining with the need to go some place but not knowing where. Why hadn't he and Al arranged for just such a thing? Why hadn't they arranged for a hideout? But they couldn't have. That was the trouble. You didn't talk about such a thing. If you did, you were asking for everything in the books to happen. So you talked only of success. That was Al, the smart guy. Al had it all worked out in his head. There was nothing to worry about. Little Al had it all worked out in his head. And now where was Al? Was he dead? Was the cop dead? He hoped they were both dead. He prayed they both had died before anybody had got to them. He wondered: if Al had just been wounded, and his shots hadn't killed him, and if somebody had got to Al before he died—would Al squeal and say that he, Nick Robey, had been on the job with him? Would Al rat on him?

Al, he cried inwardly. He could feel his whole being rear up before his plea. Please, Al. Please, please, please, Al, be dead before anybody gets to you.

But until he knew what had happened to Al and what he might say, if he were still alive, he knew that he had to stay out of sight. But where could he go? Where could he hide?

He was near the sandy part of the beach again, among the thicker crowds of people. He felt it strange that nobody had bothered him so far. He felt as strange as the immense heat of the sun shimmering over the water and waving over the people about him and burning through the top of his head. He had to lie down. He had to take a rest. He had to get into the water and take a drink and cool off. He had to look like a right guy in place with everything. He had to get a pair of trunks and get out of his clothes.

He passed two men with trunks swinging from their hands. He reached to grab a pair and to start running. But he contained himself. He couldn't start running again. This time, for certain, he would be pursued. People, crowds, yelling, being pursued. Always, it was that way. You chase yourself, people chase you, you chase the people, a dog sweeps around to bite his tail, and sweeps and sweeps around, until . . .

"Hey, bud, you're walking in the water. Want to get your shoes wet?"

Yes. He didn't even know he had stepped in the lake. He jumped onto the hard-packed sand. Now he was on the beach, and there were so many people, so many many people.

"You ain't feeling sick or woozy, huh?"

He began walking faster. He began to walk away from that voice.

"Thought you was going to spin right in, plop."

Don't run, he told himself. Don't run. Just walk. Just walk. The beach was a cockeyed maze of people, one leading into another, one color patched up against another like a crazy quilt. But he was getting lost among them. They were tall fences hiding him. And if he could lie down and bury his face in his arms, nobody would see him: nobody.

"Hey, you're stepping on my clothes."

He jumped away, startled. The beach was also full of clothes.

"Why the hell don't you watch where you're going?"

He stepped over somebody lying down, paused, and walked around a group of standing boys and girls shrill with laughter.

"Watch it, mister. Ouch, my toes."

A pair of hands came up against his chest and pushed him. He flung the hands away from him and stepped for-

20

ward. He had to get set. He had to sit down and stay put before he got into a fight. Then he saw a kid swinging a pair of wet trunks. He walked up quickly to the kid, who was about his size.

"Hey, Mac," he said. "The trunks."

"What about the trunks?"

"I'll give you a buck for them."

"What are you, crazy, a buck?"

"Two bucks."

"What is this, an auction?"

"Here's a sawbuck."

He fumbled in his pocket for some of the money he had put in there and handed the kid a ten dollar bill.

"Okay, okay, don't grab," said the kid.

"Shut up and here's the ten and let go the trunks."

"Okay, okay. I guess if I had a sweat-up like you, mister, I'd be dead for a swim, too."

He wanted to kill the kid. The kid might talk. He might talk to anybody. He might say: a goof, he gives me a tenspot for a pair of cotton trunks ain't worth a buck, but he's suffering from the heat or shock or something. And maybe the kid would say this to a cop and the cop would say: shock, suffering from the heat, did you say—where is that guy?

He grabbed the trunks from the kid's hesitating grasp and walked away rapidly. When he turned about the kid was out of sight. He stopped at a section of the beach that was very crowded and sat down. He took off his wet jacket carefully so as not to expose his pistol. He put the paper bag of money inside his jacket. Then he wrapped the wet tails of his shirt around his groin and very quickly slipped out of his pants and wriggled into the trunks. He took off his wet shirt and laid it out to dry and placed his shoes and socks on top of his clothes pile. Then he rushed into the water, dived under, jumped up, leaned over and drank until his stomach felt bloated, and rushed back to where his clothes were. He rolled over on his belly and lay on the sand a long while, sighing and trying to calm his shuddering insides.

21

Chapter III

NICK lay on his belly facing the lake. He couldn't hide his face in his arms. He kept glancing about constantly, his body geared to jump up in a second. His clothes were bundled beneath his head and he had one hand inside his jacket fingering his pistol. He was close to the water's edge and the beach was still crowded. Behind him the sun dropped slowly, coming closer to the tops of the buildings.

He tried to think of what to do. He knew if Al had been picked up alive and had talked he would be finished. There would be no place for him to go. He had a record and his picture might be put in the papers. Then he would be recognized. Where could he go? he wondered. Start traveling? Where? Besides, the cops always looked for a guy at a railroad or bus station. And it would be even more dangerous to ride the freights. He was not going to run away. He had always been caught before, running. The cops expected that. He was not going to do what they expected. He would do like Dillinger and stay right where they least expected to find him. That's where he was now, where nobody expected him to be. That's why he wasn't being bothered. But how long could he stay at the beach? Soon, the crowds of people would start leaving. It would get dark. And then the cops would come around and chase the people off the beach. Then where would he go? Where *could* he go, if Al was caught alive and talked and his picture got in the papers? He knew that he could not go home and that he could not be seen anywhere in his neighborhood. He bet that the cops might now be looking for him all over, if Al talked. And if Al was dead, or didn't talk, then he could go anywhere. Nobody would know anything. He could even go home. He could go home with money. He could change his whole life. He could change his mother's life. He could be a magician and change everything. If Al was dead and didn't talk. Otherwise he would have to get a set-up where he would not be seen and recognized. Where? How?

Out of the corner of his eye he saw the dark pants. The cop was down aways, moving slowly, looking around, peering at faces. He clutched at the handle of his pistol, rolled to the side away from the cop, and watched him. The cop moved very slowly in and out of the crowds of people, studying everybody, coming closer. He saw the murky water and the splashing people in it. He drew his hand away from the gun, rose casually with his back to the cop, and walked slowly into the water. He sank to his knees, and in a glance he caught the cop's searching movements, then ducked under, pushed off from the sandy bottom, and swam beneath the water, avoiding the standing legs that suddenly came to vision, until there were fewer people and there was no more breath in him. He came up slowly and peered above the surface of the water. The water was still shallow and warm, without any life to it; but with bent legs he could just keep his head above the surface and watch. The cop was near his clothes now, looking about and at the people in the water, and he prayed: don't step on the clothes, don't feel the gun and the paper bag of money with your feet, just move on, move away to the breakwater, just move. He thought the cop saw him and he ducked under water again. He swam away from the cop's line of sight until he began to feel a slow fire start in his chest. He was about forty yards away when he came up for a breath of air. He pushed under again and swam still farther away. Then he rose and sighed. The cop was moving away from his clothes, away from him, toward the breakwater, but still searching. He kept watching him, his mouth just above the water's surface, his heart beating hard and his muscles tensed.

He didn't see it come. His face became dazzled and his eyes smarted and he jumped up and grabbed the fleshy part of an arm. He had been struck by a girl's hand. She came up against him as he lifted her and she began choking and rubbing her eyes. When she caught her breath she began spluttering and laughing. She had even white teeth with water rilling into her mouth from her freckled face.

"I'm sorry," she said.

He saw the cop jump up on the breakwater and walk away from the beach. Then he stared at her—her white bathing cap pressed against her forehead, the freckles on her body and face, her snub nose and round face, her flat chest and boyish hips.

"My arm," she said. "Let go. It hurts."

He let go her arm.

"I'm just a beginner," she said. "I always bump people. I'm sorry."

"That's okay," he managed to say.

"I can't see under water." She began laughing again. "So I bump people. I can't get out in the deep water where there are no people. But I've got to learn how to swim. So I sometimes bump into somebody."

"That's okay."

She turned around and flung herself against the water, her eyes closed, her arms flailing and splashing, her head straining for a breath. He stepped over and grabbed her under the shoulder and lifted her as she still struggled.

"I'll learn you," he said.

"No, that's all right," she said, rubbing her eyes and gulping.

"No, I'll learn you."

"I've been trying to learn a long time."

"All you got to do is relax. Look."

He shoved off from the bottom and went into a dead man's float. When he stood up he said: "It's hard to sink if you relax. I'll show you."

He doubled up and clasped his arms about his knees to go into a jellyfish float. Then he stood up and wiped the water from his face and asked: "Did you see my back on top of the water?"

24

"Yes. It just came right up in a curve."

"It's easy like anything, if you relax."

"It looks hard."

"It's easy, I'm telling you. You learn that jellyfish float and you'll be able to swim as easy—as easy like this."

He pushed off the bottom and stroked about twenty yards, his long, loose arms sweeping above the surface and dropping in effortlessly. He whirled about and swam back to her.

"Gee," she said.

He smiled self-consciously, and said: "Come on, let's try it."

She tried to do the floats but was very tense and timid. Then he held her around her waist as he got her to practice kicking and stroking. He got to feeling peculiar. There was in him a strange mixture of vague plotting, a sense that he was going to use this girl for something, a feeling of gratitude for keeping his mind off what had happened and what might happen, a sense that he was not alone and that he somehow belonged now, and also a timid passion and a wonder of how it would be if he was in bed with her.

She scrambled out of his arm and said: "I'll never learn."

"Sure you'll learn."

"I'm tired. I'm going in."

"Don't go in yet." He felt safer in the water and less troubled.

"I have to. I'll get blueberry lips if I don't."

"Come on, I'll learn you some more."

"Some other time. And thanks."

"What other time?"

"Oh, some other time," she said coyly.

"Now. I'll learn you now."

"Please, some other time. I'll get a cramp if I don't go in."

"Then I'll save you. Look, I used to be a lifeguard. I'd be nuts about saving you."

"Please let me go."

He saw that he was holding her arm. He let it go. He

25

restrained himself from grabbing it again. He wanted to be very close to her. He wanted her to hide him. He looked at the beach. There were no police on it. He picked out his clothes. There were people nearby but the clothes appeared untouched. He found himself being pulled by the girl. She didn't even turn around as she walked ahead and he followed her. When she stepped on the sand she turned about and glanced at him but didn't say anything. And then he felt like smashing her. He felt that he had followed her like a dog and that she had taken it for granted that he would.

"Hey, you're a wise babe, aren't you, babe?" he said.

"Why, what do you mean?"

"I mean pushing me around like that."

"Like what?"

He saw her eyes narrow, become pleading, almost searching for help. He became frightened at his lack of control. All she had to do was to start screaming . . .

"Ah, I was kidding," he said. "Don't take me serious."

"You're a very peculiar person, you are. One minute you're as nice as nice can be. And the next—gee, you're a funny person."

"I told you I was only kidding."

"All right, you kidded me. Now go kid someone else."

She turned away from him and took off her bathing cap. Her hair fell down to her shoulders. It was red hair. Her freckles came out to him and he suddenly saw that her eyelashes were reddish but hardly noticeable and her brown eyes had a pinkish tinge. Her shoulders were small away from her hair and her breasts mounded very slightly above her flat stomach. Her legs were slim, with thin ankles and tapering calves and firm thighs. She was not a big girl, but her legs looked long and not quite full. He felt big beside her and he felt her diminishing before him. He wasn't afraid of her.

"What's your name, Red?" he said.

"See what I mean? First you're nice, and then you scare me, and then you want to know who I am. You're a funny person."

"I didn't want to scare you, Red. I just got mixed up. For a minute I just got mixed up."

"Why?" He didn't answer, and she asked: "What's the matter?"

"Nothing. Nothing's the matter."

She glanced at him quickly, trying to figure out what was wrong with him; the way he looked became like a hand that reached inside of her and clutched her heart and then released it.

"I'm Peg," she said simply. "Peg Dobbs."

"Swell."

"And you?"

He hesitated a moment.

"Joe," he said. "Joe Martin."

"Two first names." She laughed.

"Yah. Two first names."

She sat down and crossed her legs. Nick looked down at her, then walked away to where his clothes were and carried them back to where she sat. This time he was no dog following her around. He was Nick. Nick Robey, now known as Joe Martin. He sat down beside her and for awhile neither of them said anything.

"What are you looking for, Joe? Expecting something?"

"Nothing."

"Do you come here often?"

"Sometimes."

"I promised myself I'd learn how to swim this summer."

"It's good to know how to swim."

"I kind of always like to promise myself something. And then I try to make it come true. Do you do that ever?"

"When I was a kid."

"And then?"

"Nothing came true."

"That's too bad, Joe." Then she smiled. "Maybe you don't live right."

"Maybe I don't."

"How do you live? I mean what do you do, Joe?"

He didn't answer.

"Maybe I shouldn't ask. But I like to know about people."

"There's nothing to know."

"You're very cynical for a young man. There's a lot to know." After a pause she said: "You're a strange kind of person, Joe, always looking around, not saying much."

He smiled wryly. There wasn't much he could say. He was too busy thinking, watching. But he'd have to say something. He had to keep talking to her and make her stay with him until darkness came. He had to figure out a plan of getting away. And maybe she could help him. A guy with a girl looked like he belonged. A guy with a girl never looked suspicious. Nobody would expect him to be with a girl. Nobody would even expect him to be out in the open. He had to hold on to her.

"I'm hungry," he said. "I was looking for a hot dog stand."

"There's one on the walk."

He saw the hot dog stand and also a cop nearby.

"You hungry?" he asked.

"Kind of. I came straight from work and didn't eat."

"Here's a dollar and buy us some."

"Say, who do you think you are, Humphrey Bogart? Do you think you can just look at me with your dark eyes and make me do anything you want me to?"

"Then forget it," he said. "I got a strained tendon, else I'd go."

They sat silently for awhile before she rose and walked away to buy the hot dogs. She wondered what was wrong with him. Perhaps he had some physical defect which she hadn't noticed and which made him the way he was. But there was something about him that touched her: something about his eyes, their pained expression, their sense of backing away, of being hunted. Perhaps the war had done that to him and he hadn't got over it. She shrugged her shoulders. She wanted to be with him. She felt good within the image of other girls glancing at him. She bet the other girls on the beach were asking what she had that they didn't have. Her body felt strong as she moved. She hadn't

28

felt this way in a very long time. Joe was a good-looking man, she thought. There was danger in his eyes but, like in the song, she didn't care. Maybe he would offer to take her home. And maybe she would see him again. She wondered what he saw in her that made him want to know her and stay with her when there were so many good-looking girls on the beach. She hoped he would offer to take her home but she would try to make it difficult for him.

CHAPTER IV

THE beach was less crowded and seemed worn out. The sand was dirty and cooler and the horizon was darker and very close. Nick had decided to go home with Peg. Perhaps if his picture wasn't in the papers, and if a good description of him hadn't got out, and if Al had died or had refused to talk, he would be able to get home with her safely. He felt that if he could get past this day he would be all right. Peg became a link between the night and the next day that he had to get into; then the affair of his dream would no longer hold up and it would become an untruthful omen of the past. So Peg was not a woman to him. She had become his life. And so, when the exhausted day became lit up by the lamp posts on the boulevard and the darkening sky blotted up more and more of the lake, Peg shuddered, smiled, and began to put on her clothes over her bathing suit. Nick began dressing, too.

"I'll take you home," he said.

She wanted to play with the desire of his wanting to take her home, but he was too abrupt.

"Where do you live?" he asked. "Is it far from here?"

"A thousand miles from here."

"Where?"

"An island in the Pacific."

"Where?"

"Supposing I said I had a date and I couldn't let you take me home?"

30

"Come on, I'll take you home."

"Why don't you ask me first whether I'd like to have you take me home?"

"All right. I'd like you to have me take you home."

"Did you ever take no for an answer, Joe?"

"Sometimes, when I couldn't do anything about it."

"Supposing I said no now?"

"You can't."

"Supposing I just walked away?"

"I'd follow you."

"Then I'd call a policeman and say: Officer, this man's bothering me."

"You couldn't, Peg."

His forehead seemed to press down on his eyes, and she felt that she had hurt him with her teasing. He seemed to be beyond her and yet surrounding her on all sides, and she knew that she couldn't get away; she did not want to get away.

"I'd be glad to have you take me home, Joe," she said. "You're very kind."

She told him where she lived. Then they stood up and faced the lighted boulevard. Nick became tense with the idea of escaping into the city. He had his jacket on his arm. He put his hand inside his jacket and gripped his pistol. He pressed the bag of money against his ribs. He knew that he wouldn't take a streetcar; it was too long a ride and too risky. The bus didn't go that way. And the walk to the El was too far. A cab wasn't too good, either. Cab drivers always remembered fares; at least they did in the movies. But there was no other way. He could lean back in the seat of the cab and hide from sight until he reached Peg's house. He saw a long line of cars and cabs stopped by the red light.

"Come on, Peg."

He grabbed her hand and started running along the boulevard, away from the intersection and the cop on its corner, until he found an empty cab. He opened the door and got in with Peg.

"Turn west on the next corner and just keep driving west," he told the driver.

"No special address you want to give me?" the driver asked.

"No, just drive and I'll tell you when to stop."

He settled into the seat, sank low into it so that he couldn't be seen through the window.

"I didn't mean for you to take me home by cab," said Peg. "We could have gone by streetcar or El."

"This is the only way to travel, Peg. When I like a girl I like her to travel nice."

He glanced at her. She looked better in clothes. Her rounded face was soft within the shadows of the cab. He liked the way she stared tenderly at him for a moment. Maybe he was an all right guy with her. Maybe now, because he was all balled up, he was an all right guy and a girl could kind of go for him. But he had to be careful of her. He had to use her some way and he had to be nice to her. And being a nice guy wasn't bad. It made him feel different. It made him feel warmer. It was the way a mother could make you feel before she went bad on you.

Now she was quietly singing a song. She was singing a song wholly within herself and not paying any attention to him.

"You like to sing, huh?" he said.

"Yes. Especially when I'm tired. It's like taking a warm bath."

"You got a good voice, kid."

"Good. Good for selling furniture polish."

"That what you do?"

"Yes."

"You got a voice for the stage."

"Yes, yes," she said, smiling coyly.

"No kidding. And maybe I'll put you on the stage. I got connections. I got money."

Her smile spread.

"That's all right, Joe. You don't have to give me a line. That's what I liked about you and why I let you take me home. You didn't hand me a line."

"But it's no line, kid. I got plenty money."

"Then save it, Joe. I don't want to go on the stage."

"What do you want?"

"That would be telling." She winked at him and sighed. She sank deeper into the seat.

Nick looked out on the street. The cab was stopped by a red light. There was a newsstand on the corner. He told the driver to wait a minute. He rushed out and bought a newspaper. Then he told the driver to go up a diagonal street in a southwesterly direction. He opened up the newspaper, holding it away from Peg and clicked on the rear light. And there it was, right on the front page: his picture, one of the cop lying dead, and one of Al holding his leg, his face looking crazy with pain. He saw his name under his photograph, but it didn't look like him; it was an old picture of himself as a kid taken four years ago; nobody, he was sure, would recognize him from it. Then he read the story:

Two gunmen in a daring payroll robbery during broad daylight today shot and killed Patrolman Michael Shaughnessy at Municipal Pier. One of the killers was wounded during the running battle, while the other escaped with a payroll of slightly over $10,000.

Al Molin, one of the gunmen, was wounded in the right leg during the shooting fray. He identified the other killer as Nick Robey, 22, of 918 Throop street, who had escaped. Police headquarters say they have put out an extensive dragnet to capture Robey, who has been described as being about six feet tall, heavy-shouldered and well built, with dark eyes and hair.

Under questioning, Molin said Robey did the shooting, as well as the slugging of Sam Grayson, 44, paymaster of the Great Lakes Steamship Co., who was taken to the Presbyterian Hospital suffering from concussion.

At first Molin said he was only a passerby who had been shot when he wandered upon the scene of the crime. But later he admitted that he was one of the two hold-up men. However, he said Robey did the shooting and slugging. Molin claimed he didn't have a gun with him and that Robey was the only armed one of the two.

Later, police found a gun nearby with two empty

33

chambers and with Molin's fingerprints on the weapon. Police are now checking the type of bullet that killed Shaughnessy . . .

Nick flung the newspaper out of the window.

"Burn," he said without sound. "Burn, you rat sonofabitch. Burn."

"What's the matter, Joe?" Peg asked. "Anything wrong?"

He paid no attention to her.

He could have got away if Al had died. He could have been free if Al hadn't talked. Why did Al talk? Why didn't Al say he was alone and take the whole blame? Why?

You're going to burn anyway, Al, he said silently. You should have known you couldn't have got away by putting the blame on me. You were with me. That makes you guilty of murder, too. So why did you turn rat, Al? Why couldn't you have kept your mouth shut? Why couldn't you have said: I'm going to let Nick live, I'm going to let Nick live, I'm going to let Nick live? Or why couldn't you have died? You're going to die anyhow. You're going to die bad. You're going to die thinking about it. You're going to die with your head making the death a million times worse. The worst way to die is the way you see it in your head. So why didn't you die nice, like the cop, easy? Damn it, damn it, damn it, why? And why did you talk, Al? Jesus, why did you let Al talk, and why did you talk, Al?

Peg held her breath. She wanted to hold his hand, or stroke his hair, or pat his back. She wanted to do something to comfort him. She saw his wrinkled forehead crush tears out of his deep-set eyes; bubbles of sweat cropped out of his face and neck and slid down. Nobody had ever touched her so deeply.

Tell me, Joe, she wanted to say. Tell me what's wrong.

She wanted to hold him in her arms and watch his face become calm and smooth.

Tell me, Joe, she wanted to say. Let me help you, Joe.

34

CHAPTER V

THE cab shot up Ogden Avenue and wound through Douglas Park and continued along a lawned one-way drive until the park system ended; finally, near the suburb of Cicero, it stopped in front of Peg's house. Nick paid the driver, then stooped out of the cab with Peg. Off the curbs the street was lined with fully-leaved trees of all shapes and sizes. And farther down was the structure of the elevated bridged over the street. The sky was bright and clean with stars and a half-moon.

"I was born in that house," said Peg. "Nineteen years ago."

Nick looked at the two-story frame house for a moment. It was wedged between two three-story brick buildings. He faced away from some people who were sitting outdoors on a bench.

"When I was little there were prairies all about," said Peg. "There were only a few houses. There was ragweed all over. And the crickets—they sounded like waves. It was like living in the country, not in Chicago. Then the city moved in on us, little by little, until now you can hardly see the sky, or the stars at night, until you can hardly breathe."

"Let's get in the house, huh?" He took her arm and compelled her to move faster. He wanted to rush up the wooden stairs leading to the door of her house. He was afraid of the people sitting outdoors. He knew that they were staring and he kept his face away from them.

"It's going to be pretty warm indoors," she said, and stopped to greet the neighbors. One of them said it was a nice night but warm; another got Peg laughing shyly when she was asked if she was going partying tonight; and a kid made her quicken her steps and blush when he started chanting: "Peggy's hooked a fellah, Peggy's hooked a fellah." And Nick felt as though he would never make it to the door atop the wooden porch steps. But finally she opened the door and he followed her up another flight of a musty staircase to where she lived.

As soon as she opened the door Nick sighed. He felt safe. He had stopped running.

Peg said: "Hello. Hello." She was greeted from the kitchen by her mother and father. Then she announced: "I've got company." She sounded light, victorious, momentous. "Please sit down, Joe, and make yourself comfortable," she said, pointing to a couch in the living room. "I'll be right back."

Nick wanted to reach out and hold on to her as she walked away down the foyer. Alone now, he felt unsteady and shaky and found that he couldn't sit down. He felt something inside him take off into a run again and, to keep up with what strained to rush beyond him to safety, he found himself pacing about the rooms off the doorway.

There was one bedroom which faced the street. It was fixed up daintily, with a large double bed, a dressing table draped in pink embroidered lace, a backless stool covered in pink cloth which ruffled to the carpeted floor, and a mahogany bureau. Opposite the hallway door was the other bedroom, where all the furniture was mahogany, from bedposts to dressing table. The building across the passageway blocked out most of the light. The living room was immaculate, as though no one ever used it. There was a fake fireplace with an iron gratelike structure piled with glass coals above a red bulb. Three windows, facing the street, were heavily draped in gold patterns on a reddish-brown background. The broad couch and three easy-chairs were covered with flowered slip covers. And the rug was an imitation Oriental, whose peacocks and smaller birds and curling patterns wound in and out of the deep brick-red background.

Nick was studying a model sailboat set on top of a table when Peg walked in.

"You hungry, Joe?" she asked.

"No."

"That's what I told my mother. I told her we had some hot dogs at the beach. But my mother said you must be hungry and she wants to fix something for you."

"Tell her I don't want anything. Tell her I ain't hungry. I couldn't eat a thing."

"Swell. It's too warm anyway." He noticed a few bubbles of sweat on her upper lip, as she added: "Come on in the kitchen and we'll tell her. She won't believe me."

She grasped his hand and led him out of the living room, past the bedrooms, and into the long foyer. There, she apologized for the way the house looked. He insisted that she had a swell home; he had never seen one so swell. But she told him to wait until he saw the dining room where her mother worked: she was a seamstress; oh, in a small way, just for the neighbors, and just to keep herself busy, but also in a small way it was sort of like her life.

Nick saw a studio couch in the dining room, and Peg explained that Mickey, her younger brother, slept on it. There was also a mahogany table with high-backed red plush seats around it, which was littered with pieces of cloth and straggled threads. And in one corner stood an old-fashioned dummy with a wired bottom, which was draped in a dress that was in the process of being made. Against the window wall, whose view was obstructed by the brick building next to it, stood a sewing machine. Then they stepped into the kitchen of white walls and a glaring porcelain-topped table surrounded by chromium chairs with red seats. Mrs. Dobbs was at the sink, washing dishes, and Mr. Dobbs was drying them.

The first thing that Nick noticed—while he was being introduced and while Mrs. Dobbs was very pleased to

37

know him and while Mr. Dobbs nodded warmly—was that they were punks, little people that he could handle without effort and for whom he should feel no fear.

Mr. Dobbs was about five feet four, with narrow shoulders, a slightly protruding stomach, and small-boned fleshless arms. His face was very ruddy from all the time he spent outdoors; his receding hair was lank and black; and his forehead was white in contrast, since he always wore a cap outdoors and that part of his face was never exposed to the weather. The corners of his gray-green eyes were lined from squinting in the sun.

Mrs. Dobbs was heavier and broader than Mr. Dobbs and Peg. But she was a little woman, more freckled than Peg, and with fading red hair that almost had a pinkish tinge. Her mouth seemed puckered and lined around the edges from the way she screwed up her face while holding pins in her mouth as she worked. Her motions were quick and effective, as against Mr. Dobbs' leisurely movements.

She asked Nick if he didn't want something to eat, she knew that he must be starving, and she would be happy to fix something for him to eat as soon as she finished with the dishes, for it would be a pleasure, she just knew that after a swim and an exhausting day he must be starving, and she wanted to know whether this wasn't just one of the most exhausting days he had ever known, but wouldn't he have even a little bite or perhaps something cold like lemonade with a piece of cake; but after he said no and shook his head, and Peg told her mother that she had told her so, and Mr. Dobbs stood by smiling with his gentle eyes, Mrs. Dobbs wondered then why Peg had brought him into her dirty kitchen and through her messy dining room, she had to apologize for that, and she asked Peg to please get him into a comfortable room, the living room, where it wasn't so warm and where he could sit down and where he wouldn't have to look upon sights that could make a pair of eyes sore.

Peg took Nick back to the living room, leading him by the moist grasp of her hand, and sat down on the broad couch. Nick kept standing, staring at the windows but seeing nothing; his eyes finally focused on the sleek-hulled, two-masted sailboat resting on the occasional table.

"Slick," he said.

"Sit down, Joe. Make yourself comfortable. Sit down here. I won't bite you."

He sat down beside her, leaned over, his feet firm on the rug, his fist kneading into his palm.

"That's my father's," she explained. "He's made hundreds of them. It's his hobby. I used to help him when I was little."

"You still help him?"

"Oh, no." She smiled shyly, and added hesitantly: "I— I kind of grew up."

"What do you mean, you kind of grew up?"

"You see, there were lots of stories connected with the boats my father and I built. Stories and stories, like dreams. Then I kind of stopped believing them, didn't find time for them, I suppose, and I stopped helping. But my father, he still gets a kick out of making them. He's got Mickey, that's my kid brother, to help him now. And together—Joe, you ought to hear them and see them together."

"Sounds like you got a good old man. What was he, a sailor?"

"No, a cabinet-maker. He used to make them beautiful, he used to say. Then in the last war, the first one, he was a soldier and he was gassed. The doctor told him making cabinets was bad for his lungs. The doctor said he had to get an outdoor job. So with the help of my mother he bought a newsstand. That was a long time ago. That was before I was born. I sound like I was right there, huh?"

"Yah. Who else is in the family?"

"Well, there's my mother. You met her. And then there's Mitchell, but everybody calls him Mickey."

"How old?"

"Ten."

"That's all in the family?"

"That's all. Just me, my mother and father, and Mickey. How about you?"

39

"Me? I was the only kid in my family."

"What do you mean, was, Joe?" There it was again, this constriction she felt from the things he didn't say, from his abrupt way of talking, from the way he looked, like he had never smiled in his life; and she wanted to see him smile; she wanted to see his whole face lit up with a smile; she bet that she could someday make him smile, she and her happy family could bring out a smile in him, and then a laugh, slow at first, then fuller and fuller, until his big chest would let out all the trouble in him; and she bet that when that would happen his face would light up like at a carnival, full and bright and all over.

"I'm all that's left of my family," he said. "I'm alone."

"I'm sorry."

"That's okay. I got along. I'm getting along okay. I been doing that a long time."

"All alone." It was hard for her to imagine a person being alone. She didn't know how a person could stand it.

"Sometimes it's better that way. Then you're sure nobody'll ever rat on you. Then nobody can turn rat on you."

"You talk like you've got it in for somebody, Joe."

"Let's skip it."

"What makes you so tough, Joe?"

"I don't know. Maybe I chewed nails when I was a baby."

"Like you alone can beat the world, is that it, Joe?"

"I don't know."

"Like you're alone against the world."

"I am, that's all."

She was trying to understand him. She was trying to understand why she felt so desperate when she was alone, and why, if he was human, which she knew he was, too too human, he could bear and even wish for loneliness.

"You never wanted anything, nobody?" Now she was trying to justify herself, with him, and prove him wrong, for he was with her and she had felt him reach out for her and she had felt that in some way he needed somebody, if not her.

40

"I wanted plenty," he said. "But I never wanted nobody."

"How can you want plenty without nobody to want it for?"

"Can't a guy want for himself?"

"That's selfish."

"Ah, what are you beating out your brains for? I'm okay."

"You're a strange guy, Joe. I wish I knew you."

"Yah." He smiled wryly. Then he jumped up quickly, suddenly startled. Mrs. Dobbs had entered the living room with a sigh.

She wanted to know if everyone was comfortable. She looked interested, but she wasn't, really; she didn't wait for an answer. She wanted to know why Nick didn't take off his coat, she couldn't understand why a young man just couldn't relax and sit around in his shirt sleeves and even roll them up in this warm weather, she wouldn't object, she was sure, nor would Peg object, she was more than sure, but she supposed, sighing, that people were always grinning and bearing it, no matter what their discomforts were. She stared at the packed paper bag beside Nick and wanted to know if that was his lunch which he had forgotten to eat. And Nick sat down hard against it as she stepped toward it; his insides began to coil, grow tense; and he was about to yell: don't touch it, goddamn it, you're going to stick your nose into that bag and you'll die for it, you and everybody else in the house. But she passed by and sat down on an easy-chair facing him and Peg and waved her hand alongside her face.

She wanted to know if it wasn't still uncommonly warm after a hot day and didn't the heat have a way of just wringing the life out of a person and then making one as limp as a rag. Peg interrupted by asking Nick if he wouldn't like a cold glass of lemonade. Mrs. Dobbs thought that it was a good idea and said that she would be grateful for some. And Nick nodded his head, he would have a glass.

Peg walked out and Nick squirmed as Mrs. Dobbs punctuated her talk with little gasps. She thought it would be pleasant at this moment to be on a lake cruise, way out and not caring or knowing where, but just letting the cool breezes calm you. That's the way she and Mr. Dobbs had spent their honeymoon, on a one week lake cruise. That was so long ago, soon after the world war, the first one; but she would never forget it, for the memories, the good memories, one never forgets. After that cruise, Mr. Dobbs said that someday they were going to take a cruise for the rest of their lives, but in their own boat. Just go anywhere, that's the way Mr. Dobbs wanted it. See an island, put in there, and if you like it, spend some time there, then cruise again after you got tired of the land. But she and Mr. Dobbs had never got around to that. Mr. Dobbs was too gentle a person. Gentle people never made the money they needed to do what they really wanted. But still, she and Mr. Dobbs didn't have anything to be unhappy about. And still, it was kind of pleasant to be able to sit about a clean house at the end of a day and think about these things. Kind of very nice, now that the war was over and the men were nearly all back, and the beasts of the world had been destroyed. It gave a person a sort of comfortable feeling. Now a body could sit back and relax and think of nice things without fretting. Mrs. Dobbs knew that Nick must feel that way now, for he had been overseas, hadn't he? Nick nodded. She gasped a little deeper, knowing that his experiences must have been ghastly. It had been ghastly for Mr. Dobbs, too, during the war before; more so for him because he couldn't bear killing and he had died a million times every time he had to handle his rifle. However, he was saved by the horror of being gassed, an experience she was glad to know the boys of this war didn't have to endure. But Nick looked all right to her. She bet that Nick had come out of the war without a scratch. He said, yes, without a scratch, he had been lucky.

Mrs. Dobbs was glad to know that. And now that he was back, back for good, alive and unscathed by the horrors of war, she wanted to know what his plans were.

Well, Mrs. Dobbs guessed, when Nick didn't answer, that sometimes the best laid plans of mice and men often go astray and leave us nothing but grief and pain for promised joy. Anyhow, she explained, that's what Mr. Dobbs was always saying.

Mr. Dobbs came in with Peg at that moment and he wanted to know what he was always saying. Mrs. Dobbs smiled sheepishly and Peg poured the lemonade she had made into some glasses which she had brought in on a tray. Mr. Dobbs had a pipe in his hand and he tamped the bowl as he said:

"Mrs. Dobbs, I hear you've been complaining about the heat."

"Well, no more than usual."

"I've got a fine remedy for it, Ella."

"Yes?"

"It's at the Apex theatre. They say it's sixty-six degrees there, cooler than an off-shore breeze. And they've got a movie there that you've been aching to see."

"What are they showing?"

"I don't know. But it's bound to be good. It'll work out the way we want it to because Hollywood understands us. And that'll make it good. So, Mrs. Dobbs, let's go and get our eyes and ears massaged while we enjoy the soft cool breezes of the Apex. We'll pick up Mickey down the street and take him along. Okay?"

"Well, if you insist."

"Then please get ready and don't be long."

Nick stood up as Mrs. Dobbs rose and minced out of the room. He patted his coat where his gun rested and felt safer knowing that it was there. But he couldn't stop the spinning that went on inside of him. He felt himself straining to take off in a wild run again. He saw a huge man leap high into the air before crashing down upon him and pinioning him still. That was the way he would have to stay until he knew where he wanted to go and what he wanted to do. He couldn't afford to make a mistake. He couldn't afford to take any chances.

He knew that in this house he was safe. Nobody would

43

ever think of looking for him here. The police, he knew, would be scouring his neighborhood. His house would be watched. The police would be at every flat he had ever visited trying to seek out some clue to where he could be hiding out. But they would never suspect his coming to this house. Anybody who ever knew him would be under constant watch; but these people had never known him and nobody would think of watching them. And should he decide to run, where could he go? The police would be looking for him at the railroad and bus stations and freight yards. And if he stole a car, how far would he get? He knew that he had no way of getting anywhere, and he had no place to go. So the man who had leaped out to hold him still whispered: "You're safe here, Nick. Here, you've got to stay. Nobody'll come to look for you or catch you here in a million years. For the first time since you got up this morning you felt safe only here. So where are you going? How are you going? This is the spot, Nick. Here, you've got to stay."

"But how?" he asked. "How am I going to stay here without them knowing, without them finding out, and without my killing them, if I want to live, when they do find out? How?"

Supposing, he thought, I just say to them: "Look, I'm the guy that's wanted for the killing of the cop. I'm Nick Robey. But I didn't kill him. I never killed anybody in my life. Al Molin killed him. He was shot and wounded killing him. And he framed me. Will you help me? Will you help me for just a little bit until the heat's off and until I can get away?"

What would they say? How would they act?

But supposing he said to them: "Okay, you don't believe me. But this talks. This talks plenty. I've got ten thousand bucks. It's yours if you keep your mouth shut and if you keep me until the heat's off."

Could he buy them? Would they agree?

Could he trust them?

And supposing he said to them: "All right, here it is. I'm Nick Robey. Yah, that's it. I'm the guy that's wanted

44

for murder. Now that you know it, I'm staying here. And you're staying with me. From now on, it's going to be one big happy family here: me, my gun, and you."

But he knew that he couldn't keep all of them prisoners. Somebody would get suspicious if the old man didn't show up at his stand. Somebody would get suspicious over a lot of things. And besides, one of them would have to go out when they'd get hungry for food. And then where would he be? And besides that, when the time came to escape, he knew that he would have to kill them all before he left so that nobody would know he had been there and where he had got away from and how close he was to the house.

So what should I do? he asked himself. Should I lam out of here and take my chances? But where could I go? What could I do? How could I hide out? . . . Or should I stay? . . . How?

Please, God, he begged. Please, God and Jesus and Mary, please tell me what to do. Let me know what to do. Make it easy for me. Don't drive me nuts. Jesus, make it easy for me.

Then Mrs. Dobbs entered the living room in a freshly ironed summer dress, the straggling wisps of her faded red hair now pinned down.

"All right, Casey," she said to Mr. Dobbs. "I'm ready."

"Wait," said Nick. "Do you have to go?"

"Well, no, not exactly," said Mrs. Dobbs.

"Why don't you stick around and we'll talk?"

"But we thought if we went, why—"

Mr. Dobbs interrupted her.

"Ella, it's getting late," he said. "And if we don't go soon, we'll never get there."

"However," said Mrs. Dobbs, "if you'd rather we'd stay—"

"Sure," said Nick. "I'd like you to stay."

"Well—" Mrs. Dobbs hesitated.

"I see you build sailboats, Mr. Dobbs," said Nick.

"It's a hobby of mine."

"Good. They're real good."

"I just make them to keep my hands busy in my spare time. It sort of helps me think."

"What do you think about, Mr. Dobbs?"

"Oh, nothing very important. My thoughts don't amount to a row of beans."

"Did you ever want to own a real sailboat? Is that what you think about?"

"All my life, Joe. All my life."

"Could ten grand buy you one?"

"Yes, I suppose it could."

"Supposing a guy walked up to you, Mr. Dobbs, and he said: here's ten grand; then stuck it in your hand? What would you do for ten grand?"

Mr. Dobbs thought a moment.

"Probably nothing," he said.

"Nothing!" said Mrs. Dobbs. "How you talk, Casey! Why, it would make your dreams come true."

"That's the point, Ella. I don't want my dreams to come true. If they did come true, why, I'd only be forced to think up some more. And soon I'd have to stretch my imagination beyond all limits. And then I'd be forced to hurt people to get what I want.

"A thing few people understand, Joe, is that you can ache and ache for a dream to come true and the ache never stops, if you've got it bad and if you've got it big. But let us say one of your dreams does come true. Well, you're satisfied with it for a time, certainly. But you might still feel hollow inside, so you're led into another dream, a more expensive one. You ache a little harder with that. But let us say that comes true. And afterwards you feel a little more hollow inside, because sometimes something happens to a man that pushes him beyond himself and he begins to drive himself beyond reason. So you dream up a still bigger dream, until finally you're in the realm of power. And then, well, you might want the whole earth, and even the sun.

"Ever watch a kid, Joe? You give him a rattle. He rattles it and gets a big bang out of it. Then he throws it away. He's had the experience. He wants a new one. Well,

46

some people never grow up. They want one thing after another in a world of gimme, gimme, gimme. It takes a smart man to know when to stop saying gimme. It takes a big man to be able to say take me. That's the way I sometimes think, Joe, but how I seldom talk. At any rate, I'm satisfied with what I've got. And even my dream is just big enough for me to handle and I'm satisfied with that, too. So ten thousand dollars wouldn't help me at all. I think I'd rather imagine my sailing boats than really sail them."

"I was just talking," said Nick. He also thought: this old duck is queer; he can't be bought; he is even too queer to live.

Mr. Dobbs took Mrs. Dobbs by the arm and started walking out of the house. Peg grasped Nick's hand as he almost rushed to stop them. And in his indecision about what to do he muttered goodbye as they left. And inwardly, alone now with Peg, within a closed door, he prayed: don't let anything happen; don't, for Christ's sake, let them suddenly get wise to who he was. For if anything happened, if the police came, he would shoot his way out with Peg in front of him. She would die first, before he died.

So don't let anything happen, he begged. I don't want to kill anybody else. But I will if I have to. Just give me time and don't let anything happen and just give me time.

Outside, while walking to pick up Mickey on the way to the theatre, Mrs. Dobbs said:

"He seems like a nice fellow, doesn't he, Casey? But he's definitely not a very talkative person, not talkative at all."

"You know, Ella, it seems to me that I've seen Joe before."

"He seemed sort of nervous," continued Mrs. Dobbs, "a sort of nervous type, like he was in trouble, or something was troubling him. But maybe he was in the army a long time and he hasn't adjusted to people yet, especially women."

"But I'm sure I've seen him somewhere before, some time today," continued Mr. Dobbs.

47

"But how could you, Casey? He was at the beach all day."

"That's what puzzles me. I wish I could think of where I'd seen him."

"You're always seeing things, Casey."

"Well, I'll think of it later, I suppose. Then it'll come to me like that—" he snapped his fingers—"and I'll feel as though I've had a good bowel movement."

"How you talk, Casey!"

They glanced at each other and smiled, then saw Mickey and called him, and then walked on to the theatre.

Chapter VI

NICK felt as though there were a thousand little men within him, scratching, picking, and tearing up his insides. They kept him in constant motion. He looked out of the window. The trees were motionless in the earth between the sidewalk and the curb. The lights from the lamp posts glimmered in yellow arcs. There were still some people sitting on the bench outside. Occasionally, people passed by; he didn't know who they were. The street, with the dark passageways between buildings, became unreal and dangerous to him. On it lurked somebody who was out to get him. He had a wild desire to rush outside and search out this somebody who was out to get him and kill him. Then he would be all right. Then he would have nothing to worry about; for the rest of his life he would be safe and without a worry. But a sudden fear overwhelmed him and he backed away from the window deeper into the room, felt Peg beside him, and saw her look at him in a puzzled but trustful way, the slender freckled kid. Here, he had to stay.

But how?

Outside, there was danger. There was himself scurrying down a maze of streets. There was himself dying as he ran. There was himself running into a burst of gunfire. There was himself scattered on the streets.

But here he was safe.

How could he continue to make himself safe here?

49

But supposing Mr. and Mrs. Dobbs knew who he was? Supposing they had seen his picture in the paper and had recognized it, even though he was hardly able to? Then, maybe, they didn't go to the movie. Then they got out of the house to get away from him and to tell the police. And supposing the house was surrounded now? Supposing there was a cop in every dark passageway on the street just waiting for him to step out of the house and down the stairs? But he would never leave the house alone. Peg would go out with him, if he left. She would go out with him, directly in front of him, right up against him, leg moving with leg.

So don't try anything, he yelled inwardly for Mr. and Mrs. Dobbs to hear. Just don't try to rat on me!

"Don't you want to take off your coat, Joe?" said Peg. "Your face is kind of wet. It's awfully warm in here. You ought to take off your coat. It'll be more comfortable."

"That's okay," he said.

"And you ought to relax, too. There's nothing like relaxing when it's warm. Nobody's going to bite you, you know. We're alone, just you and me."

"I am relaxed."

"Or maybe you feel restless and you want to do something?"

"Like what?"

"Like anything. Like going dancing or to a night club. Or we might even take a walk, if that's what you want."

"No, I don't want to do any of that. I don't know what I want to do."

"Then what would you like to do?"

"We can dance here, can't we? You got a radio. We can dance here."

"Certainly."

"Okay. Let's turn on the radio and dance then."

Peg tuned in a jazz orchestra. She glided, the way she did in her dreams, toward Nick, her arms outstretched, her body feeling warm and big in lazy movement, her head upturned. Nick circled his arm about her small waist, his arm so strong, and she felt as though she wanted to bend into it, wilting, and to be glided away. The warmth and strong beat of his body gave her a strange feeling, which turned into a slight fright, for the sense of his physical closeness sent peculiar shivers through her.

"What's the pushing for?" he asked.

She strained away from him and pressed her hand against his shoulder.

"You just hold me so tight I can't breathe," she said. "Relax a little, Joe. Glide a little."

"That's the way I dance."

"Then let me teach you another way."

"That's the only way I ever danced."

"But there are other ways, Joe. Nice ways. Let me teach you."

"It's too late for that."

"Why, you talk like an old man, Joe, like there's no use in your learning because you're going to die tomorrow."

"Don't say that." He let her go and stepped back from her.

"Why, what did I say?"

"Die tomorrow."

"You know I didn't mean it, Joe. I was just talking. Why—" she laughed slightly—"how could a person as young and as strong as you die tomorrow, or even for the next fifty years? It's ridiculous."

He shook his shoulders to loosen them from a cramped feeling he had and he tried to get out from under a tremendous pressure on the back of his neck.

"Let's cut out the dancing," he said. "I don't feel so hot."

"All right."

"And let's turn off the radio. It's too noisy."

She dialed off the radio. It became very quiet. Voices could be heard indistinctly from the outside.

"Is anything wrong, Joe?" she asked.

"No. Do I look like anything's wrong?"

Yes, she wanted to say; but instead said: "I mean, did I do anything wrong?"

"No. That's a crazy idea."

"I'm glad to hear that. I hate to do anything wrong. I hate to hurt anybody."

"You're okay, kid. You're nice. It's me. I don't feel so hot, that's all."

He felt her eyes linger over him before she sat down on the couch. He sat down beside her. And for a while they didn't talk. Nick liked that. He went inside himself, started moving again within the dark mazes of his mind, groping and hurling himself at the high walls and tight corners of his life.

But Peg didn't know what to make out of him. He was deeply disturbed; she knew that, could feel it almost as though he had reached within her and was shaking her insides. He disturbed her with his warm, strong, violent-moving body that nearly always seemed ready to pounce upon her, which kept her poised but from which she couldn't flee. And he disturbed her in the way that her mother and Mickey did the few times she had seen them cry. She wondered what was troubling him and why she was touched so deeply.

Could it be, she asked herself, that he was a psychoneurotic, whatever that really was? Could it be that he was all mixed up from having spent too many days in a fox-hole, or from having been a prisoner of war, or from having been wounded? She took it for granted that he had been overseas and had been discharged recently. But whatever it was that troubled him, she remembered that the papers and radio had warned her to treat a veteran in a normal way and to act with him as though he were the most undisturbed person in the world. These men, she remembered reading and being told, were not insane; they were just a little tired; they just had to get adjusted again. But she was a little tired. She hadn't had any breaks, either. You met somebody and before you knew it he was drafted. Or you met somebody and before you knew it he was going somewhere else. Or you met somebody and there was something wrong with him. But always, they all had seemed to want only one thing. It seemed as though she had gone through a whole lifetime of this in the few years she had grown into what she thought was a woman. She had been denied what older girls had and what younger girls were going to get. How long could she wait? she wondered.

Still, she had to be sympathetic. She would not be the one to aggravate his malady. For despite everything, he seemed like a nice person, generous, too, in the way he had taken her home in a cab and hadn't even tried to maul her as other men had. He didn't undress her with his eyes as other men did, either. And he had such nice eyes, deep and dark and burning in a face so strong, so smooth. But she wished he was more romantic. She wished he would try to make himself more appealing to her. But she knew that he couldn't. He was unhappy about something. She wished she knew what.

Could it be that he had been jilted by a girl while he was overseas? she asked herself. She knew that a person like Joe could have a lot of girls if he wanted them. But perhaps he was the type that didn't want a lot of girls. He wanted only one. Yes, she could hardly breathe saying it to herself, he was the true blue type, not a sometime thing, a one-woman man. . . . Or perhaps a girl friend hadn't jilted him; a wife had, a sometime thing who had left him for another man. He had said he was alone; he got by alone; he had nobody. He said it angrily and said you couldn't trust anybody, and like a fool, fool that she was, her mind sang limply, she said if you trust you love and if you love you trust; but he could have said, and didn't, if you trust you can be betrayed; but she would never betray him, she would never betray anyone, she would die first.

Yet she wished she knew what was troubling him. She wished she knew a lot of things. She wished she could ask a million questions and that she would get a million answers, true ones. Because she wanted to know. She wanted to help Joe. She wanted him to feel the way he had touched her and to let him know that he could trust her. And then . . . this was the way people fell in love. This was the way you became wrapped up in each other, if you were not the light, bouncy type; and Joe was not that; she was not that. She was—the lyrics of a song twisted through her mind—*nothing to look at, nothing to see, just glad I'm living, lucky to be, got a man, crazy for me, he's funny that way*. But she wished that were true, to have a man crazy for her. The desire ran through her with an exquisite ache. And she did not know that the song had floated softly out of her throat.

"You sing nice, Peg," he said.

"Oh," she said, surprised.

"What is it?"

"Oh, an old song. There's not much sense to it."

"I like a girl that sings."

"I sing all the time, mostly inside."

"Let's hear."

"I can't. I'm embarrassed now. But if you'll sing with me, that'd be nice."

"I don't sing. I never sing. I don't know a single song."

"Singing is good, even if you haven't got a voice. It's good for what ails you. That's what you ought to do, Joe, sing a little more."

"If I started singing you wouldn't like it, Peg. Believe me, you wouldn't like it."

"Ah, you're modest."

They paused a moment and became entangled in each other's glances. Then Nick said:

"I like you, Peg. You're a good kid. You don't put on an act."

"What's the good of putting on an act? Where would it get you—in the end?" She laughed at her joke, and he smiled.

"I like your ma and pa, too," he said. "They're nice people."

"They are, Joe, real nice. And I'm glad you like them."

"I like the neighborhood, too. I'd kind of like to live around it."

"You would?"

"Yah, sure."

"That'd be nice, Joe, real nice."

"We could be neighbors." He felt her eyes linger over him. "We could even be better than neighbors. You wouldn't have room for a boarder, would you?"

54

"Goodness, no. We even need another room for Mickey."

"I'm kind of looking around for a place to live, Peg. I don't have any place to live now."

"There are a couple of hotels nearby," she suggested.

"Where?"

"A couple of miles from here."

No, he thought. That wouldn't be any good. Police might check on hotels. A guy had to live some place, so they'd check on hotels, and maybe even rooming houses. And besides, if Peg recommended one, she would know where he was. And then if she found out who he was, he would be trapped. Peg was a danger to him. Sooner or later she was bound to find out who he was. She might tell somebody. Her folks might tell somebody. They were trapping him. He should never have met her and gone home with her. Now they had seen him and they were dangerous to him. He should have been alone all the time. He would not have so much to worry about, then. Now they were a menace to him. He had to watch out for them. Even if he left now, this minute, perhaps in a few hours or the next day they might suddenly realize who he was and they would tell the police and the police would then start picking up his trail from this house.

"But my mother," said Peg, "might know of a neighbor who has a spare room to rent. She knows everything. Do you want me to ask her?"

"No," he said. "Forget it."

That would be no good, either, he thought. Peg and her folks would still know where he was. And then somebody else, the neighbor, would see him and perhaps recognize him. He felt a trap slowly being set for him. He had to get out of it some way. He had to remain as safe as he was. He could not expose himself to any more people. He wished he knew of only one person to whom he could go for help and who would hide him out until the heat was off. If he had only one place to go to. But he had only the outdoors to go to, unfriendly landlords, hotel clerks, restaurants; only places where he would be seen and recognized and captured. He had to figure out an angle to be able to stay here and not be caught. But how? Supposing he told Peg who he was? Would she help him? But then her folks would have to know. Would they help him? Supposing he put it up to them and they refused to help him, then what would he do? But that was no good. For supposing they said they would help him; could he trust them? No, he had to figure out a plan so that he would have control over them, so that no matter what they decided to do, he would be safe. But how?

"Where will you sleep tonight?" Peg asked.

"I don't know."

"But where have you been staying until now?"

"With a friend. He got married today."

"I'll bet that's what has been troubling you. I don't blame you. I'd feel plenty uneasy myself."

"Yah, I'm kind of on the spot."

"Have you tried any hotels?"

"Filled up."

"Rooming houses?"

"Them, too."

"Well, you can't sleep in the park or on the street."

"It'd be lousy. But if I have to—"

"Maybe you could sleep on this couch, Joe. I'll ask my folks when they come home. I'm sure they'll say okay. They can't say no to anything. That's the way they are."

"Where are your folks? Shouldn't they be home soon?"

"Oh, no. They're seeing a double feature."

"What time will they be home?"

"Around midnight, I guess."

"What time's it now?"

"You don't have to worry, Joe. It's all settled. You're going to sleep here tonight. So stop your worrying."

"But what time's it now?"

"About ten, ten-thirty."

He was sure now that they were in the movie house. If they had suspected him, they would have informed the police long ago. The police would have come for him some time ago. And then the battle would have started. Because he was not going to give himself up. He was

56

going to die fighting before he would die a million times in his mind the way Al Molin was going to die.

He had tried to make it so easy for Al. Why hadn't God done Al a favor by making his bullet find Al's head and giving Al a good death, bang, without knowing it? Why? And then he would be free. And he wouldn't have to think about dying and killing. And he could even know Peg now in a good way. And he wouldn't have to be wrinkling his brains for a plan. He wasn't good at making plans. That had been Al's department. Al was good about those things. Now he was alone. He was going crazy trying to make things come out right. Something might happen. He didn't want anything to happen. But if Peg's folks didn't get home by midnight he did not know if he could stop himself from making something happen. The longer he stayed, the more trapped he felt. Now Peg was telling him he could sleep here. He knew that he couldn't sleep here, that he would never be able to fall asleep, not until he had control over them, not until he knew that he could stop running and that he was safe. He had to have a plan. Come on, Al, he called inwardly, tell me the plan you had, in case something happened. Come on, Al, give me a little little little idea. I've got to have a plan. I'm safe here now. But I've got to stay that way.

"You're sweating again, Joe," said Peg. She gently wiped his forehead with her palm and looked at the wetness of her hand. "You ought to take off your jacket and relax. You haven't a thing to worry about now."

"That's okay. I'll wait till your folks come home."

"That won't be for a while."

"That's okay. I feel more comfortable with it on."

Peg stood up and Nick clutched at her hand.

"Where you going?" he asked.

"I'm going to make some coffee. Maybe there's some cake to go with it. Would you like that?"

"Sure, sure. That's a swell idea."

He followed her into the kitchen, afraid to lose sight of her, and watched her make the coffee. The smell of it was good. The taste of it, together with some cake, was better.

He felt more alert. They went back into the living room. But still a plan would not come to him. His thinking began to exhaust him. The whole day began to catch up with him and he gave himself over to his exhaustion for a moment. He leaned back into the couch and began to feel himself drift. Peg was beside him and the warmth of her body was like a live thing wrapped about him and he felt safe within its glow. Suddenly, he saw himself lifted up and brought gently against the broad bosom of a woman with the face of a saint. He saw himself wilting against the warmth of her body and being held tenderly in her arms. Then he looked up and saw her lips almost upon his and for a moment he thought he was sucking from the juices of her being, when suddenly his whole body recoiled from the full impact of their lips and he sprang away from Peg, not noticing the shock and bewilderment on her face.

"What were you trying to do?" he asked.

She didn't seem to understand and she couldn't answer.

"What are you, like all of them, like my mother, like every hooker on the streets?"

He didn't know what else he said. She buried her face in her hands and began to cry. His legs got jittery and he had to sit down. And after a time, the exhaustion came over him again, but his stomach began to churn, and he rushed to the bathroom and got sick.

When he came back to the couch, Peg was still crying. He sat down limply and, as he felt his body drift away from him again, he prayed: hold it, hold on to yourself, don't don't don't let yourself go. And then he felt the tears washing down his face, tasting salty on his lips. And when he felt her hand on his head, he felt soothed. He gave himself over to the strain that had overwhelmed him and abandoned himself to crying.

CHAPTER VII

NICK hadn't cried in years. He hadn't reached out for comfort, for tenderness, for love, in so long a time that he was not able to recognize it. The last time he had felt a warmth, a family relationship, a unity of strength, was when he was a kid. But that hadn't lasted very long. For even as a kid he had had his first contact with the police. It had happened in a way he did not like to remember. It had happened in a way that perhaps made him the way he was now.

Nick did not remember much of his father. He only knew that his father had seemed to him a big man with big muscles, and he used to like to watch the way his father's biceps jumped about as he moved them. But what he remembered most about his father was that he had gone away and left him and his mother. Nick never knew why he had gone away, and without saying a word to him. But before his father went away he remembered how he sat around the house without ever talking. He looked like a blown up crumpled paper bag waiting to be banged out of usefulness. The only time he seemed to grow alive was when he coughed; his whole body trembled and jerked with what seemed like chains rattling through him. Then he had gone off one day, his back stooped and round. And he had not returned. Nick had heard him talking to his mother before he had left.

"I'm a dead man," he said.

59

"You should never have taken that job in the sewer, with your weak chest."

"I had to."

"Every day you worked I saw you getting a hemorrhage in your lungs, and you were gone. It wasn't worth it."

"That was life."

"What do you mean: was?"

"I can't hold out any longer. You'll get some insurance money soon. I took care of that on my last job."

Nick's mother began to cry. Nick was only seven years old then and he could not understand why she cried. She had cried a lot lately, and each time he felt himself swimming through her tears, boiling and choking in them.

Nick knew only that his father had a cold. That was why his father always kept him at a distance. But having a cold was nothing to bawl about. Nick had had many. It was practically nothing.

When his father did not return after a week, his mother seemed to wait around the house for something to happen. Whenever there was a knocking on the door she ran to it quickly. If it was a neighbor or a salesman or a bill collector, her eyes lost their expectancy.

Then his mother began to curse his father when she thought Nick could not hear. It seemed she had been cheated out of something. Nick did not know what.

When the kids on the street asked him about his father he felt bewildered, not knowing what to answer. Finally he said: "He went to buy me a pony. He went far away from here for it."

"Jesus!" the kids said. "You got a real old man."

But when he asked his mother where his father had gone, she yelled, "Don't bother me! Get away and don't bother me!"

And he thought she was going to hit him. He had to stop asking her, because when he did she no longer looked like his mother. She would stop looking big and soft and warm.

One day, not long after his father went away, Nick was hungry. He had not eaten the day before, except for a couple of apples he had hooked from a fruit stand. He was so hungry he sat at the kitchen table waiting. His mother walked restlessly back and forth from the empty pantry. Nick had said he was hungry, and watched her move silently on her sprawling bare feet. Her heavy black hair was uncombed. She looked very big and fleshy in her apron. There was a wrinkled expression on her forehead, like crying, but she wasn't. She sat down at the kitchen table and her eyes gazed upon him without seeing. Finally she stood up and put on a pair of worn, bulging shoes.

"I'm going to get something to eat," she said.

"I'm hungry, ma."

He followed her into the dank stairway. Creaking down the dampened stairs, Nick inhaled deeply the faint lingering smells of cooked food.

"It hurts in my belly, ma."

"Soon it won't hurt, I hope."

Outside the sun glazed the dusty street and the trolley rails looked like rippling cellophane ribbons. Niggy and Al Molin, both a couple of years older than Nick, sat on the curbstone. They were what Nick called the big guys.

"You play with them."

"All right, ma."

"I'll be back soon. So don't go away."

Nick walked slowly to the curbstone and picked up a rain-soaked stick on the way. He sat down beside them, with his feet in the gutter.

"Where'd your ma go?" Al asked.

"She went to get something to eat."

"Why don't she go to the corner grocery like my ma goes?"

"She don't have to do everything like your ma."

"Where'd she go then?"

"I don't know."

"You're a dumbsock. You don't know nothing."

"Your pa home yet?" Niggy asked.

"No."

"My ma said to my pa he went away and left you," Niggy said.

"He went far away from here." Nick said. "It takes a year to go up and back."

"Go on," Al said. "No place is a year away from here."

"Yeah?" Nick said. "What about heaven? That's more'n a year."

"That's bushwa," Al said. "Ain't it, Niggy?"

"Sure. 'Cause now you can go by airplane and you go like sixty."

"So where'd your pa go a year away?" Al asked.

"In the West, see. He's a cowboy there and when he comes home he's going to bring me a pony from that horse he got there."

"I don't know," Niggy said. " 'Cause in my house my ma looks at my pa and she begins throwing her fist around and she says: don't let me catch you trying to leave. And my pa says: don't go giving me ideas. Yeah? my ma says."

"Your ma and pa must be nuts," Nick said.

"I'll kill you, you say that again," Niggy said.

"You can't hit a baby like that," Al said.

"He got to take back what he said."

"Go on," Al said. "Do it."

Niggy was standing and his knuckles were white and from under his baseball cap his eyes glowered.

"I take it back," Nick said.

"You better," Niggy said. His body relaxed and he sat down again.

An automobile whizzed by and Nick was glad. Al was excited and said it was a Packard. He could tell by the radiator frame which shone like a diamond in the sun, and by the red spinning square on the hub cap. Nick said, how could Al know? He had never seen one before. But Al said Ace Gordon, the best wheelman in the world, drove one. Niggy said that was right, and bragged how he saw Ace turn corners on two wheels with the cops right behind him. Nick was awed, hearing about Ace Gordon and about seeing a Packard for the first time. Niggy and Al decided to see who was a better guesser of automobiles. Niggy and Al bet thousands of dollars guessing, and Nick envied them.

When they tired of their game they took Nick's stick

and threw it on the trolley tracks. Niggy said maybe the stick would make the car fall over. Nick was grateful for being allowed to get in the game, but was soon sorry when the trolley-car wheels splintered his stick to pieces. Niggy and Al were a couple of dirty guys. "Go on, punk," they said, "you ought to be lucky we let you hang around."

As they were urging Nick to find them a big board or a brick in order to really make the car fall off the tracks, his mother came down the street with a few bags of groceries pressed against her big breasts. There was a splotch on her dress.

"Here comes your ma," Niggy said.

"Hey, Nick, what'd your old lady do?" Al shouted.

"Where, Al?" Niggy asked.

"There, Niggy. There. See?"

"Yeah, Nick, what'd she do?" Niggy asked.

"Jesus, it looks like, ho, ha, ha!" Al laughed.

"Haw, ha," Niggy bellowed.

"Oh, what'd your old lady do?" Al yelled.

"Nicky," she called. "Come here."

Nick was bewildered. Niggy and Al were embracing their bellies, singing, taunting, "Shame on Nicky's mother, shame on Nicky's mother."

"Come here, Nicky!"

He walked to her side. Up the stairs she kept muttering, "Little snots, little snots!"

In the house she became silent and busied herself in the kitchen. Nick kept looking at her dress as she moved about. He wanted to ask her what was on it but was afraid she would not look like his mother. But the food was good and he forgot about everything and his mother was big and soft and warm. He jumped on her lap and felt her breast soften under his head, and when he looked up her eyes were watery and he felt himself strained through her tears and flowing within her breasts.

That night he went to sleep on the couch in the living room, which was next to the bedroom and off the kitchen. He was suddenly awakened by loud knocks on the door. He saw his mother's naked body bulge from the darkness.

"Who's there?" she whispered.

"It's Mike!"

"Please go away. It's too late."

"Let me in!"

Nick thought the door was going to whang to the floor, such hard knocking followed. She ran to the couch and he squeezed his eyes tight. He was afraid to breathe. Then as he lay there stiff and tense against the bulgy cushions, he could hear his mother saying shhh, and her feet hissing across the bare floor, and the man saying, "What's a matter? You don't like to eat no more?"

He heard the door to his mother's room close, then talk, then no more words, just heavy groaning and breathing, and he fell asleep in the hush that followed. He awoke feeling a smile on his cheeks after dreaming his father was back, who was also his big brother, and he ran into his mother's room. And it *was* his father there, he was so happy, until he heard the voice.

"What's the kid doing here? Beat it."

Nick stood there in the darkness.

"Go back to sleep, Nicky," his mother said quietly.

He walked out and dressed and ran outside and walked in the yellow-orbed streets and finally slumped into a store entrance. He was awakened by a policeman lifting him to his feet.

"What you doing here, sonny?"

Nick did not answer. He rubbed his eyes with his dirty hands. His eyes looked feverish and frightened.

"What's the matter, boy, you dumb?"

Nick nodded.

"You lost?"

Nick shook his head.

"Where do you live?"

"Home."

"Where's home?"

"Don't know."

"You ain't got a home, sonny. Tell me."

"Honest I got one."

"If I don't take you home, I got to take you to jail."

"I can go myself home."

"I'll take you."

The policeman followed him. Nick did not want to go home. He saw Niggy and Al, and he could not go back. He did not want the cop to go up to his house. Somebody was going to get in trouble. Then he forgot where he lived. No matter what the policeman asked, Nick did not know anything. When Nick began to cry the policeman said he shouldn't be afraid of being lost. He wanted to help Nick. Nick felt the tears on his cheeks, and tasted them. When the squad car came, Nick got in.

That's how the police had first picked him up.

At the station the police asked him many questions. But he stared at them without focus, without answering. They offered to take him home, give him a ride in an auto, pull the siren, anything, if he would let them take him home. But he said he wanted to go home by himself. He pressed his bloodless lips together determined that nobody was going to take him home. The police didn't want the responsibility of letting him wander about in the darkness alone. They wanted him to stay overnight but he wouldn't fall asleep.

"Ah, let the kid go home," said one of the policemen. "The punk knows where he lives, all right, but he's just too scared about something. Maybe his old man's drunk, or his mother's whoring around, or they're both whoring around and drunk in the same house. Who the hell knows about these people?"

Nick glared at the cop and his eyes began to burn from the intensity. The cop shrugged off Nick's bright glistening stare by shaking his shoulders and tousling Nick's hair.

Finally, he was released.

Nick ran out of the station. His side ached and his chest seemed to fill up with hot coals and the air seemed to grow thinner and thinner and his legs became like stilts upon which he jounced with every step, but he didn't stop running through the dark streets until he reached his house. He lingered outside a while looking up at the unlit windows of his house, where he knew his mother was but where he knew he could not be alone with her. He walked

65

through the passageway to the back yard, and under the porch steps on the hard ground he whimpered himself to sleep.

In the morning he went upstairs. And his mother was alone. She clutched him to her and cried, but he pushed her away. After that, he always pushed her away. But at night he had strange and disturbing dreams about her. And sometimes in his deep loneliness and from the vague images that groped through his mind he cried out, "Ma! Ma!" But she never heard him.

After that night he and his mother ate quite often. There were also different men who came around who, he was told, were his uncles. But sometimes after eating he got sick. His mother said tenderly that he ate too fast, or that her little boy wasn't used to eating so well, or that the food was too rich but he would get used to it.

And he, himself, did not know why he got sick. He only felt strange after that. He felt that he didn't belong and that nothing belonged to him, and he felt himself ducking from something that he never saw but which was always behind him. He felt very strange.

Chapter VIII

NICK stood up suddenly from the couch, with a peculiar spinning in his stomach.

"What time is it?" he asked.

"It's late, I guess," said Peg.

"How late?"

"Ten minutes past midnight."

"Where's your folks?" He had to stop himself from yelling. "You said they'd be home by now. Where are they?"

"They'll be along, Joe," she said appeasingly. "Don't worry. You won't be turned out. I told you you'd be able to sleep over here."

"It ain't that."

"What is it, then?"

"Nothing." Jesus, nothing, he added to himself.

They better come soon, he thought. If they didn't, something was going to happen. He didn't want anything to happen. He wanted to be left alone and for the world to stop still for a moment and for the spinning in his stomach to stop. Then he would be all right. But as it was, nothing was all right. Mr. and Mrs. Dobbs weren't home yet, and so long as they were out anything might happen.

He shoved his hand inside his coat pocket and tightly gripped his pistol. Now nothing could happen to him, so long as he had the gun. From the first time he had ever felt a gun, he felt that he was reasonably safe. Instead of his fearing anybody, people feared him. He had a sense, then, of reaching out and of holding anybody he wanted close to him and under his power.

Peg noticed him relax slightly. That was peculiar. Every time he put his hand in his pocket and sort of held something tight he began to relax and the pressure of his forehead upon his eyes seemed to ease up; it was like he was swallowing a drug that he knew would make him feel better. She followed Nick to the window. He watched the people and the automobiles that went by occasionally.

"What?" she asked timidly. "What's wrong, Joe?"

"Nothing."

"Something's wrong, Joe. Why don't you tell me? Maybe I can help you."

"Nothing. Nothing's wrong."

Above the lamp post lights and the tree tops outside there were a few scattered stars in a clear sky. A wispy cloud floated across the half-moon. She remarked that it was nice out, and he agreed without looking upward.

"A night like this," she said. "Have you ever been out on the lake in a big boat on a night like this, Joe?"

"Sure. Plenty times."

"It gets nice and cool out there. And the moon, it looks bigger and milkier there. And the stars, they dance more."

"Where is your folks?" he said tensely.

"They'll be home soon. It must have been a long movie. But what's troubling you, Joe?"

"What would you do," he asked slowly, feeling his way, "if you knew a guy who killed somebody?"

"I knew that was it."

He felt himself tighten up, and he said slowly, "You knew what?"

"But what can a person do?" she said evasively. "Didn't millions of our men kill somebody? Didn't we at home hope and pray for killing and more killing so's the war could end quicker and so's less of our men would get killed? And didn't we make the stuff for killing? Don't worry about that, Joe." She took his hand and squeezed it gently. "Please don't worry about that. It's all over, Joe. It'll never happen again. It wasn't your fault anyhow. It's all finished."

"But suppose a guy killed another guy personal?"

"You mean, like with a bayonet?"

"No. I mean, like on the street, to keep himself from getting killed."

"I don't know. What could I do?"

Yes, he thought. That was it. What could she do?

"What are you trying to tell me, Joe?" She felt herself growing cold, distant, and she shriveled within the fear of what he might be getting at.

"Would you be for him?" he asked.

"I don't know. I don't know what you're talking about." She found her eyes growing as watchful and as restless as his.

"I was talking about a guy who killed another guy personal."

"How could I be for him?" Now she no longer held his hand but he was holding hers. She felt her breath cut short as his hand clutched hers tighter when she retreated slightly. "I don't know what I'd do," she added. "He killed somebody, didn't he? He committed a crime against God and the world, didn't he?"

"Supposing the world tried to kill him? Supposing the world committed a crime against him?"

"How can that be? How can the world try to kill one person? It doesn't make sense. It's funny kind of talk, Joe. What are you trying to tell me, Joe? What are you trying to do?"

"Then how can one guy commit a crime against God and the world? He just knocks off one other guy who's in his way, like in a holdup."

"What are you driving at, Joe?"

"But supposing a guy didn't kill anybody and the police think he did and he is wanted for something he isn't guilty of? Would you stick by him?"

"If he wasn't guilty," she said hesitantly. "If he was important to me."

"Would I be important to you?"

"I don't know, Joe. You've got me all mixed up. I don't know what you're talking about."

His body became very stiff for a moment. His hand

became a rigid vise around her hand and it sent a sharp ache through her whole body. Then he stepped closer to the drapes, pulling her with him, and continued scrutinizing the sidewalk outside. His other hand clamped over her mouth and stifled the scream that came to her throat.

Mr. and Mrs. Dobbs and Mickey were coming toward the house. But with them were two big men with rounded black shoes. Nick knew they were detectives. The spinning and the tension in his stomach stopped. He felt himself being lifted, then soaring high, and then somebody else seemed to step inside of him, and he became ecstatic with the sense of having overwhelmed himself and of still stepping forward as a conqueror. His mind felt released and the threatening pressure above his neck was thrown off. He took a deep breath. This was it. He knew what he was facing now. The threat was before him and not behind him, the way it always was. Only his legs quivered.

"Okay, Peg," he said. "I didn't want this to happen, but it has." He watched Mr. and Mrs. Dobbs and the kid stop in front of the stairway leading up to the first floor of the house. The two big men, one in a gray and one in a black suit, wearing hats and the unmistakable shoes of detectives, stood with them, talking, nodding toward the house, and looking upward occasionally.

"I'm going to take my hand away from your mouth," he continued. "When I do, don't scream. Be very quiet. If you want to live, be very quiet. I got a gun in my pocket. My fingers are nervous. They're nervous as hell. When I pull it out, I'll start shooting, if you're not quiet. I'll start shooting outside, too, and get your mother and father and kid brother, too, if you're not quiet. You won't scream then. You'll keep quiet."

She nodded her head and mumbled against his hand. He released her mouth.

"Those two big guys out there, who are they?" he asked.

"Neighbors."

"They're dicks. I can spot them a mile. Tell me the truth. Who are they?"

"I'm telling you the truth. They're neighbors."

70

"Okay, they're neighbors. But they can still be dicks. A dick can be a neighbor, too."

"What are you going to do to us?"

"Nothing, if you'll do like I say, if nothing happens."

"Nothing will happen, Joe. Don't you see, we don't even know who you are. Be good, Joe. Nothing will happen, you will see. Trust me, and leave us alone, and don't hurt us."

"We'll see."

One of the big men walked to the passageway and turned in.

Okay, Nick thought. He's covering the back of the house.

The others started climbing up the stairs slowly.

"Okay. The big dick coming up doesn't get in this house. Your old man must of seen a late paper and saw my picture and got wise. It's too bad. The police want me for killing a cop. I didn't kill the cop, but my partner, Al Molin, did in a holdup we was on. He ratted on me and said I did it. So I'm wanted for murder, too. But I'll never burn like Al will. Nobody'll ever catch me to make me burn. And I'll kill anybody who stands in my way. That's the way I am. I'll do it. I'll do it in a second. So I want you to be for me. I want you to do like I say. Then maybe nothing will happen. Then maybe all of us will be all right. Are you going to do like I say? Are you going to be for me?"

"I'm going to be for you," she said quietly.

Nick pulled out his pistol and backed away, pulling Peg along with him, into the living room and to the front door. He put the metal latch into the slot so that when the door was opened from the outside it would make an opening of but a few inches into the house before the chain would catch the door.

"When the door opens," he said, "tell your folks to send the big guy away."

"He won't come up."

"You just make sure, any way you do it, nobody but your folks and the kid come in the house. Then everything will be all right. I just hope for my sake, for everybody's sake, you're right and that ain't a dick. Somebody's going to get hurt. But I won't burn."

Nick heard the key being put into the door lock. He stabbed Peg's back with his gun. He took a deep breath and held it. Then the door was caught on the latch.

"Say, what is this?" said Mr. Dobbs. "The latch on the inside? That's funny."

"I wonder what Peg's up to."

"Shhhh. Don't let your mind wander. Mickey's here."

"The way you talk, Casey." Then Mrs. Dobbs called softly, "Peg? Peg?"

"Yes, mama."

"Anything wrong?"

"No, mama. Are you all alone?"

"Certainly we're all alone."

"You didn't bring Mr. Kribovitch along for coffee or something, did you?"

"What a foolish question!" said Mrs. Dobbs.

"What's all this hush-hush?" Mr. Dobbs wanted to know.

"Come on, Peg," said Mrs. Dobbs. "Open up and don't act so strange."

Nick got behind the door and nodded for Peg to let them in. He placed his foot and body against the door so that only one person at a time could walk in. He saw Mickey step in first, then Mrs. Dobbs, and then Mr. Dobbs. He slammed the door shut and latched it. Everything was all right now. He was still safe. The big guys were really neighbors. Now, more than ever, he could not leave this house. The way Mr. and Mrs. Dobbs stared at him and at his pointing gun made everything all right.

"Okay," he said. "Come on in and keep quiet or I'll shoot."

Their mouths opened as they looked from his gun to his face and back again.

"We better do what he says," Peg said. "He's a killer."

Mrs. Dobbs gasped. A breath died short in Mr. Dobbs' lungs. Mickey looked on with great curiosity. They walked into the living room, with Nick following them behind his leveled pistol. He motioned with his gun for them to sit

72

down on the couch. Nick lowered the shades carefully, then stepped into the center of the room and stood tall over them, watching their furtive eyes, speechless mouths, and cramped bodies.

"If you got something to say," he said, "you'll say it quiet. I don't want nothing to happen. I don't want no noise. And I don't want to shoot. You, kid, remember that." He swallowed hard and saw the kid nod his head. "I don't want anybody to make a break for the outside. I'll start shooting if that happens. I don't want nothing to happen. I don't want you to get hurt. But I don't want to get hurt, either."

He stopped talking. His legs quivered so, that he tried to stand more firmly upon them. Then he tried to lessen his weight by letting out his air and holding his breath. Neither worked. He did not know how long he could stand above them.

"What do you plan to do?" asked Mrs. Dobbs nervously in a high whisper.

"We're not rich people," said Mr. Dobbs. "But you can take what you want. Rob us and get out. But get out."

"I don't want your money," said Nick. "I've got plenty. Ten grand. More money than you ever saw in your whole life."

"But," spluttered Mrs. Dobbs.

"If it's not money you want—" said Mr. Dobbs.

"I'll let you know what I want," said Nick. "Just sit still. You, kid." He motioned for Mickey to come to his side. "Come here."

Mickey walked cautiously toward Nick, who grabbed Mickey's bony hand and yanked his slender body to his side. Mickey turned his freckled face upward and stared open-mouthed at Nick.

"What does he want, Peg?" asked Mrs. Dobbs. "He must be—" She gasped and clapped her hand over her mouth to keep "out of his mind" from coming out.

"I don't know," said Peg. "I wish I knew." Her throat was choked, and she was bewildered and disappointed.

Now he had them, Nick thought. But he couldn't keep them under his control all night and into the next day

73

without falling off his feet. How could he keep them under his control? How could he stay in this house safely and still control them, keep them from telling the police? He knew that he couldn't leave now without killing them. As soon as he would step from the door, they would pick up the phone and call the police. How far would he get? How long would he live? If he left now he would have to kill them, unless he wanted to die himself. But he didn't want to kill them. That would be noisy. That also would bring the police. How could he stay and keep them within his reach, no matter where they were? But the first thing he knew he had to do was cripple the phone.

"Sit still," he said. "I'm taking the kid with me to knock your phone out. If one of you moves, tries to leave the house, does anything funny, the kid's going to get it. Stay where you are. Come on, kid."

He pulled Mickey into the dining room where the phone was. Nick yanked the cords of the phone out of the wall. He felt strong doing it. He took the kid into the kitchen with him and drank a glass of water. He felt better, less dry. On the way back something stirred within him; a great weight was lifted from his pained, planning head; his mind became clear. He picked up a newspaper lying on the dining room table. It had his picture and the story of the killing. He brought it into the living room and threw it on Mr. Dobbs' lap.

"Read it," he said, "and weep. It's about me, Nick Robey. The picture of me is a lousy one, but if it was better maybe I wouldn't be here now. Then I'll tell you what I'm going to do."

"Now," said Mr. Dobbs, staring at Nick's picture. "I know where I saw him. I never forget a face. I was right on the corner when I saw this and I didn't remember."

"If you had only remembered, Casey," said Mrs. Dobbs.

"If he remembered, Peg would of been a dead pigeon," said Nick. "You're lucky you didn't remember and didn't tell anybody. There'd of been some dead people around. Because nobody's taking me. Nobody."

74

He watched them read the paper anxiously. When they looked up, he said:

"Now you know the story. But you don't know it all yet. Here's the finish. From now on, I'm staying here. You're going to be my prisoners."

"For how long?" asked Mr. Dobbs.

"For as long as I want to stay."

"But we'll die here," said Mrs. Dobbs. "How will we eat? How can all of us be your prisoners?"

"You're not all going to be my prisoners," said Nick. "You're going to be my prisoners all of you at once, when you're all here, like now, or you're going to be my prisoner one at a time. You, Shorty," he said to Mr. Dobbs. "You can go to your stand like you always do. You, Pinky," he said to Mrs. Dobbs. "You can buy food and gas around like you always do, but not about me. And the kid and Peg can do what they want. But one of you always stays with me. One of you will always be with me, even when I'm sleeping, and that one gets killed if anybody comes for me, if any one of you tell the police or anybody. From now on nobody but you comes in the house. If you try to drag somebody in as your cousin or the landlord or a friend or anything, whoever's with me is going to get hurt. You got that straight? You keep your mouths shut outside. If you don't, so help me, before they get me, one of you will be killed. You got that straight?"

He saw them nod their heads solemnly.

"Okay, then we'll get along," he said. "I don't want to hurt anybody unless I have to."

"We'll do as you say," said Mr. Dobbs dryly.

"Good," said Nick.

"But how long will you stay?"

"Until I get ready to leave."

"But how long?"

"What the hell do you care?"

"A judge giving us a sentence would give us a better break. Why can't you tell us how long we'll have to endure this?"

"How the hell do I know? A week, a couple weeks, a

75

month, maybe a year. How the hell do I know? I'll stay until the heat's off, and then I'll blow."

"What if the heat's never off?"

"Then I'll stay all my life. Okay?"

"But what will you gain? You're a prisoner, too."

"The hell I am. What are you trying to do, Shorty?"

"Nothing. I'm trying to make it easier for you."

"Don't antagonize him, Casey," said Mrs. Dobbs.

"The hell you're trying to make it easier for me," said Nick. "You're trying to make me go in circles. You're a smart punk. But don't be too smart. Just don't be too goddamn smart."

"You ought to give yourself up, son. That would be the wisest thing to do. How long do you think you can go on killing people and getting away with it?"

"Long enough to outlive you, Shorty. And if I was you, that'd be long enough, too long."

"I've got nothing against you, Nick. I don't want any trouble. All my life I've been running away from trouble. My wife will tell you that." Mrs. Dobbs agreed with a nod. "Why don't you go now? Leave us alone. Go away now and be absolutely free and go right away. I promise we won't call the police. We'll never tell a soul. We'll wipe this out of our minds. You can still escape, Nick. I promise you that. But leave us alone and go away."

"Please," said Mrs. Dobbs, beginning to cry.

"Sure," said Nick. "I leave. You run downstairs, pick up the phone, and call the police. I'll be about two blocks away, running like hell and running who the hell knows where. And then you'll hear some shooting. And then you'll say: they got Nick. Nick is finished. That poor dumb bastard has got his guts splashed on the streets. . . . What the hell do you think I am, a punk born yesterday? The hell I am. I'm staying till I'm ready to leave. I'll let you know when. And when I go, I'll be free. I'll make damn sure of that. I'll be plenty free and alive."

Mr. Dobbs was suddenly unable to talk any longer. His mind became filled with the implications of Nick's plan, of which Nick perhaps was not conscious. And he became terrified at the thought, not for himself, but for his family.

For, he thought, no matter when Nick might decide to leave the house, even now, he would have to either kill all of them or carry his plan through of keeping a hostage with him and taking one of them with him when he left, threatening those left behind that if the authorities were informed the hostage would be murdered before he would allow himself to be captured or killed. Logically, then, he thought, even the hostage would be killed in the end before he could make his escape from them complete. He felt that Nick would never allow anybody to live who might know where he was. Still, he struggled against the horror that seeped about his mind and clung to the hope, like men at war facing constant death, that he and his family would get out of this all right; they had to get out of it all right. There would be a slip, a mistake, but unlike the one great hope that men at war had, he knew there could be no peace to save them; there could only be an armistice, and they had that now.

"Now I'm tired and I'm going to sleep," said Nick. "I'm sleeping with the kid in the pink bedroom. At night, from now on, the kid sleeps with me. And he's going to be tied to me, so he can't get away. If you call the cops to get me while I'm asleep, they'll have to get past that bedroom door, and before they do the kid won't get a chance to see them, he'll be dead. Tonight I'll put a chair under the knob to keep the door closed. If I hear any funny noise I'll wake up. Don't worry about that. I'll wake up, all right. And as sure as I'm alive I'll kill the kid before the cops or you or anybody can get me. I want you to know that I know I can be taken. But I want you to know that if I am taken in this house, the kid or one of you will be killed first. And you, Shorty," he said to Mr. Dobbs. "Don't get any funny ideas about running out and getting a gun or bringing a cop in with a gun and waiting for me until morning, until I walk out of the bedroom. The kid'll go out first, right in front of me, right in front of my head and chest. Just don't get any funny ideas and we'll get along okay. Okay?"

He smiled when he didn't get a response. He couldn't get over the way his brain was working. He felt strong and secure. He was in full control. He could feel his gun reaching out all over the city behind their backs, wherever they might go.

"You don't care about anything, do you?" said Mrs. Dobbs hatefully.

"Only me," said Nick.

"And I suppose the army helped that along. You've killed so many people that it's nothing now for you to invade a peaceful home like a beast with the thought of killing more people."

"That's the ticket, Pinky."

"You hateful wretch."

"Save it, Pinky, you'll last longer. Until today I never killed nobody. I never wanted to kill anybody. I don't even know if I did. My pal, Al Molin, did the killing, for all I know. And I don't want to kill anybody now. But I want to live. That I want. And if I have to kill to live I'll do it.

"I never killed nobody before today because I was never in the army. I never even registered for the draft. Nobody was the wiser. I got me a fake draft card but I didn't even need that." He saw their eyes grow shocked. "So I cheated the country. But I stayed alive. And the war stank for my dough, anyhow. Now let's get moving. I want to get some sleep."

Mrs. Dobbs went into Peg's bedroom to prepare the bed. Mickey went into the bathroom. Nick put his pistol into his pocket and his shoulders became slack, wearied from the gruelling day. Just then, Mr. Dobbs sprang from the couch and leaped for Nick's legs to tackle him. Nick jumped out of the way. Mr. Dobbs hit the carpeted floor. A smile creased Nick's face. He raised his leg and kicked Mr. Dobbs in the belly. Peg stifled a scream. And Mr. Dobbs gasped in great pain.

"You little bastard," said Nick. "Next time you try something funny I'll kick your brains out."

He raised his leg again, but let it down to the floor. Peg had her fists clenched tightly and her eyes wrinkled shut. Mr. Dobbs was doubled up, wheezing for air and groaning.

When Mickey came out of the bathroom, Nick walked into the kitchen with him and found a clothesline in the pantry. He cut off a piece of it. He pushed Mickey in front of him into the bedroom. He told Mrs. Dobbs to leave. Then he put a straight-backed chair under the knob of the door, tried it to feel how it would work, felt satisfied, and then got undressed.

"I don't want no trouble with you, kid," he said.

He lifted Mickey and got into bed with him. He began tying their ankles together.

"You ain't scared, are you, kid?"

"No," said Mickey hoarsely.

"How old are you, kid?"

"Ten."

"You sure got bony ankles. You need a little meat on you."

Mickey didn't respond.

"Nothing to be scared of, huh, kid?"

"No."

"You ain't going to say a word about this to no one, huh, kid?"

"No."

"You're going to protect your family, kid. If you keep your mouth shut, you're going to be protecting them. Get it?"

"Yes."

"You don't like cops, do you?"

"No."

"Sure. You're a tough kid, huh, and not scared."

"Yes."

"That a kid."

The line was tied securely around their ankles in a dozen hard knots. After this night, Nick thought, he would not do this. He'd send the old lady out to buy a lock. He'd fix the lock high on the door from the inside so that the kid couldn't reach it. Besides he'd have the key.

"Just tonight, kid."

Mickey didn't say anything. He laid back with Nick, who reached for the lamplight above and pulled the chain.

79

Mickey moved away from him and Nick felt the bony ankle against his ankle.

"Be still, kid," he said. "We'll be pals."

They lay flat on their backs in the warm room. There was a faint light coming in from the lamp post outside. Nick shut his eyes and thought he would fall asleep in a second. But he couldn't fall asleep. He felt his nerves skitter through his body. He kept turning from one side to another and dragging the kid's leg with him.

Now, quiet, craving to put the long night behind him and to wake up into a new day, he had a vague feeling that his life wanted to rush out of him. He was finished. If he had deliberately put the barrel of a pistol in his mouth and had pulled the trigger, he could not have been more finished. Or if he were now like the cop on the ground with a bullet somewhere in him and with his life spilling out on the dirt—or if he were like the way he wanted Al Molin to be with a bullet somewhere in *him* and with *his* life oozing out on the dirt—he could not be much worse off now. Because what he had to face from now on, mother of God, he pleaded, help him to face what he had to from now on.

But why, he thought, should he feel this way now? He was tired, he told himself. That was it. He was tired. A guy can get so tired he can go nuts. He didn't want to go nuts from that. He wanted some sleep. That would help him. That would make him new. So let's have it, sleep, he said inwardly. Come on, let me have it, sleep.

But he couldn't fall asleep.

He was safe enough, he told himself. So why didn't he sleep? The family was scared crapless. They wouldn't do a thing. He could sleep and sleep and sleep, so long as he had the kid with him. So why didn't he fall asleep? There wasn't a thing to worry about. Nobody was ever going to get him. He had the perfect plan. He had figured it out himself, too. But if he didn't get any sleep the plan would go lousy on him. He needed sleep now more than they did. He had to be more careful, more alert than the others. He had to get some sleep or he'd fall off his feet the next day. Supposing while he had one of the family in the

80

house with him he fell asleep, even for a second? He'd be through. He had to live their kind of life now. He had to fall asleep. Like the kid. He was sleeping. He bet everybody was sleeping. But they shouldn't be sleeping. They should be scared. A guy scared can't sleep. He's too scared. Only a guy relaxed, nothing on his mind, can sleep good. So why couldn't he sleep? He wasn't scared. He was as safe as could be. Safer. He had never felt so safe in his life.

He twisted and turned. He felt like he wanted to yell and yell and yell. No. He wanted to get out of bed, sneak out of the house on his bare toes, while they were asleep, and run away.

But where would he go? Where *could* he go? And how far would he get?

He began to cry weakly, squirming within the nerves that skittered through his body.

Oh, sleep, he begged. Please, sleep, let me. Come on, let me, let me, let me go.

Chapter IX

MR. AND MRS. DOBBS also lay in bed without being able to fall asleep. They stared at the walls and at the ceiling. The bed squeaked sullenly from their troubled movements. They tried not to look at each other. But from time to time their eyes met and their thoughts crossed and they glanced away silently.

"Casey," whispered Mrs. Dobbs.

"Yes, Ella."

"You're not asleep, are you, Casey?"

"No."

"Don't fall asleep, Casey. Please don't fall asleep."

"I won't."

"I'm afraid, Casey."

"Don't, sweetheart. Don't be afraid."

"I can't help it, Casey. I try to be reasonable. I try to stop what's going on inside me. But I can't. I don't know what's going to happen, Casey. I'm afraid."

"Don't, sweetheart." Mr. Dobbs put his arm about her and held her shoulder firmly. "Please don't be afraid, Ella. There's nothing to be afraid of. Not now. Not yet."

"Maybe we're being punished, Casey." Her lower lip began to tremble; her voice quivered: "What have we done, Casey? Why should this happen to us?"

"We've done nothing, Ella."

"What are we going to do?"

"I don't know yet."

"You've got to do something, Casey. Please, please, Casey, you've got to do something."

What? asked Mr. Dobbs silently. He withdrew his arm and turned away from his wife. What can I do? he asked himself.

"Mickey," said Mrs. Dobbs suddenly. "He'll be killed by him."

"He won't, Ella. He won't."

"Mickey's only a baby. He could kill Mickey, without a sound."

"But he won't, Ella. I tell you, he won't."

"Do something, Casey. Please, before anything happens."

Mr. Dobbs kicked the sheet away from him. He sat up in bed.

"Do you think he's asleep now, Casey?"

"He must be. After going through this day, he must be."

"What are you going to do, Casey?"

"I'll see."

"Kill him?"

"I'll see."

"No, Casey. Don't."

Mr. Dobbs stood up and stepped away from his wife as she crawled toward him.

"Don't, Casey. He'll kill you."

"We'll see."

"If he doesn't kill you, he'll kill Mickey, then. First he'll kill Mickey. Then he'll kill you. Don't go, Casey. Please stay here."

Mr. Dobbs walked on his toes to the kitchen. He opened the drawer of the kitchen table carefully and drew out a strong meat-cutting knife. He pressed the sharp point against the palm of his hand. He felt that with just a little dart the knife could go right through. He then stepped silently through the dark dining room and foyer and stopped at the closed bedroom door. He paused a while to listen. But the pounding of his heart seemed louder than any sound he might hear. He slowly turned the doorknob. He thought he heard somebody stir within the room. He held the knob still and tried to hold his breath. His heart beat wilder and louder. After a while he leaned his shoulder against the door. He hoped the chair inside was off the rug and that it would start sliding along the smooth floor. If the chair would slide a few inches, just so he could get his hand inside to pull the chair away before it clattered to the floor, then he could get into the room. And then . . .

He leaned more of his weight against the door, very slowly. But it would not give. He now had all his weight against the door but still it would not move open. Suddenly, he heard a mumbling from within the room, a body stirring. He leaned away from the door and slowly let the doorknob go back into place. The pounding beat of blood through his body began to subside. He stared helplessly at the door and at the knife in his hand. Then he saw Peg beside him, her lips pressed tightly together, patiently waiting, afraid to move in her fear of evoking any sound. She took the knife from his hand and stepped with him into the living room. She hid the knife beneath one of the cushions of the couch she had been lying on, then walked back with him to his bedroom, where Mrs. Dobbs was sitting up in bed, her hands clenched tightly against her breasts in agonized prayer.

They sat on the bed a long while in silence, staring at the closed door of Nick's room. Finally Mrs. Dobbs said:

"Now what?"

"Yes. If the door had opened—"

"Casey, you've got to promise me you won't do anything so foolish again."

"No. No more idle gestures."

"I almost died then. I wanted to scream and scream and scream, and I couldn't. I was so afraid to move, Casey." Her lower lip began to tremble again.

"Don't, mama," said Peg, her voice choked.

"Mickey could have been killed," said Mrs. Dobbs in a quivery voice. "You, Casey, you could have been killed."

"But we weren't killed, Ella. We're still safe and alive."

"How do we know? How do we know Mickey's safe in there with him?" asked Mrs. Dobbs.

"Mickey's safe," said Mr. Dobbs gently and firmly. "Nick is a killer but he's also afraid to kill."

"Why should he be afraid? What's one life more or less to him?"

"He's afraid because a shot will wake up the neighbors. That would attract attention. The last thing he wants to do is attract attention. We're all safe, so long as he stays here and we do as he says."

"But a baby like Mickey, he could just choke him to death without a sound," said Mrs. Dobbs. "And what would stop him from putting a knife into one of us? He could kill us without making a sound. And that wouldn't attract attention."

"Yes, he could kill all of us in our sleep," said Mr. Dobbs. "He's stronger than all of us and he could just choke us to death or drive a knife into our hearts and we could die without making a sound. But he won't do that. First, because he needs us. He needs us very much, just the way we are. Maybe this is the first time in his life that he's ever needed anybody. But he must know this, else he wouldn't have come home with Peg; he wouldn't have decided to stay. His life is in our hands as much as our lives are in his. Second, he won't kill any of us, if we're careful, because a dead body is still a dead body. It has to be disposed of. Otherwise it stinks like hell. So he won't want any dead bodies around, either."

"What are you driving at, Casey?"

"We're safe with him, because he needs us. Nick is cunning in a desperate way. But he won't hurt any of us, not yet."

"What do you mean—not yet?"

"Nothing," said Mr. Dobbs. He could not tell them his deepest fear: that before Nick left, all of them would be killed, or one of them would be taken along as a hostage, only to be killed later; this was the logic of Nick's life. "All I know now is that we're safe. As long as he stays with us we're safe. But we have to think of some way to stay alive, and together, and still get rid of him."

"But how, Casey?"

"I don't know, Ella. I wish I knew."

"You're not going to try to do a foolish thing like you did before?"

"No. I wasn't thinking. Now I am. He'll make a mistake."

"How?"

"Don't drive me, Ella. I don't know yet."

"I brought him here," said Peg simply. "I'll get rid of him."

"But how, Peg, how?" asked Mrs. Dobbs.

"I don't know yet," said Peg. "But I'll do it."

"I don't want you to do anything, Peg," said Mr. Dobbs. "I want you to let me handle this."

"But papa—"

"Why shouldn't she do anything, Casey?" Mrs. Dobbs interrupted. "I'm willing to do anything I can, so why shouldn't Peg? I don't see you doing so very much."

"Don't, Ella. Don't say anything to hurt us. Now, more than ever, we've got to be strong together; we've got to trust each other. Otherwise, we'll fall apart, we'll become corrupted, we'll begin to hate each other, and we'll have nothing, though we remain alive. Trust me, Ella. Trust me."

"God, what'll we do?" Mrs. Dobbs flung her head back and stared at the ceiling. "Please, God, help us." She buried her face in her hands.

Mr. Dobbs and Peg glanced at her and at each other.

"You must think," said Peg huskily. "I don't know what you must think of me."

"We're not thinking anything, Peg, sweetheart," said Mr. Dobbs. "You were lonely. He seemed attractive to you. He seemed nice to you. And what he had on his conscience and what went through his mind, though you didn't know it, must have moved you deeply and brought out the pity in you. So you're not to blame, Peg, sweetheart. You didn't know. You just didn't know."

"But if I'd been smarter I'd have known," said Peg. "Other girls, who've been around a lot, they know. They made their mistakes and they know. But this—this might be my first mistake and my last. Why shouldn't I have known? Why?"

"Easy, Peg, darling. It'll turn out all right."

"It has to, papa. It has to. But why couldn't I tell Nick was evil when I met him? Why didn't I know?"

"Why?" Mr. Dobbs paused, wondering: were they now caught up in a battle between good and evil? But he had to help Peg. And he said: "Maybe you couldn't know, Peg, because we're all born evil and it's hard to be able to stand aside and recognize it when we see it. Just like a weed, Peg. You see it growing from the ground and somehow it seems to belong. But it doesn't. It's the fascist of the ground and we have to tear it out to let other plants live. And we, Peg, we're a little like weeds when we're born: reaching, reaching, grasping, completely selfish. But something happens to us. We learn that other people are born like ourselves. And we learn that to live we have to compromise. Perhaps the compromise becomes what is called good, perhaps the compromise is God; I don't know. I do know that people learn to get along. And in that way we keep ourselves from killing each other off; we kill the destruction in ourselves; we keep on living. Some of us learn how to get along. But Nick never did. We'll have to destroy him so that we can go on living."

"But what if he destroys us first?" asked Mrs. Dobbs.

"I don't think he will. We're too strong together."

"And yet he's stronger than all of us."

"No, Ella. He's not. He seems to be. Actually, he's already been destroyed. His way of life has already eaten up a good part of him. He'll crumble soon. You'll see. We have to wait for that moment. We have to keep ourselves strong for that moment."

"How long will it take, Casey?"

"I don't know."

"We can't wait that long. Life is too short. Let's tell the police tomorrow."

"We can't, Ella."

"They'll work out something for us. They'll find a way."

"Somebody will be killed then, for certain."

"What other way is there?"

"Don't be hasty, Ella. Remember all the stories you've heard and read about kidnappings. When the police were brought in, how many people that were kidnapped were ever returned alive? Very few, Ella. Very few. And none I know of."

"But this isn't a kidnapping, Casey."

"It's worse. Though we'll be able to walk about at liberty, each one of us, in our hearts, will be chained to this house, to the person left with Nick. We daren't tell the police yet, Ella, not until we're sure, not until we ourselves have a plan, not until we know that all of us are going to come out of this alive. Will you tell, Ella?"

"But I'm afraid something might happen to us before then. The police might be able to do something we can't think about."

"They might. But we have to be sure. They might also be interested only in getting Nick. He killed a cop. The police will want to get him at any cost, even if it means our death. The police might not give a damn about us. But we're interested only in us. We aren't like an army, Ella. We can't give up so many lives so that so many more lives can go on. We have to go on without giving up any lives. This is our world now, Ella: Nick against us. For a little while, Ella, are you with us?"

"Yes, Casey."

"And you, Peg?"

"I won't tell."

"We'll do as Nick says until we can work out a plan."

"And if we can't?" asked Mrs. Dobbs.

"Then we'll tell the police."

"Not until it's too late, Casey." Mrs. Dobbs clutched at Mr. Dobbs' hand. "Please don't wait until it's too late, Casey."

"No, Ella. No."

Peg rose from the bed. But before she could step away Mr. Dobbs grasped her hand and looked at her for a moment.

"Yes, papa?" said Peg.

"You'll have to be careful, Peg."

"What do you mean?"

"You'll be in greater danger than us."

"Why?"

"I don't know exactly. I feel it."

"I'll be in less danger, papa. I think Nick likes me."

"That's why, Peg."

"But if he likes me he won't hurt me."

"He might, Peg. And you might hurt yourself. Be careful."

Peg forced a smile and said: "Don't worry, papa."

"You'll go to work tomorrow, won't you, Peg?"

"If you want me to."

"Yes. And don't come home for supper. Eat out and go to a movie or someplace and stay away from the house as much as possible."

"But I couldn't. I'll go crazy worrying."

"There's nothing to worry about, Peg, sweetheart. Please don't worry."

"No. Let me come home early. Let me be alone with Nick. Maybe I can get him to leave."

"That's it, Peg. Maybe you can. But we don't want that. Don't you see, if you go with him, we'll be safe; but it'll be just as if he was still with us or had taken us along, too. At least, here, we're all together; we know where we are and how we are. But if he's away, with you, we'll know nothing. We'll go mad worrying. And more than ever we won't be able to tell the police. And we would never know where you are."

"But I could write and tell you."

"Don't think about it, Peg. Please do as I say."

"All right, papa."

"Now get some sleep. You'll need it. We all need it."

After Peg left the room, Mrs. Dobbs asked:

"Why'd you talk like that to Peg, Casey?"

"I'm afraid for her."

"But she's in no more danger than we are."

"She is, Ella. Inside of her, she is. She's a young girl, Ella. She's a beautiful girl. But perhaps to others she's not so beautiful, and she might want to clutch to anything that makes her look beautiful in someone else's eyes. Nick might make her look that way if he gets to need her enough."

"Do you believe that, Casey?"

"No. I don't believe anything. I feel like my head's whirling. Nothing makes sense."

"Poor Casey."

"All our lives, Ella, we've lived good, peaceful lives. We've harmed no one and all we've ever asked is that no one harm us. Now the world is brought smack up against us and we aren't prepared for it. Peg, with her dreamy, romantic notions, isn't prepared for it. Neither am I. Neither are you. And Mickey, he's had a good start in being cut out of my pattern."

"Try to get some sleep, Casey."

Mrs. Dobbs put her arm on his shoulder and drew him close to her.

"You're tired, Casey. Just tired. You'll work things out."

Chapter X

PEG lay stiffly on the bulgy cushions of the living room couch. The night was warm and silent and she couldn't get comfortable. It seemed to pull at her, stretching her taut. She felt her insides converging in her small breasts, until her nipples became hard and aching, being sucked up into the vacuum of the empty night. She drew up her legs and wrapped her arms around her shins and dug her chin into her knees, tightly keeping herself together. She began crying silently.

Nick, she wanted to call.

Oh, Nick, she cried.

Please, Nick, go away.

Please, Nick, take me with you and let's go away.

Oh, Nick, leave us alone.

Don't make us cry any more, Nick.

If you go away and want me to go with you I promise to take the tears out of you.

I'll make you happy, Nick.

Oh, Nick, why did you have to turn out to be what you are?

Why did I make such a mistake?

Why didn't I know who you were, Nick?

What have I done?

What's going to happen to us, Nick?

Tell me, tell me, Nick.

And don't let anything happen.

She stopped crying. She unballed herself and stretched

out tensely, retreating from sudden images of the way Nick moved, the way he looked so pained, the taut awkward sense of his body as he danced, the deep loneliness in him that reached for her, the sense of his touch and closeness and the way she felt herself yearn to get closer, closer.

What if he came to her and touched her?

She cringed before the thought.

She could not feel mixed up about him. She had to hate him. He was dangerous. He was brutal. He was a beast. He was death. He was all the things she had been brought up to despise.

And she was weak.

Perhaps that was why her father didn't want her around the house. Perhaps that was why she was in greater danger. He was afraid for her. She was afraid for herself.

Why was she so weak?

Why was she so mixed up: with Nick a black beast coiled in her mind, and with her body moist and feverish, being pulled through the hard aching nipples of her breasts.

But she mustn't be weak any longer.

She must hate him, hate him, hate him. She must, she must, she must.

She felt a sudden pull at her nipples and she almost screamed from the pain.

For a dark shadow loomed over her, came closer and closer, and seemed to stretch and settle down upon her. She turned her head slightly. And there he was, staring at her, tall and stark in the dim light.

"Don't be scared," he said, and added after a long pause: "I can't sleep."

She couldn't bring herself to say anything.

"I said I couldn't sleep," he repeated.

She didn't know what was expected of her. She stared at the full darkness of his body tensed above her.

"I wish it was different," he said. It seemed that he almost flung himself at her as he continued: "Jesus, I wish I could sleep and it was different and I wasn't here and nothing would happen and everything was okay. If I could only sleep for a minute and get off this crazy merry-go-round. If only."

Her body began to quiver, waving up to the trembling of her lips, gushing hot against her throat.

"Cut out the bawling," he said, clenching his teeth. "Cut it."

She tried to grip her lower lip with her teeth but she couldn't stop crying. Stop it, she told herself. Do something, she urged. You'll go crazy if you don't.

She pressed against the back of the couch and dug her hand beneath the cushions. Her breath stopped from sudden shock. Her hand touched the knife she had taken from her father and which she had buried under the couch cushions.

"You think I wanted to kick your old man in the guts?" he asked. "You think I like that? Like hell. But something goes screwy in me and I do like I have to do. You think I like it here? Like hell. I'd rather say: to hell with you, to hell with all of you. But I can't. I'll get killed if I do. I'll be shot on the street if I do. I'll burn if I do. I'll do something, but I won't live. I don't want to die. I ain't ready to die yet."

Her throat became very dry. She had stopped crying. And, frightened, she pushed the knife into the wedge at the base of the couch. She withdrew her hand, watching him closely.

He dropped to his knees and his eyes seemed to tug at a wild desire in her to comfort him. But she also had a feeling of blackness that wanted to destroy him.

"You got to be for me, Peg," he said. "If you're for me, nothing is going to happen. We'll be all right. Nobody is going to get hurt. Nothing is going to happen. But you've got to be for me. Somebody's got to be for me. I never needed anybody for me before. But now if somebody ain't for me I ain't got a chance and nobody here has got a chance, either."

"You better go away, Nick," she said finally.

"Are you going to be for me?"

"Go away, Nick. Leave while everybody's asleep. I'll promise not to ever tell anyone about you. I'll promise nobody in this house will ever tell. I'll promise to let you get away. That's how much I'll be for you. But please leave, Nick. Leave while you've got a chance. Leave before something happens to us. Please, please, Nick."

"Like hell I'll leave."

"Don't you trust me?"

"Like hell."

"What good is staying here going to do you, Nick? Sooner or later you'll have to leave. Go now, Nick."

"I'll leave when I get ready."

"When?"

"I'll write you a letter."

"Give yourself up, Nick."

"Are you crazy?"

"You can't do anything now but kill and kill and kill, if you don't."

"That's okay by me, too."

"But how do you know you'll be safe here?"

"I'll be safe, all right."

"But how do you know we won't tell the police after you leave? Then what good would staying here do you?" She wanted to say more but couldn't. She also realized what might happen: that Nick would not leave alone, or that he might murder everybody to keep himself safe and his whereabouts unknown.

"What are you trying to do?" he asked. "You trying to drive me nuts with all them questions? You want to get me off my nut thinking angles?"

"But supposing I go away with you, Nick? If I went with you nobody here would tell on you. I'll go away with you now, while everybody's asleep. I'll help you escape. I'll keep you safe. I promise, Nick. I promise you."

"Would you, Peg? Would you?"

"Yes, Nick. Yes."

"You go for me, don't you, Peg?"

"Yes, Nick. Believe me, please."

"Where'd we go?"

"Somewhere."

"Where?"

"Somewhere. Anywhere."

"How?"

"I don't know yet. I have to think. But we can do it somehow. We can go somewhere. There must be a place that's safe for us."

"Where? How?"

"Give me a chance, Nick. I'll think of something. I'll make you happy, Nick. I promise you. But let's go. I'll get dressed. Let's go now, while we've got a chance."

He got up off his knees. The skin along his jawbones quivered. She saw his hand coming but she couldn't avoid it. Her whole body leaped to his hand, tried to clutch it, and her face smarted from the sting of the hard slap.

"You're a smart bitch, aren't you?" he muttered tensely. "Who the hell do you think I am, a punk, a guy without a brain, a jerk with his pants in heat? The next time you get me running in a circle I'll beat your brains out. You wise, smart bitch. For a minute you almost had me. For a minute I was almost a goner. But I was too smart. I seen through you. You go for me, like I go for cops. But I ain't leaving. Not you, nobody, no angle is going to make me leave, until I, I myself, say so. Here, I'm staying."

He walked out of the living room into the bedroom and shut the door.

Peg heard the chair being placed firmly under the closed bedroom doorknob. She lay quietly on the couch, biting her lip, feeling the sting in her face, trying to look away from what was going to happen, and wondering what she could do to avoid the disaster that threatened her family.

CHAPTER XI

AFTER Nick left Peg he climbed back into bed and tied his ankle to Mickey's. He watched him wake up for a moment, but the kid grumbled into sleep again, and then Nick crouched up to face the night that was already longer than all of his life; it had gone beyond time and space. He saw himself waiting, like Al Molin was going to wait, for the end of time to run out.

But Al didn't have long to wait, he thought. Al was already in a coffin. Soon they'd take him out for a little walk. Then they'd clamp him down to the chair and Al would know it was coming and, knowing and squirming and being held down, Al suddenly turned black. All of Al's red insides turned black before he was carted away. They threw the dirt over him, and for Al the night would never never end.

Nick shivered upward and stared out the window. He seemed to hear the singing buzz of electricity in the lamp-post outside. Its yellow eye was draped in a dark hood and it teared and dripped over him. He tried to look away from it but couldn't.

A minute, he prayed. Please, God, let me go for just a minute. God, let me go. Jesus, God, let me go.

He did not know how long he offered this prayer, nor how long he was held in the dark grasp of his wakefulness, but the day came without his knowing it, and when a pink glow nudged the gray dawn away Nick felt a gentle push and a slow sinking before he struggled up and awoke with a start to find Mickey trying to untie the knots around their ankles. He flung Mickey back against the bed. Mickey bounced up and stared belligerently at him; a slow flame seemed to rise out of the kid's ashy eyes, stick-like body, and pale red face and hair.

"You sonofabitch," muttered Mickey.

"You say that again, kid, and I'll tear your tongue out," said Nick.

"You sonofabitch."

"You punk kid, I told you not to say that."

"You stink, too."

"Don't get me mad, kid. I don't want no trouble."

"You're yellow. You're yellow to do something."

"Kid, I'm telling you."

"It's up and down your back. A yellow streak. A mile wide. You got crap in your blood. You're yellow."

He raised his arm to strike Mickey. But Mickey didn't duck. He didn't even try to shield himself. He just stared belligerently at Nick and pressed his lips together and braced himself for the blow.

Nick let his arm fall slowly to his side.

Now he was up against the kid, he thought. Now he was up against everybody. Well, what did he expect? That's the way it always was, himself against everybody. Nothing was going to be any different now. Only now he was going to control everybody. He could get along if he could control everybody. If he lost control he would be finished. But he wasn't going to be smashed up now. Not by a kid. Not by a punk old man and a talky woman and a girl who was trying to screw him up. He wasn't afraid of them; they were afraid of him. He couldn't doubt that for a minute. If he ever did he would be through. He would have to be tough: tougher than tough. He would have to take out his insides and never let them in. If he ever got the feeling they weren't afraid of him he would be lost. If they ever got the idea that his threat to kill all of them or one of them was a fake, he would be beat. But there wasn't anybody who wasn't afraid of death. He had proved it. That was his ace in the hole. And if they really wanted him to prove it to them he could. He wasn't fooling. They better

97

know that. He could show that he wasn't fooling in a minute. He could wrap his hands around the kid's neck, stick his finger in the dent over the kid's collarbone, and keep it there until the kid turned purple. Then he could carry the kid out and drop him on their laps and say: I ain't fooling, see. But he didn't want to do this. He just wanted to control them. That would keep him safe. That would keep him from having to leave and to start running again. And he also had to control himself. If he went wild and lost himself he would lose them, too. He had to hold them in his hands. He had to watch himself carefully. Then he would be all right.

"What makes you so tough, kid?" he asked.

"You."

"Tough punks don't stay healthy long."

"Yah?"

"Yah," said Nick.

"What are you going to do about it?"

"Listen, you punk, keep quiet."

"You're yellow."

"I told you tough punks don't stay healthy long."

"Without a gun you'd be on your knees. If you didn't have a gun I'd kill you. Any guy who needs a gun is yellow. Any guy who picks on a littler guy is yellow."

"Where do you get that noise? On the radio? In the movies?"

"What do you care?"

"Because you're a punk kid."

"And you're yellow."

"When you grow up you'll stop believing those fairy tales."

"Yah?"

"Yah. And don't act like you're tired of living."

"Do something. Let's see how tough you are."

Nick couldn't help himself. He grabbed the kid's face and squeezed it until he thought it had turned into a comic rubber face. The kid's red tongue darted out and his eyes bulged and his lips curled up from his teeth and his little hands flailed against him and his body squirmed. Then Nick shoved the kid flat against the bed.

The kid held his face with his hands. He didn't say anything aloud. But Nick could see that the kid was saying inwardly: I'll kill you. And he could not help from answering, "You and who else?"—just like the kid might have answered, just like the kid he wanted to be before his father went away and before there was no food in his house.

"Okay?" he said. "Am I tough enough for you?"

The kid didn't answer. He swallowed hard to keep from crying aloud.

"Okay, you had enough," said Nick. "You're still alive. But don't get tired of living, kid. And if you try anything funny, remember, your ma and pa and sister ain't tired of living yet. You keep them healthy. Get it?"

The kid brushed his eyes with the backs of his hands and smeared the tears over his face.

"Let's be pals, kid," said Nick. "Now we can be pals. You're always pals with a guy after a scrap."

"You yellow son of a bitch."

"Let's forget it, kid, and be pals. I'll buy you something. What do you want?"

"You whore."

"Tell me what you want: a football, a baseball, a cowboy suit, a choo choo train, a pony, a catcher's mitt, a big league bat, a pair of ice skates—" he tried to think of more things that a kid might want, of the things he had wanted—"For Christ sake, what do you want?"

"Nothing. I don't want nothing."

"I got a lot of money, plenty money. I can buy anything. You tell me what you want and I'll give you the money to buy it."

"Nothing. I don't want nothing."

"But let's be pals."

"No."

"Look. I'll let you slug me one. Go on and slug me one, all your might, right in the eye, right on the nose, any place. Slug me one and let's be pals."

The kid looked at him for a moment, clenched his fist, drew it back, studied his face; and Nick braced himself, watching the small fist, the tense body, aching to be struck

99

and to grab the kid to himself and hold him tight and to have the kid for him, pals. But then the kid's lips curled, his face and body relaxed, and he leaned forward and began untying the knots around their ankles.

Nick lay back and a door seemed to shut between himself and the kid. He saw a picture of himself as a kid on the streets playing crack the whip. He was the last one in the line. All the kids began running and he was being pulled along, clenching tightly the hand of the kid in front of him. Then the whip was cracked and he couldn't hold on and he was flung way out, away from everybody, and he wasn't able to stop himself until he smashed up against a fence, and they kept on running and playing and laughing, away from him.

Chapter XII

NICK heard indistinct whispering outside his room. He reached for his gun. Then he heard a knock on the door and Mrs. Dobbs called:

"Mickey, are you all right? Mickey, baby, are you all right?"

"Yes, ma."

"Thank God."

"I'm okay, ma. Don't worry."

"He didn't hurt my little baby, did he?"

"He couldn't hurt a fly, ma. He's yellow."

"When are you coming out, baby?"

"I don't know, ma."

"Nick, when are you going to let him out?"

"When I get good and ready," said Nick.

"Please let him out, Nick," said Mrs. Dobbs. "Breakfast has been waiting a long time. Aren't you hungry, Nick? Don't you want to eat? Come on out with Mickey and have something to eat. Mickey has to eat. So please will you come out with Mickey and let him eat?"

"Who's in the house with you?" asked Nick.

"Nobody. Just myself and Mr. Dobbs."

"You sure?"

"I swear, Nick. I swear it."

"Where's Peg?"

"She's gone to work."

"There better be nobody in the house but you and the old man."

"I swear it, Nick. Please come out and see for yourself."

"I will. I'll come out shooting if somebody's in the house."

"There's nobody, Nick. Believe me. Come on out with Mickey. He's a growing boy, you see. He's got to eat. Otherwise he won't grow up into the man he should be."

Nick began to laugh.

"What's the matter?" asked Mrs. Dobbs.

"That's a hot one," said Nick.

"He's all right, isn't he, my baby?"

"Sure he's all right, now. But he better watch himself or he won't grow up at all."

"Why? What's he done? He hasn't caused any trouble, has he?"

"Not yet. But that kid of yours thinks he's tough people."

"He's not, Nick. He's just a baby. He couldn't cause anyone any trouble. He's a nice quiet boy. He knows his place."

"He knows how to say sonofabitch."

Mrs. Dobbs gasped.

"Mickey!" she exclaimed.

"He got me mad, ma," said Mickey.

"Baby, be a good boy. Please be a good boy."

"Okay, babe," said Nick. "Beat it to the kitchen where you belong and we'll be right out there."

Nick finished untying the knots around their ankles, which were sore and red from their movements. Then he and Mickey got dressed. He lifted Mickey to his chest, held him tight about the stomach, stepped to the door with his gun in hand, and withdrew the chair from under the knob.

"Anybody out there?" he called.

"No," said Mrs. Dobbs. "Please believe me."

"Okay, I'm coming out. Don't try anything funny. If anybody's out there, or if the old man tries something funny, somebody's going to get hurt. I got the kid right up against me, right in front of me, and I'm coming out behind him. I got my gun in my hand, too, and my finger's on the trigger. So if you don't want any dead pigeons around, don't try anything funny."

He turned the knob and opened the door slightly. Mickey squirmed in his arm and kicked at his thighs.

"Cut it out, kid, or I'll break you in two," he said.

"I hope they get you. I hope my pa's got a gun and he kills you. I hope your yellow blood dies. I hope."

"Boy, you're tired of living." He crushed the breath and any more talk out of the kid's body. "I'm coming out," he said.

He kicked the door open, stepped out slowly, and saw Mr. and Mrs. Dobbs in the living room.

"Let him go, Nick," cried Mrs. Dobbs. "You're killing him."

"Let him take a breath, Nick," said Mr. Dobbs. "Let him go, let him go."

Nick released his pressure on Mickey's stomach and felt Mickey's body tremble and claw for a breath of air and he could see Mr. and Mrs. Dobbs gasp for air with the kid. He walked away to the bathroom with Mickey still in his arm.

From the bathroom he and the kid went into the kitchen. Mr. Dobbs was at the table and Mrs. Dobbs was at the stove. Neither of them looked at Nick. They glanced quickly at Mickey to see if he was all right. Nick sat down at the table where he could observe everybody.

"Okay," he said. "Let's have some food."

Nobody paid any attention to him. Mr. Dobbs nodded for Mickey to sit down beside him.

"Where's Peg?" he asked.

The house felt strange without her.

"That's right, working, you said," he added. "Polishing furniture, huh? What does she get—fifteen-twenty bucks a week?"

Nobody answered him.

"What are you?" he asked. "One of them cheap pimps who sends his daughter out to hustle for him?"

Mr. Dobbs' eyes narrowed.

"Well, that's all a dame's good for anyhow," he said,

and, after a pause: "You ain't talking, huh?" And after another pause: "To hell with you. To hell with the whole goddamn bunch of you."

He studied them a while.

"Here kind of late, ain't you, Shorty?" he said to Mr. Dobbs. "What's the matter, scared to go to work?"

Mr. Dobbs shook his head slowly.

"Oh, you ain't scared," said Nick. "You're a hero. A bunch of heroes in this family. Listen, they don't pass out medals for being your kind of a hero. Well, be a goddamn hero. But don't try anything funny. Who's sticking around with me today, the missus or the kid? . . . Who the hell cares? . . . Hey, it's a good thing the kid ain't going to school now, else you'd have no one to relieve you, huh, missus? . . . Goddamn it, ain't nobody talking?"

Mrs. Dobbs brought a glass of orange juice, two eggs, bacon, and toast to Mickey. But no move was made to feed him.

"What's the matter, missus, don't I eat?"

She didn't answer. Mickey began drinking his juice. Nick didn't like the defiant look on her face.

"Oh, you figure to starve me to death, huh?"

Still he received no answer.

"But I ain't starving to death. If I don't eat, nobody does."

He knocked the glass out of Mickey's hand and scraped the breakfast off the table and the dishes clattered and broke on the floor.

"Now make the kid's breakfast again and make mine, too. . . . I'm telling you nobody eats if I don't. . . . Shake it, missus. Shake your ass and get some food here."

There was a long strained suspended pause. And finally Mr. Dobbs said: "I guess you'd better, Ella."

"Goddamn right, you better," said Nick. "Nobody eats if I don't eat. Get that. Get that straight."

Nobody answered him.

"You're not talking, huh? You think you can make me starve for company, die of loneliness, huh? You got another think coming. You just put food on the table and keep your mouths shut. I been getting along without talk a long time. I don't need nobody to talk to. So keep your mouths shut. And be goddamn sure you keep your mouths shut outside this house."

He watched them glance at him and look away.

"Who the hell wants to talk to you jerks anyway?" he continued.

Mrs. Dobbs brought two glasses of orange juice to the table. Nick told Mickey to drink part of his juice. Mickey looked up at Mrs. Dobbs and took a few swallows. Nick took the glass away and finished the drink. When the rest of the food was ready, Nick made Mickey taste what was placed before him before he began to eat. "In case you try to monkey around with poison," he explained.

And while he ate he said to Mr. Dobbs:

"I want you to tell the kid to watch his step. He thinks he's tough. If he has any funny ideas, tell him to get rid of them, for his good and yours. I think you're a smart guy, Dobbs. I think you know I ain't fooling when I say I'll kill somebody in this house if anybody comes to get me. So make the kid get it. Get it?"

Still he received no answer. It began to irritate him. The food tasted bad. He wished Peg was around. Peg would talk to him. He would feel that he had more control. But he told himself not to go crazy for an answer. He knew what he was going to do. If they didn't believe him, it would be their tough luck. No matter what happened, he would still have a chance, so long as he had the gun. He might still be able to shoot his way out. But they didn't have a chance. They had better know it. He wasn't fooling.

"You'll get it, all right," he said. "But get it before it's too late. Don't make me prove I ain't fooling when I say you're dead ducks if somebody yaps on the outside. And that kid, he better get it. A kid can't be trusted unless he's pals with you. I don't trust him. I just hope you can trust him."

After breakfast, Mr. Dobbs and Mickey went into the living room and Nick followed them. He could not hear what Mr. Dobbs said to Mickey because they spoke quietly. He wanted to break up their conversation. But he couldn't. Mr. Dobbs, he thought, might be telling the kid what the score was. He had to let them go on. If they were scheming up something, well, it would be their tough luck. He knew what he was going to do.

"Son," said Mr. Dobbs quietly to Mickey, "I suppose you would like to kill Nick."

Mickey nodded his head seriously.

"So would I, son. But we can't."

"Why, pa? Why can't we?"

"In a way, we're helpless."

"Gee, pa, maybe me and a bunch of the guys on the street, we could come up, and when he wasn't looking we could tackle him and kick him all over and you could get the gun——"

"No, son. He means what he says. If mama is left alone in the house with him and you should come up with somebody, he'd kill her first. If I should come up with somebody while you're in the house with him, he'd kill you."

"He wouldn't, pa. I'd like to see him try."

"No, son. I couldn't take that chance. None of us can. We'll just have to wait and see how to get out of this."

"How?"

"I don't know yet. But we'll find a way. Meanwhile, you've got to promise me that you won't tell anybody about Nick, his being here. Will you, son?"

Mickey nodded his head and Mr. Dobbs put his hand on Mickey's head and stroked it.

"In a way, we're at war now," said Mr. Dobbs. "Nick is our enemy. He's dangerous and strong. We'll have to use all of our brains to outsmart him. We want to outlive Nick. And we will outlive him, if we keep our mouths shut."

"Yes, pa."

"That's a good boy, son."

Mr. Dobbs stepped to the door. He called goodbye to his wife and told her to take care of herself and asked Mickey again to be a good boy.

Nick walked up to Mr. Dobbs and said:

"Before you go, I want to warn you. Don't buy or borrow a gun and come home with it. And don't bring anyone home with you. When that door opens on the latch my gun's going to be out and my finger's going to be very nervous on the trigger. You'll be frisked when you come in. So if you want to come in shooting, that'll be your tough luck, or the kid's, or the missus', or Peg's. Okay?"

Mr. Dobbs opened the door and slammed it shut. Nick latched the door on the inside.

Chapter XIII

MR. DOBBS was known around the corner where he had operated his newsstand for twenty-two years. He had seen boys turn into young men, go off to war, and come back men. He had seen girls lose their gangliness, grow soft and full, sure and knowing and more secure; and suddenly one day their youthfulness became lost in the bigness of their bellies and they became women. And he had known the feeling of missing the sight of a man or woman whom he had seen and talked to for years. And then he would be asked:

"Do you remember——?"

"Yes."

"Passed away."

And the flow of growing and living and dying would suddenly stop still for Mr. Dobbs, would become spiked in silence and solemnity and awe: the living, made conscious of life, by death.

Yet nobody could conceive of what the corner would be like without Mr. Dobbs. If anybody were asked what would happen if he didn't appear one day at his stand, they might answer: "You just don't think of a thing like that. Things just couldn't be the same again, that's all."

For Mr. Dobbs was known as good people.

However, nobody could quite figure him out. He was a hard person to understand: that is, for anybody who had a drive, who was compelled to do something important and to be somebody.

If anybody asked Mr. Dobbs what he wanted to be and what he wanted to do, he would say: "Do? Be? I don't know. I think I'm kind of satisfied. I think I like what I do and I think I like what I am. I don't think I could want anything more."

"But there's no future in this newspaper game, Dobbsy."

"I don't know," he would say. "A future doesn't seem much to look forward to. There's no surprise in it like everybody thinks. You work yourself to death to make it come out; and after it comes out, you work yourself to death to make another future come out. The trouble with the human being is—there's something inside of him that just won't let him alone."

"But your kids, Dobbsy. Don't you think about your kids: sending them to college, getting them good things, having your girl dress up in a way to make you proud? A guy has got to leave a future behind him. Supposing something happens to you? You got no future to leave behind you."

"I never thought of that," Mr. Dobbs would say. "But," and he'd shrug his shoulders, "we'll get along. We always have."

"You know, Dobbsy, there's no money in your way of thinking. Don't you want anything?"

"Actually, I want a lot," he would say. "I just want to be left alone. I just want to live out my life full and proper, do what I have to do, perhaps like nature meant a person to do, without too much interference and without hurting anybody."

"You don't have to worry about that, Dobbsy. You'll be left alone, all right. A guy who don't bother anybody, he's good people, he's a guy you can trust, he's a guy you know isn't out after what you got or want, so he's good people, and he's left alone."

But Mr. Dobbs knew that the desire to be left alone was as difficult to attain as the dollar and cent future for which people yearn; because society was too demanding.

Somebody, or something, was always demanding that you take a stand. Even the simple function of eating was demanding. The signs rubbed forceful letters into your eyes.

"Eat!" the signs said. "Dine!" they said. "Lunch!" they said.

The world of signs clutched you, brought you right up against their chesty words:

"Smoke Camels."

"Drive a car."

"Own your own home."

"Invest here."

"Secure your future."

"Clear your conscience."

"Be right with God."

"Keep your bowels open."

"Be prepared."

The world of signs: demanding attention, decisions: telling you that you don't belong if you haven't got what they offer, that you're an outcast if you're not striving for them. But those were the simple demands close at hand.

What of the complicated things that demanded big decisions? . . . those which you couldn't possibly know were right for many years to come or until after you were dead . . . like the war, why it came about, why it was fought, and what will result from it . . . like, are you with us or against us when a strike breaks out . . . like, should we live by atomic energy or should we let it be forgotten . . . like, should we mix into Russia's business and not let anybody mix into ours, or should we build up Germany again and give China a billion dollars and see to it that Indonesians become a free people . . . ?

These made big demands upon a person, too.

And the newspapers, which he sold, reached out with gruff hands, pulled you by the eyelids to its Brevier type and bawling headlines: Bomb. . . . Ban. . . . Drive. . . . Kill. . . . Charge. . . . Rape. . . . Break. . . . the strong words asserting themselves, forming opinions with so-called objectivity, dominating you in a way in which you think you are dominating them, not realizing that before you is the daily obituary of life.

These not only made demands; they were also inciting.

110

But Mr. Dobbs had a simple formula for making decisions. He always asked: was a thing, a person, or an event, for or against people? Yet, though he was for that which was for people, it was always difficult for him to rationalize the injuries it might cause. This drove him sometimes very far away from the world, into a world of his own that was orderly and which he could dominate and rule. At these times he would lock himself in his basement and build model sailboats. He would become calm in the orderly working of his mind and hands. He would let himself be lifted by the fantasy of sailing out on the boats he made to the vague stretches of the uninhabited world. In the promise of these journeys away from the struggle against man he would see a reflection of man at ease in the world—undemanding, trusting, and belonging.

Now, alone, walking to the newsstand, Mr. Dobbs knew that there was no escape for him. He knew now that he could not escape the world by escaping from life, for they had suddenly become one. And though he felt himself strain to leap beyond the hard insistent beat of his life and the world, he saw himself diminish as he moved, creeping under a huge foot devoted to death and destruction, poised to trample him down. And as he neared the newsstand he felt himself being pulled, as by an umbilical cord, back to his house. He was not so sure now that his wife or his son were safe with Nick. He was not even certain which one of his family was with Nick. Even that seemed to force a decision from him: which one of his family would he rather expose to the danger of Nick? While in the house, though physically weaker before Nick, he had forced himself to be stronger in mind, and he had given his family courage. But now he was afraid. Now he was uncertain. Now he did not know what to do.

And when he got to the newsstand to relieve the man who owned the morning side, the man, whose name was Shiman Goldfarb, said:

"What's the matter, Casey? Something the matter?"

Mr. Dobbs didn't answer. He hadn't heard the questions, though his glazed eyes had met Shiman's.

"You got troubles? Casey, you got troubles?"

111

"Huh? Oh, troubles. No. No troubles."

"You don't feel so good, then?"

"No, not so good, Shiman."

"Then if you'll go home I'll take care of the stand for you, Casey."

"No," said Mr. Dobbs absently. And after a pause, in which he clambered out of the vagueness of his mind, he added: "No. That wouldn't do any good, Shiman. You go home and go to sleep. I'm all right."

Shiman studied him a moment, then counted up the morning papers he had to leave with Mr. Dobbs and marked them on a piece of paper. Mr. Dobbs had never checked Shiman's count, but Shiman had never cheated him. The newsdrivers had, though, for a time. But Mr. Dobbs hadn't minded. He had felt that a dollar less couldn't make a great difference in his life, but if it appeared to be important in their lives, why, he didn't feel that there was much point in accusing them of cheating, only to be called a liar and to be punched around, perhaps. Shiman would say: "You're not a rich man. You should mind." And he would answer: "I eat and I sleep." Then Shiman would say: "It's the principle." And Mr. Dobbs would not answer but he would think that it was not worth making an issue of a small principle, and the big principles seemed too far away to disturb him very deeply. But the newsdrivers, of their own accord, stopped short-counting his papers. "A guy like that," they said. "You don't take advantage of a guy like that. He's too goddamn dumb. He's like a kid. There are no kicks in it anyhow. A guy like that. He's out of this world."

When Shiman left, Mr. Dobbs watched him cross the street: a man who limped through life with one leg slightly shorter than the other, whose head was too big for his short body, whose shoulders were hunched in a constant shrug; a man who didn't need or ask for much, except to be left alone, and who was grateful for his escape from a country of utter poverty and violent pogroms because he could overlook the more subtle poverty and pogroms of his adopted land.

Mr. Dobbs felt a violent twitch in his heart.

What was happening to him now, he thought, might have been happening to a man like Shiman all his life. Was being a Jew, he wondered, to have a feeling of imprisonment, of destruction always imminent, of fighting always against evil, of aching to be at ease in the world but being opposed at every twist and turn? Was that what a Jew endured? Did a Jew feel always as he did now? Supposing the situation he was in was transferred to Shiman? Could Shiman, because of his heritage, bear up any better than himself? Could Shiman, because of a cunning he might have developed to ward off torture and death, advise him what to do? Should he call Shiman?

Shiman, help me. Please, Shiman, you know what to do. Please tell me what to do. Oh, please.

But Shiman, his body lurching as he limped, his shoulders cramped in constant shrug, faded from sight.

However, Mr. Dobbs wasn't alone very long. People bought newspapers, and people who knew him began to come by. There was always someone around the corner who wanted to talk: the people of the neighborhood, the professional men from the offices, the workers from the nearby factories, the policemen on the beat, the streetcar conductors and motormen, and the newsdrivers. And the talk was about everything, from the headlines in the newspapers to women, but mostly the talk was about horses, for around the corner was one of the biggest bookmakers and gambling houses in the city. In order to stand firm within his circle of friends, Mr. Dobbs long ago became a student of the Racing Form, the Racing Record, the Scratch Sheet, and the handicapper's dope sheets. And the world of horses become another family to him. Most of the men and women thought of the races only in terms of winning money. But Mr. Dobbs saw how that frustrated people. So he swore that he would never bet, and his feeling about a thoroughbred horse became like a child's feeling about a baseball player he's never seen but whom he knows intimately from every base he ever stole to every batting average in his big league career. So the language of the racing sheets had the overtones of great poetry for Mr. Dobbs. But this morning, the poetry of conflict, the prophetic judgments, the weak and strong performances, the stories of new careers born and great careers ended, did not sing for Mr. Dobbs. The print dimmed before his eyes; a part of his world had gone awry.

Then he looked at the newspapers. And though he read the important articles, he always looked for a pleasant human interest story that had charm, so that at night, when his family would say, "What's new?" he could have something to tell them. But today he couldn't find anything. Nothing made any sense to him, except a story about Nick: that the police were looking for him and were expecting an early capture. The story made him feel peculiar, made him feel like a criminal himself, made him want to hide. He got a sudden urge to start running, shrink to nothing, when a police car stopped at the corner. A policeman got out and walked up to him.

"What's the good word?" he asked.

"I don't know," said Mr. Dobbs.

"What's the matter, Casey, ain't you passing out the good word today?"

"What *is* the good word?"

"I'll give it to you, Casey. But you've got to keep quiet. Don't even breathe it. Okay?"

"Okay."

"Excelsior in the fifth at Hawthorne. It's a hot one."

"I won't say a word."

"What's the matter, don't you believe it's a hot one?"

"Sure, Tim. If you say so."

"Who do you think is good, Casey?"

"I don't know. I didn't see anything good today."

"Why the hell didn't you? And what's wrong with Excelsior?"

"Nothing. But she finishes weak. The last four times out she finished very weak. But she's beautiful, strong as steel to the stretch, sired by No Wonder."

"I never saw her, Casey, and I don't care who sired her, but today I got it direct. She's in. So what do you say you run around the corner and lay a fin on the nose to win, will you, Casey?"

The policeman gave him five dollars because he was

114

afraid of losing his job if found in the gambling house. Mr. Dobbs placed the bets for all these uniformed men when he brought in the house's batch of Racing Forms, Racing Records, and Scratch Sheets.

"Of course," said the policeman, nudging Mr. Dobbs with his thumb, "if you want to book the bet yourself, Casey, you're welcome. But I'd advise you not to start today. It'll cost you a lot of do-re-mi."

Mr. Dobbs smiled faintly. He was always kidded about holding the money instead of turning it over to the bookmaker. And though everybody would have been enraged at it, for he would then have betrayed their trust in him, they still couldn't understand why he didn't book the bets himself. Nobody would be any wiser. But Mr. Dobbs couldn't, not because he was opposed to gambling, but because he knew that he couldn't bear the agonizing suspension between winning and losing; he knew that he would never be left alone again; he would become as grasping and harassed as others he had seen. So he just placed the bets, held the tickets in his pocket, and cashed them in the next day for the person who won. Sometimes he was treated to a drink or a cigar, and he would feel good within the overwhelming triumph of the people who won. The ones who lost just tore up their tickets with a curse and came around the next day with great hopes; they had a hot one, one that was going to bring in a new pair of shoes for baby, one that was going to bring in next month's rent, one that was going to pay off in telephone numbers.

"I'll be around tomorrow to collect," said the policeman. "And boy, you'll have to dig, Casey, dig deep in the guts when you shell out."

But Mr. Dobbs didn't hear this. Instead he listened to his mind: maybe he can help you, ask him what you should do, find out what *he* would do.

"Tim," he said suddenly. "You ever been shot at?"

"Who, me?" said the policeman. "You crazy?"

"It happens. A policeman was shot yesterday."

"Yah, that was tough."

"Did you know him, Tim?"

"No. He had a bum break."

115

"How does a thing like that happen?"

"Who knows? Why are there rats in the world?"

"Could it have happened to you, Tim?"

"You crazy? Me, if I see a trigger-happy punk I'd run like hell. A dead guy can't see medals, Casey. A dead guy's no good to the world, except for fertilizer. And to-day, inside a cemetery he's no good even for that."

"I wonder why this policeman didn't run away. What makes a person want to be a hero?"

"Search me, Casey. If you was to say this cop was to get a chunk of that ten grand for stopping them payroll bandits, okay, maybe he's got a reason for sticking out his neck a little; there's a payoff in it. But what happens? He gets varicose veins instead. He gets a few crumbs for pay, he gets no respect from the public, everybody looks at him like he's muscle-bound from the eyes up. He gets good sweet crap instead."

"Do you think they'll get the killer who got away?"

"Oh, sure. We always get them."

"How, Tim?"

"That's out of my department, Casey. But I don't care what anybody says, there are some smart heads on the police force. They always get them."

"Do you think they're on Nick Robey's trail, that the police are really expecting a capture soon, like it says in the paper?"

"Could be?"

Supposing the police were on Nick's trail? thought Mr. Dobbs. Supposing they had tracked Nick to the house? Supposing they were to try to enter the house while his wife or Mickey was in there with Nick? Supposing at this moment the house was surrounded and they were calling for Nick to surrender and Nick was answering with gunfire and the police were throwing tear gas bombs into the house and Nick, going blind and choking, had hold of Mickey or Ella and in his last moment of vision shot them? Supposing the police ran up the stairs and shot the door away and rushed into the house shooting with Ella or Mickey between them and Nick and one of them was killed in the crossfire? Supposing, supposing, supposing. . .

116

"Supposing," he asked the policeman, "this Nick Robey was hiding out in this neighborhood and the police were on his trail? Would you be called to help capture him, Tim?"

"Boy, if that guy was in this neighborhood, you don't think I'd be standing here chewing the fat, do you?"

"No, I guess not."

"But don't even think of a thing like that, Casey. A guy like that, he's got nothing to lose, he can only be fried once, he's going to shoot, and he might hit somebody, and me, I don't want to be around when that happens. God help the guy who's around when that happens."

"Yes," said Mr. Dobbs huskily. "God help."

The policeman started moving away. Mr. Dobbs grabbed his arm.

"Tim," he said, "actually the police don't know where this Nick Robey is, do they?"

"Maybe yes, maybe no."

"But you don't know."

"No. I don't even want to know."

"Supposing, Tim, a killer like that hides out with a family?"

"We'll get him anyhow. Headquarters knows every family this guy ever knew. And don't think they ain't being checked on."

"But supposing this Robey puts in with a family the police don't know about, a family Robey never knew before?"

"What kind of family would let him in?"

"Supposing the family didn't know who he was?"

"Don't the family read the papers?"

"Sure, Tim. But suppose they do read the papers?"

"So they tell the police. Christ sake, Casey, even one of their own kind is always stooling on them, so why shouldn't a plain good American family tell on him?"

"But supposing he forced his way in on the family, scares them to death, makes them his prisoners? Supposing he keeps one of the family a hostage, to be killed if another member of the family outside the house tells on him?"

"Brother, you've got a problem. The family's really up the creek."

"And the killer?"

"Him, too. Sooner or later the law gets him."

"But maybe too late."

"Never too late. Sooner or later the guy has to pull another job or be seen in public. How long can a guy keep himself holed up? How long could the family stand it? They know somebody's going to be knocked off, so they tell the police. And if they don't, somebody else will tip us off."

"Is that the way it always is?"

"That's it, Casey. No guy is safe from another guy. That's the way the world is."

"But the police, Tim, would they be interested in the lives of the family, or more interested in getting the killer?"

"You got me, Casey. But when a killer knocks off a cop it's bad, bad for morale, gives people funny ideas, tells people nobody's safe, makes us lose respect; so we've got to get him. And the family, well, it'd have to take its chances."

"But somebody in the family might be killed then?"

"That's right, Casey. Somebody might. But why are you so hepped up on this case?"

"I don't know, Tim. I was just thinking."

"Why, you training to become a mystery writer?"

Mr. Dobbs smiled weakly.

"Or maybe you're training to heist the book joint."

"No, just thinking, Tim."

"Let me give you a tip, Casey. Leave them book joints alone. I know there's a lot of dough in them, and if you're going to pull a job it might as well pay off big and secure you for life, but them book joints; they'll hand you fifty grand, maybe, but they'll hand you a bouquet of lilies, too."

"I suppose so."

"But you wait till after tomorrow, Casey. Wait until after they pay me off on Excelsior. My ball and chain is

118

aching for a new dress and Excelsior's going to take us out of hock. Then tomorrow I'll come home. Babe, I'm going to say, here's twenty-five bucks; go buy yourself a gold-spangled gown. That's what I'm going to say tomorrow. And brother, if she don't bring me the bedroom slippers when I get home at night, I'm sure going to kick her sweet little fanny. Hey, Casey?"

The policeman nudged Mr. Dobbs with his elbow, said he would see him tomorrow, and warned him not to spend any of his winnings. As he walked back to the squad car, Mr. Dobbs wanted to run to him, grab him by the coat, hang on to him, and cry:

Tim, come with me. This Nick Robey is in my house. Come with me and get him. Do something for me, Tim. Do something for me just once, please, will you, please, Tim. What I was talking about was about me. It's me who's scared. It's my family who's facing death. So come on, Tim. Hurry before something happens. Do something for me once, will you, please, Tim. And hurry hurry hurry before something happens.

But he couldn't move toward Tim, who now ducked his big body to get into the car. Instead, he began to count the Racing Forms, Racing Records, and Scratch Sheets, which he had to take to the gambling house; then he went to deliver them.

Big Moe was standing outside the gambling house, slouched against the building, munching a black cigar.

"Hi, pal," said Big Moe.

"Hello, Moe," said Mr. Dobbs.

"What's the good word, pal?"

Mr. Dobbs shrugged his shoulders. He opened the door and stepped into a long corridor. There was another door at the other end. A man named Willy stood in front of it.

"What do you say, Doc?" said Willy.

"Nothing much, Willy."

"Got any good ones today?"

"They're all good until tomorrow."

"Yah, Doc. You got something there, Doc."

Willy opened the door for Mr. Dobbs. He was about

the only one who ever entered without being frisked; nobody could conceive of his ever trying to bring in a gun and trying to hold up the place.

Inside, the house was built like a small garage. The day hadn't started yet and the place was almost empty. The blackboards were being marked up with the names of horses and the odds. A few men sat around a card table, holding cards in their hands and silently studying each other. One dice table was operating with a half-dozen men and one woman around it.

Mr. Dobbs placed the racing papers on a stand, then went over to the betting windows to place a few bets.

"Out to break the house, Pop?"

"As usual," said Mr. Dobbs.

"Okay."

This was almost a ritual. According to the men behind the betting windows, Mr. Dobbs was always out to break the house.

Mr. Dobbs stepped away from the windows and lingered awhile in the serious calm of the place. Should he talk to one of these men? he asked himself. Perhaps one of them might be able to help him. They knew the ways of killers. Some of them might be killers themselves. They might know what to do. But who, he wondered, should he talk to? Not the big boss. He was too important. The big boss had always said to him: "Casey, if you should ever need me for a favor, just say the word." But he couldn't say the word to the big boss; he had never felt comfortable in his presence. Should he talk to Big Moe? He had heard strange stories about Big Moe. It was said that he was a person to be very careful of; it was said that Big Moe had blood on his hands. Perhaps he could talk to Big Moe. Perhaps Big Moe could advise him.

When he got outside, Big Moe was still slouched against the building and still chewing his cigar.

"What's the good word, Moe?" said Mr. Dobbs.

"Save your money, pal."

"It isn't my money."

"Then save the sucker's money. But don't let me catch you, pal."

120

A lazy smile wrinkled Big Moe's broad face. He was a little beefy now, but it was said that he had been a clean-cut kid and had been pretty good as an amateur in the golden glove fights.

"Moe, I'd like to ask you a question," said Mr. Dobbs, feeling tense and afraid, doubtful and hopeful.

"Shoot the dice, pal."

"But I don't want you to get mad."

"What the hell do I want to get mad for? It's a nice day, you're right people, what the hell, pal."

"Supposing you killed a person, Moe?"

The laziness faded from Big Moe's face; it became still, the eyes narrowing; the cigar was held tight in his teeth.

"It's just a question, Moe," said Mr. Dobbs.

"You don't ask a question like that, pal. Never."

"I'm trying to figure something out, Moe. So be a good fellow and let me go on. It's a sort of problem in a story I read, and me and my son are trying to figure out the answer."

"Okay, pal, it's your dice again. Roll them."

"Supposing you killed a person and, to make your getaway good, you moved in on a family and made them your prisoners."

"Without a pal on the outside?"

"You're all alone."

"It's no good, pal. A guy's got to eat. As soon as he gets hungry he's got to send somebody out to buy some food. And when that happens, the guy's a cooked goose; this somebody's going to tell the cops."

"But supposing whoever goes outside is afraid the rest of the family will get killed if he tells the police?"

"Then the guy in the family, he goes and gets a gat and lets the killer have it."

"How?"

"Just lets him have it when he's sleeping, or from a window when his back is turned, or he just comes in shooting."

"But supposing the man in the family never gets the chance?"

"Then, pal, if the killer don't go nuts living with a fam-

121

ily, the family goes nuts. Either way, somebody's going to get hurt."

"Somebody will get hurt," repeated Mr. Dobbs dully.

"Sure, and if the police are brought in, somebody surer than hell is going to get hurt. Because me, if I was in that spot, and if I was stuck with a family, I'd surer than hell make them keep me safe, or else."

"Thanks, Moe."

"That clear up the problem, pal?"

"Yes, Moe, thanks."

"Yep, pal, in a case like that a lot of people are going to get hurt. It's a ratty thing for a guy to do, and whoever thought up that story must be a rat. But any way you look at it, it's blood."

Mr. Dobbs walked away slowly.

Yes, that was it, he thought. Somebody was going to get hurt. Perhaps Moe was right. If the police are called in, somebody was going to get hurt. If the police aren't informed, either Nick or he and the rest of his family might go crazy, and somebody would get hurt then. And if he tried to do something alone, everybody's life would rest in his decision, in his hands.

His body began to tremble. His legs could hardly sustain him.

"Help me," he cried. "Please, somebody, help me."

Chapter XIV

NICK sat at the kitchen table, smoking a cigarette and watching Mrs. Dobbs wash the breakfast dishes.

"Hey, Pinky," he said to her. "That was a pretty good meal you dished out." He took a deep drag on the cigarette and let the smoke curl slowly out of his mouth. "Yep," he continued, "as a cook, you're okay for my dough. Here's a tip." He threw a quarter on the table. "Yep, Pinky," he added, "I picked a pretty good spot for myself. . . . Yep, I think I'll stick around a while."

She didn't answer, didn't turn about. Her back seemed to become pinched. He hated looking at her back, her sexless legs, her shapeless body, her faded red hair.

"What's the matter, Pinky? Ain't you talking?"

He waited for an answer.

"What's the matter? Am I poison?"

He began to drum the table with his fingers.

"You ought to be glad I'm around, Pinky. You got famous people in this house. You're going to be talked about the rest of your life because you knew me."

He picked up the quarter and dropped it and listened to it chinkle and wobble flat to the table.

"Okay, don't talk. Goddamn it, don't talk. It's better that way. You got less chance of getting in trouble. Don't talk, goddamn it. Keep your goddamn mouth shut."

He continued watching her, until the back of her body and the sound of the running water began to dim. He shook his head and pulled the vision of her and the sound of the water close to him; neither of them was going to get away. He took another deep drag on his cigarette and felt relieved when he saw Mickey walk up to Mrs. Dobbs. The sight of the kid was refreshing, but the intimacy between Mickey and Mrs. Dobbs was disturbing. The way the whole family was tied up in each other disgusted Nick.

"Ma," said Mickey. "You need me for anything?"

"No, son."

"I mean, do you got to do anything outside? I mean, do you want me to stay here with him?"

"You're a good boy, Mickey. You're a—" The words caught in Mrs. Dobbs' throat. She turned about with tears in her eyes and reached for Mickey. She bent down and kissed him, hugging him for a moment to steady herself, for she had been crying without sound and without Nick's knowing it.

"What's the matter, missus?" asked Nick. And when he received no answer, he said, "For Christ sake."

"What's the matter, ma?" asked Mickey.

"Nothing, son. Nothing."

"Do you want to go out and you're afraid to leave me? Don't be afraid, ma."

"No, son. It isn't that."

"If you want to go out, ma, go ahead. I'll stay with him. I ain't afraid of him."

"No, baby. You go ahead outside and play if you wish. I'll be all right."

"I ought to stay, but. Maybe you need protection, ma."

"Ho, ho," Nick laughed dryly.

Mrs. Dobbs glared at Nick. Her whole being began to thump against her larynx and her voice, hurting and strained, broke through her clotted throat.

"Why? Why, why, why?"

"Ah, can it," said Nick.

"Did we ever harm you? Have we ever done anything to you?"

"Ah, cut out the bawling, will you?"

"We've never harmed anybody. We've always lived a good, decent life. Why should you want to do this to us?

What did we ever do to deserve this? God, why are we being punished so?"

"A bawler, just like my old lady."

"For your mother's sake, please—"

"For my mother's sake, baloney. If you knew my mother you'd never think of anything for her sake."

"Then for somebody's sake, please, why don't you go away and leave us alone? Be decent, Nick. Be a good boy. Do one decent thing in your life. Go away and leave us alone and nobody will ever know you were here. I promise you that, Nick. Do this one decent thing and we'll be forever grateful. I beg you."

"Aw, save it, missus. Relax. You'll last longer."

"God," she pleaded. "Please, God, send him away. Please, God, we've never harmed anyone and don't punish us so. All our lives we've been quiet people, good people, neighborly people. We've never done anyone a wrong. We just wanted to be left alone. Please, God, don't punish us so. Please, don't let anything happen. Please, send him away. Make him go away, God.'"

There was a long silence. Mrs. Dobbs gasped for air and struggled to stifle her sobs. Then Nick said awkwardly:

"God ain't talking, missus. God ain't saying a word. God ain't moving. Missus," he said tensely, "save the tear-jerking. I ain't moving an inch."

Mrs. Dobbs wiped the tears from her eyes with her apron, blew her nose, and steadied herself. She turned away from Nick and spoke softly to Mickey:

"You better go outside and play, baby."

"Yah, kid," said Nick, "go on to hell out of here and keep your mouth shut."

"Yah?" said Mickey.

"Yah," said Nick.

"I won't be far, ma," said Mickey.

"That's all right, baby. I'll call you when I need you."

"You sure, ma? That's a promise now."

"Yes, son. Better go and enjoy yourself, while you have a chance."

Mickey glared at Nick. He started walking out, watching Nick leer at him, and he said: "Ma, if you need me, call me. Don't forget, I'll be near, I won't be far. Don't forget."

Nick stood up and latched the entrance door after Mickey had gone. When he got back to the kitchen, Mrs. Dobbs was finished with the dishes. He followed her into the cluttered-up dining room, sat down at the table, and once again began to watch her.

She placed some pins between her puckered lips and began to pin together the loose ends of a flowered print that was draped on the dummy. Nick's hands grew nervous as he watched her small nimble fingers smoothing and pinning the cloth. He drummed the table with his fingers. By the time she lifted the would-be dress from the dummy and began basting it, Nick's eyes became glazed and heavy from the glare of the overhead lights. It seemed for a moment that she began to drift away, but his drumming fingers became like tiny legs that rushed after her; they pulled her back to focus, and he held her once again in the grasp of his eyes. He had to watch himself. He had to keep a tight hold on himself. If he fell asleep for a second he would be finished. And the lights being on weren't helping him much. Whoever heard of lights being on during the day?

"Hey, missus, do you have to do this sewing?"

She didn't answer.

"What do you want to do, ruin your eyes? You got all the daylight and sunshine in the world in the front room. What do you want to bury yourself here for? It's daytime. It's morning. What do you want to be like in a coffin for?"

"I like it here," she said. "This is where I work. This is where I've always worked. If you don't like it, you know what you can do."

"I know. I can lump it."

"Yes."

"I'd sure like to lump you one. Every time I look at you my eyes get sore."

"If you don't like it, you know what you can do."

"You goddamn right I know what I can do."

"Nobody asked you to come here. Nobody wants you here. Nobody is forcing you to stay here. And we're not going to change our lives because of you. Get that through your head. And leave."

"Don't get snotty, babe. If I want to change your life I can. The hell I can't."

"The only way you can change our lives is by killing us."

"And I can do that too, missus. Just keep on talking and it'll be a pleasure. Then I'll be able to blow in peace."

She looked away from his glaring eyes and continued basting the dress.

Nick watched her pull the threaded needle in and out of the cloth. His eyes felt hot; there was a dull throb in his head.

"You can't stand to see a person work, can you, Nick?"

"No. Work is for suckers."

"Work is for a good life."

"Crap."

"Work is doing things for people and doing things for yourself."

"You sound as simple as a school teacher. I had that kind of line tossed out to me once. I was in seventh grade grammar school. The teacher left her purse on the desk. She walked out. I took what she had in it. And I was caught. But she didn't turn me over to the cops. She talked to me. She talked to me like you. And you know what I said to her? I said: screw you, teacher."

"You would."

"You think I'm simple like you? What do you sew for?"

"Because I like to."

"Because your old man can't support you."

"He can support us, all right. I sew because I want to. I do it for people. What I do makes me happy and makes other people happy."

"Yah, yah. What's Peg working for?"

"She didn't want to go to college."

"Because your old man can't support her and he's making her hustle for him, that's why."

"You don't believe anything, do you, Nick?"

127

"I believe only what I see, missus. I see you got a simple old man. What's he build them small boats for, that kid stuff?"

"You wouldn't understand."

"That's what I call knocking yourself out."

"Nick, you're twisted."

"That's what they all say."

"Then all of us are right."

"Yah?"

She didn't answer him. She lowered her head and shook it in pity and concentrated on her work.

Nick's fingers twitched as he watched her nimble hands. He started up to tear the needle away from her. He wanted to lift her up and carry her into the living room and throw her on the couch and make her stay there doing nothing. But he was stopped in the middle of a step from her. The doorbell rang.

Mrs. Dobbs looked up. She placed the dress on the table and stood up, but Nick blocked her way.

"Don't answer it," he said.

"But I have to."

"You don't have to. You're not going to answer it."

"But it's Mrs. Gerhardt. She said she was going to drop in for a minute to see about a dress for her little girl."

"She'll see you later, after I leave."

"But if I don't answer the doorbell, she'll think something happened to me. She'll think something's wrong. She'll get suspicious."

The bell rang again, longer. Mrs. Dobbs tried to step toward the foyer. But Nick pushed her into the chair.

"Don't move," he said. "I don't want no trouble, missus, so get back to your work."

"But it's my business, Nick. Please, let me answer the door. What harm would it do if Mrs. Gerhardt comes up? She wouldn't even have to know you're here. You could hide in the bedroom or bathroom. You wouldn't have to worry about a thing. I'll give you my solemn pledge I won't do a thing against you. Otherwise, Mrs. Gerhardt will get suspicious. She knows I'm home. I told her I'd be home this morning. Everybody knows I'm home every morning. Let me answer the bell, Nick."

"Shut up."

The bell rang again, insistently. Mrs. Dobbs listened to it anxiously. Nick towered above her, as though he were on his toes, his heavy fists seemed to pull his arms taut, and the ringing of the bell seemed to ripple along the furrows of his forehead.

"You're through, missus," he said. "You ain't got a business no more. You ain't got nothing no more. Nobody answers doorbells. Nobody comes up here. Get that. Get that good."

"But what will I say to my friends when I meet them on the street, when they ask me to make a dress for them, when they ask to come up for a visit?"

"Nothing. You'll say nothing."

"But they know we're not like that. They know they're always welcome here. They know somebody's home. People know that."

"You ain't home. You're never home any more. You're out shopping. The doorbell's on the fritz. I don't give a damn what you tell the people, but nobody comes up here. Get that."

The doorbell rang again. They glared at each other in the pause that followed. Then came two sharp irritated rings. They waited silently for the next ring, strained almost to exhaustion.

"I guess she's gone," said Mrs. Dobbs finally.

"Then go back to work."

Nick sat down heavily and wiped his forehead. Mrs. Dobbs glanced at him, sighed, and went back to basting the dress. Her hands moved quickly and nervously. They got Nick to drumming the table again. He did not know how long he would be able to watch Mrs. Dobbs and her busy hands without jumping up and grabbing her fingers to pull them out one by one and throw them out the window. How long?

"What time does Peg get home?" he said.

"That's no concern of yours."

"I said what time does she get home. I ain't asking you if I'm concerned. I just want to know when she gets home."

"It depends what her plans are."

"What do you mean, it depends? You mean you got no control over her? You mean you don't care what she does?"

"I mean we trust her. Peg's a fine girl. We trust her."

"Jesus, I'd like to take your face and throw it up for grabs. I'm sick of the sight of you."

She stared at him steadily.

"We trust her," he mimicked bitterly. "You never trust a woman. They can't be trusted. They turn rat on you every time."

"Thanks for your opinion. But keep it, keep it for yourself."

"I'm just telling you, babe."

"You're not telling me anything, Nick. You're twisted. You're not true. Nothing you say or think is true. You've never said a straight thing in your whole life. Even your mouth is crooked. You're not human, Nick."

"Yah?"

"When you love people you trust them. But you've never loved anybody, you've never trusted anybody, your heart is a piece of coal, it pumps soot instead of blood."

"Aaah, blow it, babe," he drawled.

"I feel sorry for you, Nick." Her head became unsteady with pity as she stared at him, watching his discomfort, his drumming fingers. "In a way I feel very sorry for you."

"Where do you get that noise, you feel sorry for me?" He slammed the table with his fist and stood up. "Where do you get that way, standing way up on top like a goddamn saint? You button up, babe. Don't get to make me feel sorry for you. Why, I could just walk over and put my thumb on your nose, twist it, and rub you out in a second. So shut up."

He walked toward her threateningly. Mrs. Dobbs was unable to suppress a frightened gasp. He stepped around her and she held herself rigidly, her eyes following the

130

movements of his tense body. He moved down to the other end of the table and sat down again.

"You was sounding off about love," he said. "Suppose I tell you Peg likes me. Suppose I tell you Peg goes for me. Suppose, babe, I tell you Peg laid for me."

She looked at him as though a knife had been stuck in her chest.

"And you, missus," he continued. "You kind of went for me too, before you knew who I was. You was kind of spreading yourself all over for me, before you knew who I was."

Nick's words cut deeper.

"But don't worry, babe. I fluff you both off. Right now I don't need nobody. I never did need nobody. The only guy I ever liked, the only guy I ever trusted, he turned rat on me. But I got along. I'll keep on getting along, plenty all right. I don't need nobody. I fluff the whole bunch of you off."

"Nick," she said, struggling for words, her throat hard and hurting with hatred; "you've been dead as long as you've lived. Only live people need somebody, need other people. But you don't. You were born dead. You have no soul. You are very very dead."

Nick laughed uncomfortably.

"Supposing," he said, "I go get me a soul? Supposing I tear your insides out and get me your soul? Supposing I go get me Peg's soul? I can get it for a penny. She goes for me. And she's got a big enough soul to work for me, too. Supposing I get me that soul?"

"You filthy, rotten devil."

He laughed again.

"Squirm, babe. You know a woman can't be trusted, that's why you squirm. Not even your own Peg can be trusted, you know that. So squirm."

She turned away from him and began working on the dress.

"Should I tell you how Peg went for me?" he said. "Should I tell you how it was? Do you want to hear if your daughter is any good? Do you want to know if she got what it takes?"

131

No, she shouted inwardly. No. No. No. Please, Nick, NO.

Her inward pleading drowned out whatever else Nick had to say.

Her fingers moved quickly and nervously, working the threaded needle in and out of the dress. The cloth became wrinkled. She tore the thread with her teeth, pulled it out, smoothed the cloth, then re-basted it; but it wrinkled again; nothing was coming out; yet she had to keep working, tearing, fixing, jabbing, smoothing; everything was going wrong.

Nick was wrong, too, she said to herself. He was just talking. How could it have happened? When was there time? Where was the opportunity? While they were at the movies? At the beach? In the taxi? There had been plenty of places. There had been plenty of time. But Peg couldn't. Peg could never do a thing like that. Nick was a liar. Nick had never said a true thing in his life. Nick was twisted. Everything he did came out twisted and untrue. He was just talking. But supposing he had spoken an inkling of the truth? Supposing in some uncanny way he was right? Supposing Peg did go for him? Or supposing Peg went for him later? If nothing had happened before, there was still plenty of time for something to happen. If Nick stayed in the house much longer anything could happen. But could this happen to Peg? Could Peg be carried away? Could she really go for him? Would she let him? God!

Up to this moment she had accepted Peg without question. You are what you are, she had always said, and your husband is what he is. Together you plant the seeds and from your roots a child grows. And you take it for granted that it will grow strong and fine and that it will become what you want it to become.

But now, suddenly, there was so much about Peg that she didn't know.

There were so many things about which they had never talked. She was sure that she and Peg had never talked and gossiped with probing curiosity the way Peg had with her girl friends. She remembered that sometimes she would walk into the living room or Peg's bedroom when Peg was with a girl friend. She knew by their intentness, the way they seemed huddled, that they had been talking confidentially, pulling at each other with secret feelings and desires, exposing their aches and joys. But when she would walk into their midst, their faces would change suddenly, they would sit differently, more composed, more prim, more conscious, more restrained; she had intruded, a mother had intruded, and the conversation would halt red-faced and then would turn to ordinary talk, about things not close to a person, things that didn't go inside, things that fluttered about.

A mother, she thought, never really knew her daughter. Somehow, the world outside suddenly stepped between yourself and your daughter. And then the child was no longer there. Instead, you had a grown woman. You had somebody before you who no longer needed your care but of whom you had to be careful. You didn't like this. You knew that a grown woman was separated from the child you had nourished and had known. And you knew suddenly that a stranger was in your midst, with aches and desires you had once endured and which you deliberately shoved away from yourself. When you thought of this you went inside yourself and hoped that everything was all right, you trusted with all your might, you told yourself that you couldn't possibly have raised a child that wasn't all right, and you said: nothing is going to happen to her, she will never shame you, you will never be violated; she is and she will be a fine person, because you are her mother and she stems from you and therefore she is you. Nothing had happened to her. Nothing will happen to her. Nick was a liar. Nick was a devil. He was purposely trying to fill her with doubts. He was trying to pit everybody in the house against each other. He was trying to destroy her family. He was trying to destroy their lives. But she wasn't going to let him. She wasn't even going to remember what he said. He had just been talking, that's all. Now that Peg knew who he was, now that Peg recognized him for the beast he was, Peg couldn't possibly feel anything toward him but the violent hatred that she felt. Peg was her daughter. Peg could not feel differently. And Nick was a liar. Liar. Liar. Liar.

She looked up from her work. Nick was staring at her. The skin along his jawbones quivered from time to time. He seemed to be munching himself, agonized by an insatiable hunger. Soon he would consume himself. There was no telling what might happen after that. He was already clawing at Peg, at her, at Mr. Dobbs, at Mickey. How could she make him let go? How could she tear him away and keep herself and her family alive? How?

If she killed Nick, she asked herself, would she ever be the same again? Did she have the power to sit in judgment over him, to decide whether it would be right to kill him, if she could? And if she did, how would Mr. Dobbs, how would Mickey, how would Peg look at her? Would they gratefully say: mama, oh, mama! Or would they just look at her, stare at the blood on her hands, never come close to her, kill her with their fear of her?

But how could she kill him? He always faced her. He always followed her. If she went into the kitchen to get a knife he would break her arm before she could take one step toward him. Besides, she wondered, did she have enough strength to drive a knife fully into his heart? She couldn't even try poison without taking the chance of poisoning one of her family, the way he made Mickey taste the food before eating it. What was there for her to do? Please, she pleaded. Before I go out of my mind, before Nick destroys us, help me to find a way out. Lead me out of my darkness. Please give me strength and help me. Oh, God. Help me.

She became conscious of working on the dress. She didn't know why she was so impatient to finish it. It was for Mrs. Kupperman. Soon Mrs. Kupperman would come for a fitting. How would Mrs. Kupperman get a fitting if Nick would not let anyone in? What was the use in working so fast and so hard? After this dress she might not have anything to do. She would be faced with the tasks of cleaning the house, washing the dishes, and getting the meals ready. And then there would be nothing to do. Nobody would be around to talk with her. She would be denied the pleasure of making dresses and of watching the nice reactions of the people for whom she made them. She would become like an empty sack, sitting around and waiting. She would have to become a liar, too. How was she going to explain to the neighbors that she couldn't do any more work for them? How was she going to explain to Mrs. Gerhardt why she didn't answer the doorbell? What reason could she give Mrs. Kupperman that she couldn't finish her dress? How would she explain these things without becoming a liar? Soon she would be faced with this. Soon she would have to go shopping. And there he sat, his jaws working, his fingers drumming the table, his mouth tight, his eyes almost feverish. God, she wished that she could kill him!

She laid the dress away. But she had to keep busy. She had to keep from thinking. She had to calm the disturbance within her. She started to clean the house.

Nick followed her from room to room, from corner to corner, watching her sweep and dust and mop and make the beds. When she began to mop the bathroom floor he saw that the window was a way of escape. If he was alone with Mrs. Dobbs or Peg and they went in there and locked themselves in, they could open the bathroom window and jump out. They might kill themselves doing it, jumping from the second story, or they might just break a leg, but they might try it, and so long as there was a possibility he would have to secure the window.

He told her he wanted a hammer and nails. She said she didn't have any. He said she had them, all right. He grabbed her arm and twisted it behind her back. Her body bent from the pressure but she didn't move. She winced with pain and gasped as he jerked her arm upward. He said he wasn't fooling; he'd wrench her arm off. She felt her arm being torn at the shoulder. She turned slowly and led him to the pantry and pointed with her eyes to where there was a hammer and nails. He released her arm, took what he needed, and poked the head of the hammer into her back as he prodded her to the bathroom. He locked the door and told her to stand still or he would throw the hammer at her head. She stood still, while he secured the window with the nails. The only way they could get out now, he thought, would be by breaking the frosted window. He would be able to hear that and he could run in. He hammered the lock on the door until it came off. Now the door could never be locked against him. Now he was pretty safe. Now, even if one of them got tired of living and tried to open the window to jump out or call for help he could run in and stop them. Yes, he was pretty safe. He was pretty smart, too. All he needed now was a lock for the bedroom.

"When you go out, Pinky," he said, "you buy a good lock for the bedroom door."

She didn't answer.

"If you don't get the lock, it's okay with me, too," he said. "But if you don't, the kid will be tied to me again tonight. He'll stay tied to me until you do get the lock. So you'll get the lock."

He knew that she would. Then with the bedroom door locked on the inside, and with the key tied on a string around his neck, and without the kid's bony ankle digging into his ankle, and without the worry about the chair slipping and somebody coming in, he would be able to sleep once again. Boy, he thought, how he could use some sleep! How nice it would be to lay down on the couch and stretch out and shut his eyes and go right out of this world. But he couldn't. He had to keep his eyes on the old lady. He had to keep from going nuts watching her. He wondered how long he would be able to keep his eyes on her, on all of them. Always, he would have to be in a position where he could face them. That way, he could control them. He also had to get enough sleep from now on. Otherwise, he would be through. But if he knew that his door was locked at night, that Mickey couldn't get out, that nobody could get in, he would sleep. Well, the old lady would fix that for him. She would get that lock. He would be closed out from everybody with the kid. He would be able to sleep. All he had to do now was to get through this day. Then he would be all right. He'd be able

136

to keep his hands still. He'd be able to relax. He'd be able to stop the twitchy feeling he had.

He sat down on the living room couch. But in a few moments the nerves in his legs began to skitter. He dug his feet into the carpet and leaned hard against the couch. He tried to hold himself down by putting his fists into his pockets and he yelled inwardly: stop it, Jesus, stop it; but he couldn't sit still. He jumped up abruptly and Mrs. Dobbs stopped sweeping the carpet and shuddered. He paced up and down about her, moving heavily and breathing hard. She began to push the sweeper over the carpet, watching him stealthily but trying to concentrate on how clean her rug was becoming so as to shut him out of her mind. And to him, the sound of the sweeper and the sight of her jerky movements made his hands open and close.

"How long do you keep this up, you?" he said.

She didn't answer him.

"When I talk to you, say something."

She continued sweeping the carpet. He grabbed the handle and wrenched the sweeper out of her hands and flung it away.

"Missus, you talk to me, you hear?"

She straightened up very haughtily. The wrinkles about her mouth converged and pulled her lips tight. Her head trembled slightly as she faced him.

"Goddamn it, the walls don't talk but you do," he said. "Answer me, you little pink-eyed bitch. How long do you keep this up?"

Her heart started pounding from the look on his face. There was a deep frown on his forehead. Something seemed to be pressing the wrinkles closer, like a vise crushing his head, and his eyes looked like they were being squeezed very slowly out of their sockets.

"You going to answer me?" His voice was grim.

"I don't know," she said finally. "I don't know how long it will take."

"Then cut it out. Get back to sewing or something."

She backed away from him timidly, circling toward the foyer. He circled with her, leaning toward her. She stepped into the foyer and he followed her. She walked into the dining room and sat down at the sewing machine. She picked up the dress she had been basting and fumbled nervously trying to straighten out a seam under the foot of the machine. Nick stood above her. She felt him very close to her. She placed her foot on the treadle and began to operate the machine, holding the cloth in position for the jabbing needle. The cloth wrinkled; she couldn't seem to keep it smooth; nothing was working easy. If only he would step away from her, she thought. If only he would stop hovering over her. She glanced up at him. Her foot worked the treadle harder. The needle jabbed up and down faster. Her fingers became bunched in the cloth. And before she could pull her hand away, the jabbing needle drove through her finger. Her whole body became paralyzed. Her head twisted and Nick could almost see the scream coming out of her guts as her face writhed and her mouth opened. He clamped his hand over her mouth and felt her screams smash against his hand. And then her body collapsed against the chair, her mouth sagged against his hand, and her head lobbed to one side.

"For Christ sake, missus," Nick said, his heart hammering, his nerves twitching his legs. "For Christ sake, for Christ sake."

She was limp against his arm and it got quivery holding her. He looked about madly to find the cause of her attempted scream and the fainting. And then he saw the needle sticking through her finger. A trickle of blood oozed out from around the buried needle.

He tried to pull the needle up but couldn't get at it. He tried to pull the needle up by the thread in its eye and the thread broke. He put his hand back over her mouth, afraid that when she would come to she would start screaming again, and stood helplessly over her, staring at the machine.

When he felt her body stir he pressed harder against her mouth. He muffled the whimpering against his hand. Her arm reached for the wheel at the side. Her hand fell limply on it. Her whole body was atremble. She twisted weakly, the pain screaming out of her face, her eyes wide open

138

with the eyeballs rolling slowly upward and pulling the taut bloodshot veins.

"Do something," he said. "Do it quick, missus."

He wanted to withdraw his hand from her mouth so that she could tell him what to do, but he was afraid that her screams would rouse the neighbors.

"Tell me what to do, missus. Tell me."

But he was afraid to take his hand away. He was afraid that she might die on him if he didn't do something quick. He didn't want her to die. That would bring people around, people you couldn't keep out, the cops, too. He didn't want her to die this way.

"Show me, missus. Jesus Christ, missus, show me what to do. Hurry, missus. Hurry, show me."

Her eyeballs rolled out of sight suddenly, and for a moment, before her lids closed, it seemed that her taut veins had burst and had splashed blood all over. Then her body sagged against his arm and her hand fell away from the wheel.

Perhaps, he thought, the wheel had something to do with the needle. He turned it. Her finger was pulled up to the metal foot of the machine and the needle drove her finger back against the base. He stopped the wheel before it began to pull her finger up again. He moved it carefully. Her finger rose upward, pulled by the needle, but the needle wasn't coming out; instead, the finger was lifted higher as he turned the wheel, until it came up against the foot of the machine. Then as he turned the wheel he saw the needle press her finger downward. The needle wouldn't come out; it stayed through her finger in its upward and downward course from the foot to the base of the machine. Finally, still holding her mouth, begging her to come to but afraid that she might start screaming, he pressed her finger down away from the foot. More blood oozed out, but her finger was drawn away from the needle slowly until it was freed. He pulled her hand carefully from the machine, then lifted her small body and carried her into the bedroom. He stood looking at her, his hand over her limp wet mouth, wondering when she was going to come to. He slapped her chin and cheeks and forehead.

139

Her body stirred. Her eyes opened, red and pierced with pain. Her hands pawed at his hand over her mouth. Her eyes became a pool of blood but her tears turned white on her lashes and cheeks. He could hear her whimpering and he could feel the quivering of her body.

"You won't scream?" he asked.

Her eyes filled with more tears. Her face was very warm and wet.

"If you don't scream, I'll let go," he said.

She wagged her head weakly.

"All right, missus, I'll let go," he said. "But if you even make a peep, so help me—"

Her hands pawed harder at his stifling hand.

"Okay," he said.

He withdrew his hand slowly, tensely, poised to pounce back upon her mouth. Her head rolled to one side. Her body doubled up and trembled more violently.

He stood over her a long while. Then he opened the closet and took out a blanket and covered her. After that he sat down on the bed and kept watch over her. She was conscious, turned away from him, gasping, whimpering, crying words he couldn't make out, and the bed vibrated from her quivering. She seemed to have gone inside him for a moment and he felt his guts go hard, crying too. He wanted to crawl beside her and hold her firm and ease the pain; it would be so nice to cut the rock out of his guts, let it melt, become yellow and sunny; it would be so good to lay down and feel the trembling uncoil from his body and to close his eyes and drift, drift, drift until he stretched out as big as a swelling lake. He shook his head, swallowed hard, braced himself, and instead became locked in the pattern of his life.

Don't go soft, he told himself. Be careful. Don't let her get at you. Don't let these people get set. Don't let them pound their fists into your guts. Stay away. Get on the bicycle. Pedal. Stay out of the clinches. Stay far away and you'll be all right. And say: to hell with them. Say: to hell with them. Say it all the time and nothing will happen to you. You'll be all right. To hell with them.

He looked away from her. He found himself aching to

do something. Maybe he would wind up building boats, he thought. Maybe he would wind up putting shots in his arm, like the old man. He needed to focus his attention on something. He had to keep the old lady out of his eyes and out of his mind. He needed a change. He wished the kid would come back. That kid was gone a long time. He wondered what the kid was up to. It was about time he had come back. That kid better show up soon. Then he would tell the old lady to blow out of the house for a while. He'd tell her to go to a doctor, get bandaged up, and do what she had to do. He didn't want to see her for a while. He didn't want to see her ever again. For his money she could go out and fall in front of a fast auto. He almost heard the brakes screech, saw her knocked down and crushed, and she lay bleeding and dead with different parts of her body strewn all over the street. She was picked up and rushed to the morgue. The police found her identifications. They came to the house. And he began to yell inwardly: don't, don't; look out, missus; watch out for that car; look out! And he dived at her and knocked her out of the way: safe.

He shut his eyes and shuddered.

Jesus, he thought. I'm going squirrly. These bastards are hitting me from all sides. I got to get hold of myself. I got to stop thinking. I got to stop seeing pictures in my head. I got to keep these bastards away from me. They'll gang up on me and I'll never have a chance. I got to stop going like nuts.

He heard the lock of the front door click. The door opened and banged tight against the latch. He jumped up, excited, his face flushed, thrilled to action. He drew out his gun and stepped behind the slightly opened door. He looked through the crack. It was the kid.

"You alone?" he said.

"Let me in, will you, scaredy cat?" said Mickey.

"Sure you're alone, kid?"

"Yes."

"You better be."

He unlatched the door and let the kid squeeze through. He quickly latched the door again and locked it. Then he frisked the kid, put his gun away, and smiled. The kid had a surly look on his face, but Nick had never been so glad to see anyone in all his life. He tousled the kid's hair playfully. Mickey slapped his hand away. Nick didn't mind. He was just glad to see the kid. Now he could tell the old lady to fluff off. Now with the kid around there would be less chance of getting into a jam. Maybe he and the kid could even play some cards, some two-handed pinochle or rummy. At least the kid wouldn't play with needles and get him all screwed up.

"Hyah, kid," he said.

"What do you care? Where's my ma?"

"In the bedroom."

"Ma," Mickey called. "You all right, ma?"

"In here, Mickey," Mrs. Dobbs said weakly from the bedroom. "Right here, son."

Mickey rushed into the bedroom. He saw her crumpled on her side. She rolled her tear-stained face toward him and smiled weakly.

"What happened, ma?" said Mickey.

"Nothing, son. Nothing."

"She just hurt her finger sewing, kid," Nick explained.

"You hurt her." Mickey backed away from Nick, his face enraged, his fists doubled up. "You hurt her. You hurt her. You dirty—" Mickey's throat choked, then the tears came, and he rushed at Nick, who grabbed Mickey's wrists and lifted him from the floor. Mickey tried kicking Nick's shins and Nick began laughing at the futile attempt to hurt him.

"Take it easy, kid," he said. "Come on, kid, take it easy. Your ma hurt herself on the machine. It was her own fault. So take it easy."

"Don't, son," said Mrs. Dobbs. "Don't hurt him, Nick. He's only a baby. Don't hurt him, Nick. Please let him go. Please, son, stop it. Please, Nick, let him go and don't hurt him, he's only a baby."

"Relax, kid," said Nick. He lifted Mickey high and flung him on the bed. Mickey glared at him a while, then snuggled close to his mother and patted her shoulder gently. Mrs. Dobbs stroked his hair.

142

"It's all right, son," she said. "It's all right."

"I wish I could kill him."

"It's all right, son."

"I wish I was bigger. When I get bigger I'm going to kill him. I wish I was bigger now, but. I'd kill him in a minute; him and his whole family." And to Nick he said: "You'll get yours yet. You'll see. You'll get yours, plenty."

"Ah, shut up, punk," said Nick.

"I'll shut up. I'll show you I'll shut up. You'll see I'll shut up and you'll get yours."

"It's all right, son," said Mrs. Dobbs, holding Mickey's head close to hers. "Leave him alone. Don't pay any attention to him."

"Was it bad, ma? Did it hurt bad?"

"For a little while, son. Just a little while. But now I'm all right."

"Ah, why don't you shut up?" said Nick. The closeness of the mother and son disturbed him. He turned his back on them. "You slobs," he said.

"It's bleeding, ma," said Mickey.

They both stared at her punctured finger.

"I better see a doctor," said Mrs. Dobbs. She moved slowly out of the bed. Mickey jumped up and held her about the waist as she stood up.

"I'll help you, ma," he said. "I'll take you out."

"All right, son."

Nick followed her and Mickey to the bathroom, where Mrs. Dobbs bandaged her finger. Then she and Mickey walked to the foyer.

"Where do you think you're going?" asked Nick.

"I'm going to see a doctor," said Mrs. Dobbs.

"Yah, get lost, missus. But the kid's going no place. He's staying right here."

"Couldn't you let him come with me? I don't feel very strong."

"Are you kidding, missus?"

"Let me go with my ma," said Mickey. "We won't say nothing. And we'll be right back. Honest, Nick. We'll go away for a minute and we'll be right back, you'll see, and nobody will know nothing, honest, but let me go with."

"Relax, kid," said Nick. "Take a load off your feet and sit down on the couch. Let go his hand, missus, and blow out of here, alone."

Mickey held on to Mrs. Dobbs' hand. Nick reached over to separate them. Mickey held on tightly and tried to kick Nick.

"Now let go, kid," said Nick evenly.

"Better let my hand go, son," said Mrs. Dobbs.

Nick yanked Mickey's hand away and carried him over to the couch and dropped him on it.

"Now blow, missus, and keep your mouth shut, or the kid'll never know what hit him. Now blow."

She walked out of the house and he latched the door. When he stepped into the living room, Mickey said:

"You sonofabitch. You dirty yellow sonofabitch."

Nick laughed. He sat down on an easy chair, stretched out with his heels dug into the carpet, and sighed. He smiled faintly, watching Mickey glower at him.

"Want to play some cards, kid?" he asked.

"No."

"What's the matter, don't you know how?"

"No."

"You mean to say you're such a punk you don't know how?"

"No."

"Come on, I'll learn you. It'll put hair on your punk chest."

"You'll learn nothing."

"Rummy's easy. Or casino. A little game of rummy or casino, just to pass the time, and we'll be pals, and it'll put muscles on you."

"No."

"Okay, be a punk."

They sat looking at each other, the kid glowering, and Nick wondering how long he could keep on looking, looking.

Chapter XV

THE day had been long for Peg, filled with a great ache and weariness. She did not know how she had got through the day at the store. She sat down in front of her locker and opened it. She felt like the inside of the tin locker: vacant, dark, and oppressed. Her hands lay limp on her lap. She did not know how she had managed to demonstrate the furniture polish in the basement of the store, talking, polishing a plank of wood, dirtying it, shining it again, selling, while Nick throbbed hard and dark within her.

There were times when he seemed to grasp her wrists and yank her toward him; she bumped against him, bounced away; then he jerked her up, making her dangle, with her feet squirming to touch the ground and with her stretched arms burning from the tautness. Sometimes she felt her heart pound, as though she had suddenly stopped from a long run, and she let him carry her a while before she began to struggle against him; then she tore away from him and began running, terribly frightened, but the ground slipped past her and she made no headway, when all at once she turned into a crazy ride at an amusement park, dipping and twisting and turning and spiralling and spinning, until her insides were sucked out of her, and she was suddenly free; she was flung out over a million miles of space and landed gently on a great cushion of grass and she became calm and walked off like springtime: oh, crazy, crazy, carefree in the spring. And then the sky darkened.

"What's the matter, Peg?"

Peg looked up wearily. It was Marge Dubovic: darkhaired, cheeky, hot-legged without stockings, uncomfortably moist in a light summer dress. She walked a few steps, swinging her broad hips, a sinuous movement, loose and lurid, activating the pent-up dreams that she could not let herself fulfill.

"Nothing, Marge," said Peg.

"Let's punch out. This is putting in overtime we don't get paid for."

"Yes."

"Got your bathing suit here?"

"Yes."

"I got mine, too. Today's a day for the beach. Today's a day for a lot of things. Today's a day. Let's go for a swim."

"I thought I'd go home."

"Why? You got a date?"

"Sort of."

"Where'd you meet him?"

"At the beach. Yesterday."

"Well, good going, kid."

"But it isn't a definite date." Peg felt that she should go home. She was worried. She wondered if the family was still all right. She couldn't know that unless she went home. With the phone torn out, there was no way of reaching her mother or Mickey. But her father made her promise not to come home until late. Perhaps her father was right. She was afraid to go home. She was afraid to face Nick. She was afraid of what went on within her when she looked at him. She hated herself for that. She was tugged between going home and keeping her promise to her father.

"What do you mean, it isn't a definite date?" asked Marge. "Have you got a time and place to meet, or did he say he'd call you and let you know?"

"No. I said I'd call him and let him know."

146

"Oh, you're giving him the dangle. That's smart, Peg, if you can get away with it. You going to call him?"

"No."

"He ain't worth calling, huh, Peg?"

"No."

"Well, what can you expect from a pickup? Either they're tall, dark, and handsome, but strictly wolves, from the word go, and you wind up playing push all night; or they're silly, sad, and dopey, and you want to lose them the minute you start up, but it's hard to lose a dog, sometimes very hard, Peg."

"Yes."

"You're plenty talky tonight, aren't you, kid? But if you feel sad, call him up, or don't call him up and wash it out in the lake. That's what I always say."

"I'm sorry, Marge. I'll try to be better company."

"That's all right, kid. Company's company. I like it."

They punched out at the time clock and walked out into the sultry street. The sky was clear and blue, and the pre-evening streets looped by the El were in deep shadows. They walked east to Michigan Avenue and caught a bus. They climbed up to the second deck and sat down. A few men turned about, stared at them, looked away, and Marge moved her hips sullenly.

These men, Marge said. She had to laugh. She had been sitting next to a very peculiar guy one day. Oh, he looked all right, all right. It was his attitude. He started talking to her. Who did he think she was, a cheap pickup or something? But he wasn't talking to her, exactly. He was talking like to himself or to everyone in general. He talked in a way so that you couldn't give him an answer. He never asked you a question like a regular guy would so that you could give him an answer and go on from there. He was the kind of guy you couldn't get next to he was so far away in the way he talked. So he must have been a very peculiar one. He said buses are the sidewalk cafes of Paris and Brussels. How do you like that for a queery? In Paris, he said, a person sits at a sidewalk cafe and watches the world in motion, only there he has a good drink and good food to lull him. But here, he said, a person sits on top of a stinking bus and catches a glimpse of the world in motion. Chicago buses, he said, the ersatz sidewalk cafes of Paris and Brussels. He said a lot more but that's what she remembered, he was such a very peculiar guy. Sitting next to him, she said, was like sitting inside of a travel magazine. He was an interesting guy, but he wasn't interested in anybody, so he must have been pretty queer. Didn't Peg think so?

Peg guessed that maybe Marge was right. But inwardly she thought that this man was somebody she might want to know, saying a thing that was so romantic and cute but yet so sad. Perhaps he was a man like her father, except that he had done what he had dreamed about. He was probably a man who did things, while her father was just content to dream them. And that, for Peg, was the difference in men: those who acted, whom she admired; and those who dreamed but who could never become the pirates to carry you away.

She remembered herself as a child when she went into the basement with her father to watch him build model sailboats. She remembered the tender careful way in which he built his boats and the way he sometimes whittled out little wooden people and stood them on the decks. Then her father became the skipper and she was his mate as the vessel grew to life-size proportions in their minds.

"Where we going, skipper?"

"Ah, matey, must you always be going some place?"

"Aye, aye, skipper."

"But that's the beauty of this ship, matey; it has no destination. It just goes, like clouds, unworried."

"But can't we dock any place, skipper?"

"Ah, matey, right now you see only sea and sky and the way they meet in the distance. But soon you will see a little speck on the horizon. It will grow larger and larger. And the speck will become palm trees and soft clean sand and coconuts on the ground and people to greet us. We will drop anchor, matey, and we will row ashore, and there we will find paradise: waterfalls, big trees lying across rivers like huge combs, the sound of birds making music, the sound of people in love; and the breezes, matey, they will be as soft as your mother's touch; and the nights, matey, they will be as big and as milky and as kind as the virgin Mary; ah, matey, you will see, you will see."

His eyes seemed to go beyond the whole world and his soft speech was a song that made her sing, too.

But later the singing stopped. She felt that nothing was ever going to happen to her unless she became practical. Still, her father continued making boats and dreaming, while she stopped going down to the basement with him to listen to her heart sing as he sang, unless she felt that something terrible was going to happen to her, or something had hurt her, and then she would go down with him and become soothed within the sight of his careful tender hands and within the warm voice of his singing of a dream that for the moment was as real to him as anything could be.

A man like her father, she thought, if he could be a pirate, too; if she had a man like that crazy for her, oh, God, oh. And God, she thought, how she wished she could be in the basement with her father now, away from Nick, away from everybody, safe, floating, looking at beautiful pictures, and singing, safe.

Marge interrupted Peg's thoughts.

"Hey, dreamy," said Marge. "We get off here."

They clambered down from the top deck. On the street, Peg said she had to make a phone call.

"Oh-oh," said Marge. "You're going to leave me in the lurch and make that indefinite date definite, huh?"

"No," said Peg. "I'm going to call my father."

"Oh, that's what they call them now: father."

"Will you wait?"

"Sure. But ask him if he's got a boyfriend for me?"

Peg went into a drugstore and telephoned the cigarstore on her father's corner. After a long wait somebody answered and she asked for her father. And after another long wait her father said hello.

"I called to find out how you are, papa," she said.

"I'm fine, fine," he said.

"And everybody at home?"

"Don't worry, Peg."

"Were you home yet? Is everybody all right?"

"Everybody's all right, baby."

"Do you still want me not to come home early?"

"Yes."

"I'll come home in a second if you say so."

"Stay away, Peg. Stay away."

"But what will I do, papa?"

"Go to a movie. Relax. Do something."

"I can't. I can't sit still."

"But stay away, please, Peg. Stay away late enough so that he's asleep when you get home."

"It's so hard, papa. I worry."

"Don't worry, baby."

"Will everything be all right?"

"Yes."

"You sure?"

"Yes."

"Let me come home now, papa. I can keep him from hurting us. If anybody should get hurt it should be me. It's all my fault."

"It isn't, baby. You couldn't help it. You didn't know."

"Gee, papa, I wish I could talk to somebody. It's like I'm choked."

"Yes, sweetheart, I know, I know. Better hang up now. I'm busy."

"What's going to happen?"

"Nothing. Don't worry now, Peg. Go to a movie. Forget everything for a while and don't worry. I've got to hang up now. Goodbye, baby. Goodbye."

"Did you tell anybody yet? Do you know what you're going to do?"

"No."

"Gee, I feel like I can't stop talking. I wish I could talk to somebody. I wish I could do something. I wish. I wish."

"Don't, Peg. Don't. And goodbye. Please say goodbye."

"Goodbye."

She heard a click.

"But, papa. Look. Let me."

Her voice got no response. She hung up slowly. She felt

alone and choked and cold. She walked out into the traffic-jammed street.

"What'd you do?" said Marge. "Have a fight? It took you long enough."

Peg did not answer.

"No soap, huh, kid?" said Marge.

They had the green light and they walked across the street.

"Ah, to hell with them," said Marge.

They stepped onto the sandy beach, meandered in and out of the crowds to the locker room, where they got into their suits and checked their clothes.

"Wash it out in the lake," said Marge. "You got a bad feeling, drown it in the lake. That's what I always say."

They stepped into the murky water, walked a way, then Peg dived under, beat hard against the water, splashed and struggled for a breath of air, and after a few strokes she stood up, choking and wiping her eyes. She watched Marge glide effortlessly and lazily on her side. Marge circled back to her and they walked ashore.

Peg sat down near the water's edge. For a moment she watched Marge stand in the full glory and consciousness of her body, with her plump breasts, curved hips, slightly mounded stomach, and strong legs, charged by her restless head and eyes. Then Peg stared out at the great expanse of shimmering water, beyond the lifeboats, beyond the cribs, beyond the white sails against the sun-flecked sky, and even beyond the horizon.

It had been only yesterday, about this time, she thought, that she had met Nick. Her whole life, to that hour, seemed diminished. And since then she had lived more than a lifetime. Nothing, she felt, had happened to her in nineteen years. Then suddenly she had tripped and had fallen spluttering into a chasm to which there was no bottom and through which she was still falling as in a bad dream.

What was there about Nick, she wondered, that tugged at her, compelled her, until she could almost feel herself squirming and urging him? And then what made her suddenly feel completely dark and doubled up and aching to

151

smash? What made Nick the way he was? What made her the way she was? Why was he with her so much, not only as dark danger and death but also as an animal she was seeking out and whom she knew was lying in wait to pounce upon her and carry her away? From where? From whom? If she could just wipe from her mind his face and body and the things he had done! If she could just feel free of him for a moment! Was that how it happened: somebody digs so deeply into you that you can't escape and you have to carry him about with his claws hooked into you for the rest of your life? Was that what people mean when they say love and hate are the same: you start with one and end with the other? She had never felt real hate before. She did not know what it was, unless it was what she felt now. But what she felt now was fear, not of death, somehow, just fear. Was that why, without knowing it, Nick compelled her so? But she had always been told that love did this, the love that was about her all her life.

God, she screamed inwardly, I'm so mixed up!

She strained with her whole being to talk to someone. She couldn't talk to her mother and father. They were too much involved. They had given her all the answers they knew. They had no answers now. Oh, if she could talk to someone. If she could talk to a priest or a girl friend. If she could talk to the kind of man Marge had met on the bus. If she could just talk to somebody. Then perhaps she could get Nick out of her system and she could find an answer and she could then figure out how to save both herself and her family.

God, she asked. Why don't you talk to me? Why are you so silent? Why don't you just give me a nod, a brush on the cheek, something, and let me know you're listening? Jesus, make a miracle for me. Open up my eyes, please, and let me see. Let me have an answer.

She looked out over the lake. The sky was a deeper blue. The white sails seemed to be still against the sky. In the water the lifeboats wobbled and the people swam and splashed and made a great continuous sound. She felt herself waiting, lonely. She sighed finally and the world about

152

her blanked out; she went into her cavernous head and began to wander.

She wondered about the thought that had entered her mind the previous night, of Nick, not leaving the house before killing everyone or taking one of her family with him to make sure the others wouldn't talk. She knew that he would have to do one or the other. He couldn't just leave and trust them not to say anything. Nick trusted nobody. He was too afraid to trust anybody. He was so strong, so violent, so sure of himself in a way, yet so afraid. He would leave, she knew, with everybody dead behind him or with some member of her family. And those left behind would live in fear the rest of their lives for the one who was taken by Nick. But that's the way it was going to be. Nick was going to leave without killing anybody. Nick was going to leave with somebody. He was going to leave with her. She had to make sure of that. She had to make sure that the rest of her family would be left alone, alive. She would have to make him leave some way. She would have to make him fall for her some way. She, then, would take him away. Then her family would be safe.

And herself? she thought. What would happen to her? Perhaps Nick would force her to stay with him all his life, all her life. How long would their lives last? Or perhaps, once Nick made his getaway, he would kill her, so that he could be alone, safe. But would he kill her if he got to love her and trust her? Could she make him love her and trust her? Could she drive the fear from him? She, herself, would have to love and trust him first. Could she do that? And afterward, would she ever be able to escape him? But that didn't matter now. First, she would have to get him to leave the house, some way. Then they would have to escape together. And after that—perhaps there would be no afterward. She tried to imagine their escape. She saw themselves fleeing in an automobile. The roads became blocked. There was no escape. They had to face it. Nick would shoot it out rather than be captured. She might be shot in the battle. But supposing this didn't happen? Was

153

it really possible to get away, or would they be running and hiding and dying all their lives? Or would she be killed by Nick anyway, later, so that he could run and hide and die alone? But that did not matter now. She did not matter. What mattered was that her mother and father and Mickey must go on living. She must go on living, too. But later. Now she knew that her terrible secret, though it ached to where she wanted to scream, could not be told to anyone without endangering many lives. She knew that she would have to make Nick leave soon, and with her. It was the only way. But how?

Suddenly she became afraid and she felt herself begin to tremble.

"What's the matter, babe, you cold?" It was a man's voice. "Here, I got a sweater. You want to put it on?"

She shook her head.

"You're biting your lips, too," he continued. "I been watching that. I been watching that quite a while. Don't you like the lips you got? You're going to bite them off if you're not careful."

He was on his knees beside her.

"I'm with the guy that's with your girl friend," he explained.

She looked up. A man was standing near Marge and they were talking and laughing. The fellow beside her moved closer. She retreated. He was light-haired and nicely tanned and blue-eyed. He didn't look like Nick at all. But she was afraid; she retreated; she tried with all her might to stop her trembling.

"Kind of a nice day, huh?" he said. "And it's going to be a nicer night." He paused and added: "Ah, you don't want to go on biting them plenty nice lips."

He came closer to her. She moved away from him and turned from the sight of his tanned skin, soft lips, light hair, blue eyes, and what was in his mind and in his look and what he might be that she didn't know about.

"Oh, the talky type," he said. "The hard to approach, the still water runs deep type."

She shriveled further away and looked to Marge for relief, but she turned away from the way the other fellow

154

was staring at Marge and the way Marge stood on one leg with her hands on her full curved hips and with her plump breasts rising and falling before his eyes and the way her half-shut eyes and half-smile responded. Peg's eyes became filled, instead, with the motion of flesh and brightly colored trunks and suits on the beach.

"Nice lips," he said. "And turning them away to bite on them some more. What's the matter, babe?"

"Nothing," she muttered. "Nothing."

"Oh," he laughed. "You talk. You really got a sound box."

The sand was coarse under her and it hurt her hands and thighs as she scraped along it further away from him.

"Jesus," he said. "What am I: poison?" Then to Marge, he said: "Your girl friend, she acts like I'm poison. What's the matter with her?"

"My girl friend's all right," said Marge.

"That's my sentiments, too," the fellow agreed. "But she still thinks I'm poison."

"Then that's tough luck, sonny," said Marge.

The fellow that was with Marge laughed loudly and mimicked: "That's tough luck, sonny. Oh, sonny, go and get a T.S. slip and give it to the chaplain."

"Try again, sonny," said Marge. "Better luck next time."

"Turn on the charm," said the fellow with Marge. "Give what it takes."

"Gee, you've got pretty red hair," said the fellow beside Peg. "You don't want to go and get scared and uppity just because a guy tries to make a little conversation."

Peg felt like she was being mauled. She didn't know what was happening to her. She didn't know why she didn't trust anyone, why she looked upon this fellow with suspicion. Before yesterday, she wouldn't have minded; she would have welcomed it; she would have liked it; she would have felt good. Now she was afraid. Now she did not know what to make of anything.She was all mixed up.

"We thought," he continued, "my friend and your friend, they hit it off pretty good, and it's a nice day, and it's going to be a nicer night, and if we could hit it off, me

155

and my pal we always go together, we could make it a foursome."

She glanced at him quickly, then stood up and began to walk away. And as she walked, she heard him say: "The dog. A dog like that. Who the hell does she think she is? What the hell does she think she's got, a dog like that I wouldn't even take to a dog show?"

"Ah, you cover her face with the American flag and forget the rest," his friend said. And they both laughed and asked Marge if she didn't agree. But Peg didn't hear any more. She rushed into the water, fell and struggled up, felt the water like ropes tugging against her legs, and fell again. She labored upward and pushed against the water until it reached her chin. A swell lifted her off her feet and she fell back struggling until she thought her chest would burst, but her feet found the bottom; she leaped up and caught a breath of air and splashed to safety. She stood a while with the water lapping at her breasts, breathing hard, her eyes water-soaked and tight, her stomach knotted with the horror of almost having drowned and of leaving her mother and father and Mickey to the mercy of Nick.

Later, the gentle swells of the lake calmed her, and seemed to ease the heavy weight and pain in her. The sun was almost down now and there was a huge red glow above the buildings across the boulevard. The sky was a deeper blue with tones of purple in it. When she walked ashore, the sand was cool and softer-looking in shadow; there were fewer people, and there was less noise, and the papers strewn about the beach were like bloated sores. Marge was sitting alone with her hands twined about her raised knees.

"I got rid of them, Peg," said Marge.

"I'm sorry, Marge."

"They were a couple of heels."

"I'm truly sorry, Marge."

"The jerks."

Peg sat down and looked out over the lake, where the water swelled and was all one color and darker while the sky at the horizon seemed to have the night in it.

"It's a good thing you ran off, Peg," said Marge. "They were a couple of no good bums. They were guys in too much of a hurry. They were the kind of guys who see, feel, conquer, and run away. Boy, did they want to know what the score was, but fast. No preliminaries. Do you or don't you, they almost said. There's no time, there's no time for nothing with them kind of guys. So I told them to go away and sell their headlines somewhere else. I really told them. And like good little boys they went away."

"I'm sorry I spoiled it," said Peg.

"Ah, you didn't spoil a thing."

They were silent for a while before Marge said:

"Yep. So now we're alone. In a twilight night and on a Saturday, with a whole lifetime before us until tomorrow morning, with not a thing to do but eat and think and wait, them heels. Ain't that life, Peg?"

Peg didn't answer; she swallowed hard.

"Yep, that's life, all right," Marge assured her. "But so is eating life. My belly is groaning. So let's eat, Peg."

They ate and went back to a section of the beach opposite the Drake Hotel. They lay down on the grass and watched the night grow more intense. The blue beacon light from a nearby skyscraper slashed across the sky. Music floated down from the roof garden on the hotel. The constellations in the sky began to array themselves. And then, for Peg, the stars began to dance and a trumpet rising above the reed ensemble was a silver twinkle in the great motion of the plush night.

"Them jerks," said Marge suddenly.

Peg looked at her tenderly.

"Them lousy lousy jerks," said Marge more intensely.

Peg looked back at the sky. The music came down to her again. The trumpet solo had died down and the full voices of the reed instruments became packed in her throat. She felt herself twisting and rising. And then she herself went into a sweeping dance along the great path the blue beacon light made for her.

"Or maybe I'm a jerk," said Marge. "Maybe I ain't facing the facts of life. Maybe you can't make life the way you want it. Maybe you got to let life make you the way it wants to. Maybe you've got to just let yourself be made. And maybe if I keep talking like this I'll wind up trading my brains in for pretzels, they'll get so twisted. What do you want to do, Peg?"

"Nothing."

"You mean you don't want to do a thing? You want to just lay here?"

Peg nodded her head.

"Aw, we got to do something."

Peg sat up and said, "I should go home."

"Home. That's no place to go. This is Saturday night."

"We're not dressed for it."

"Dressed. It's summer. It's hot. Anything you got on on a night like this, you're dressed."

"But I should go home. I'm worried about my folks."

"What's the matter, they sick?"

"Not exactly. But in a way, yes."

"You're making plenty of sense, too."

One part of Peg said: you should go home; no matter what your father said, you should go home; you should be there; you should be there all the time; your mother and father and Mickey might be in terrible danger; you should be there all the time and keep Nick away from them; you should make Nick go away with you; you should get inside Nick and make him trust you and make him go away, far away, some way, some place. And another part of her said: no, Peg, don't go; Nick, he'll do strange things to you; your father is right; trust your father and let him work things out; Nick will tear your insides out; he'll stick his hands inside your stomach and he'll pull your guts out and he'll throw them away; you'll beat your head up against a black wall; don't go, Peg; stay where you are, safe; Nick is going to kill you; he's going to kill you in the house or he's going to kill you outside of it; so stay where you are, safe; stay with Marge.

She threw herself to the ground and said aloud: "I don't know what to do. Tell me what to do. Please, tell me. I don't know. Oh, I don't know."

She could no longer hear the music from the hotel. She saw the dark uneven ground instead of the starry sky. The acrid smell of the automobiles on the boulevard stifled her. And when she looked up the rounded lamps were no longer moons necklaced about her but were yellow ugly heads leering vacantly at her.

"Let's get away from here," said Marge.

Peg lifted herself slowly from the ground as Marge put her hand under Peg's armpit and urged her upward, and they walked away from the lake front. Peg felt limp and as though she were being dragged along the walk. She did not want to decide on anything. She did not want to think. She did not want to even want. She just wanted to feel empty. She just wanted to get away from the constant tugging at her insides. She did not care where she went, so long as she could get a rest, so long as her stomach could stop feeling so exhausted.

She boarded a bus with Marge and stared without seeing at the dark shoreline of the drive and at the dark stretches of Lincoln Park through which the bus wound. At Belmont Harbor Marge poked her to get off and they walked westward through dimly lit streets until they came to a busy street corner rioting with flashing signs and sounds.

Peg felt vaguely that she had done this before, as she faced the entrance of a dance hall, but she didn't know when. She had once been a part of this Saturday night ritual: the quest, the wild hunt before the night ended, and finally the lonely humiliation, the tight loneliness of an early morning night, the self hurt and turning into the self but finding no security, no assurance, until you became hard and small, shriveled into a dried pea in the huge night of desire.

And she paid her price, too, as she had done once before, when she had walked up the mirrored stairway with a dollar full of hope, thrilling to the smell of perfume, toilet water, powder, rouge, cigarettes, cigars, urinals, turning away from the smells of exhaled beer, whiskey, digested food, getting the first shock from the roar of many people together, the loud laughter, the blaring music, the springy floor, fading down to the subtle rustle of skirts, the shuffle of feet, the soft murmurs, being urged by the moving bodies, the close embraces, the intimate motion of lips

159

and hips, the lewd stares, the quickened glances, the coy movements, the shuttering of eyelids, and being surrounded, dressed, undressed, pinned down, forced, by the men, tall and brave and gallant, small and lecherous and swaggering, but all confident, all victorious, all seeking one victim for a final conquest.

This soon overwhelmed Peg. She felt moist, strained to the yearning lyrics to which the singers gave voice, aching to be yanked away from her clinging self and to be tossed into the abandonment about her. She noticed a pair of eyes: dark, measuring, considering, timeless in the making of a choice; and finally there came the decision, the sure movement, the undenying demand: dance with me. And Marge looked at her.

"All right, Peg?" said Marge. "You sure you won't mind?"

"Sure, she won't mind," said the voice with the measuring eyes.

"No," said Peg. "Go ahead, Marge."

"Then I'll see you later," said Marge. "I'll meet you here by the post. Don't forget."

Peg glanced at the marble-like pillar against which she was leaning and mistily watched Marge and the fellow move out on the floor, and soon they became lost in the gliding whirl of bodies. Yet when she was measured up a few times before the big decision and bold demand was made for a dance, she felt herself shrink and she shook her head, no, until she became confused and weak. She sat down in a corner and wanted to go home but couldn't get herself to leave. Later, a fellow walked up, grabbed her hand, pulled her to her feet, and said: "Come on, let's dance." She got onto the floor somehow and she couldn't seem to move into the fellow's jagged way of dancing. As soon as the number was over, the fellow said, "Thanks," and left her standing in the middle of the floor. The music started up again. She walked off blindly, bumping into the moving couples, feeling diminished, and leaned heavily against the pillar where she was supposed to meet Marge.

She stood there until the last dance. Then Marge appeared, sweating and excited, followed by the fellow she had been dancing with and his friend. Marge wanted to know where Peg had been and was she all right and was she having a good time. Marge was having a good time, a wonderful time. And the fellow she was with agreed with a wink of his eye. But Marge had found her, finally. Now they were all together. She introduced the friend to Peg. Peg didn't get the name but she didn't care. She squirmed, instead, at the way he seemed to finger her dress with his eyes, the way his hands seemed to spread over her body, the way he seemed to peel off her clothes little by little. She retreated slightly as he placed his arm around her waist, put her hand in his hand, drew her closer to him.

"Hi, Peg," he said. "Hi, Red."

He whirled her out on the dance floor, squeezed her tightly to himself, and she strained away from his hard body; but she made no dent against his command.

"Take it easy, Peg," he said. "I'm leading, not you. Just relax and follow. Relax and follow. Make this last dance count."

He held her close. Suddenly she yielded and felt all loose and limp against him, so nice and easy and gliding, and she heard the music as a soft murmur about her, and the harshness of the hall died away, and his breath against her ear was hot and moist and quivery, and she didn't care, she just didn't care.

After the dance, he said he had a car and he would like to drive her home. He would also drive Marge and his friend home. They drove along the dimly lit Chicago streets to where Marge lived. Marge and the fellow she was with got out and the fellow driving the car said he would pick him up later, after he took Peg home. He shoved the gear into first and sped off, saying: "Ah, what the hell. Let them do what they want to do. We got time, plenty time. Tomorrow's Sunday. Plenty time. And we'll be able to do what *we* want to do." He winked at her and added: "Huh?" Then he put his hand on her knee, slid comfortably against the seat, and drove on.

Chapter XVI

NICK paced back and forth across the living room, his head jutting out and jerking suddenly and dreadfully about, his hands clenched, his body strained. He walked hard. There was no end to the motion of his legs. They would not let him alone. There was no stillness in them.

Then he sat down and stared at the blank walls, at the overstuffed furniture, at the wrinkled carpet. He got up and looked into the room where Mickey slept. The kid was sound asleep. He stepped into the room where Mr. and Mrs. Dobbs lay in bed. He peered at them in the darkness. They weren't making a sound now. They were still. They were hardly breathing. He knew they weren't asleep. They talked too much. He had heard them. Buzz buzz buzz. Now they were silent. But he had heard them. Buzz buzz buzz. He had wondered what they were talking about. Then he had stopped wondering. He knew. They were plotting against him. They were trying to figure out a way to get rid of him. They wanted to turn him over to the police. They wanted to kill him. But if they tried, he thought, so help him if he wouldn't murder them if they tried.

He started walking around again. And then came the buzz buzz buzz. But he didn't care. He could take care of them, all right. He didn't care what they buzzed about. He knew what he could do. He knew what he was going to do. He didn't care what they buzzed about. His head felt heavy. But his legs wouldn't let him alone. He was very tired. He wanted to sleep. He wanted to lay down and close his eyes and say to hell with them and go to sleep. He wanted to just lay down and never wake up. But he couldn't. His legs wouldn't let him. He felt something inside cry out against him. It came out of his guts. Don't, Nick, something inside cried out, Don't, don't, Nick. Don't do this to me, Nick.

He gritted his teeth. He punched his fist into his palm. His eyes pained him. There was a steady throb in the back of his head. He sat down again but he couldn't sit still. He closed his eyes for a moment. He couldn't keep them closed. The heat of his eyes began to burn inwardly. Then he saw a picture of himself running. He was running like hell. Somebody was chasing him. He couldn't elude him. He heard the hard beat of his feet and the thump of his heart. The ground tore up beneath him as he dug and pushed it away from him with his driving legs. But he couldn't get away. He leaped with his whole body strained forward. His feet were off the ground and his legs were moving without effort. But when he glanced around he saw that he was still being pursued. He couldn't shake him off. He began growing tired. Then his pursuer flung himself at him and coiled himself around his back. He kept on running, wriggling his shoulders, shaking his hips, jarring to a stop and leaping forward, but he couldn't fling him off. He turned about to yell and his twisted mouth froze as he stared into the face of his pursuer. He had looked at his own face. The pursuer was himself. He stopped running. His heart seemed to stop beating. He fell to the ground and was bruised by the weight of his pursuer. Then in great fright and pain he began running again, not knowing that he was chasing himself.

"Oh, Christ," he muttered. "My sweet Jesus Christ."

He stood up and began walking again, back and forth, back and forth, round and round, round and round. He felt better in motion, more assured. But he couldn't stop from jerking his head about suddenly, peering to the sides and behind him. Nobody was following him. He was alone. There was no sound, only his feet on the carpet. There was only the emptiness and silence of the house late at night. It was better walking. It was better moving. That made him feel that he was all there.

Then he stopped for a moment. He listened. No. He had heard nothing. The buzz buzz buzz had even stopped. The silence was complete. He had heard nothing. Everybody was asleep. Everybody in the whole world was asleep but himself and Peg. He wondered how everybody could sleep. Weren't they scared? Didn't they worry? How could everybody sleep but he and Peg? And what had happened to Peg? Why wasn't she home? Did she pick up another guy? Is she going for somebody else? He'd kill her. Did she run away? He'd kill her. Was she never coming back? He'd murder her. Was she going to leave him alone with the family? He'd kill them all. Goddamn it, he was going to give her another half-hour to get home. He had given her all night. He would teach her to make him wait for her. He would teach her something she would never forget. If she didn't show up in a half-hour he was going to kill her.

"Did you hear that?" he said. "What I just said?"

He was in the bedroom of Mr. and Mrs. Dobbs. They didn't answer. But he knew that they were not sleeping. Nobody was going to be asleep while he was awake.

"I said I'd give her a half-hour to get home," he said. "If she don't show by then I'm going to kill her."

"You couldn't," said Mrs. Dobbs.

"The hell I couldn't," said Nick.

"You'd bring the police if you did," said Mr. Dobbs.

"I'll bring the police, then," said Nick. "But I'll kill her."

"You wouldn't dare," said Mrs. Dobbs. "You'll be caught. You'll be electrocuted."

"Who the hell cares?" said Nick. "Al. My pal, Al, he's going to burn."

"You're safe here, Nick," said Mrs. Dobbs. "Don't make any trouble and be safe. Don't do anything to harm yourself, Nick."

"I won't, don't worry," said Nick. "You're the one is going to get hurt. I'm going to knock you all off," he said evenly. "One by one. First Peg."

164

"Keep us alive, Nick," said Mrs. Dobbs. "We'll keep you safe. You'll see, Nick. We'll keep you so safe, Nick. So safe."

Her mouth began to quiver. Mr. Dobbs put his hand over her mouth. He didn't want her to talk. He didn't want her to antagonize Nick. She lay there, grateful for not being allowed to talk, trying to clutch her husband's hand with her trembling lips.

"Don't get nervous, Nick," said Mr. Dobbs quietly. "Everything is all right."

"The hell it is."

"Relax, Nick. You're safe with us. Relax."

"You're damn right I'm safe. I better be safe. I'll knock you off if I ain't. You know I will. You know I will, don't you?"

"Yes."

"Goddamn right I will. Now where the hell is Peg?"

"She'll be home soon."

"She better. She ain't got long to live if she ain't. I'm going to show her. I'm going to show you, too. Where the hell did you send her? What the hell is she doing?"

"Don't raise your voice, Nick. You'll arouse the neighbors. They'll think something's wrong. They might call the police."

"To hell with them. I ain't scared. I'll wake up the whole goddamn neighborhood. I'll bring every crummy cop in the world to this door. But I'll get you first. You and the old lady and the kid. And in a half-hour I'll shoot the guts out of Peg if she don't show. I'll shoot the guts out of you, too, you lousy bastards."

Mr. Dobbs sat up and braced himself against the back of the bed. Nick leaned closer and closer to him.

"Telling me I'm safe with you," said Nick. "You dirty lying bastard, telling me I'm safe with you."

"Think, Nick. Think of what you're doing. Don't lose control, Nick. Relax. Relax, Nick."

"I'll relax. Over your dead body, I'll relax."

"Shhhhh, Nick. Why don't you go to sleep and rest up? All you need is a little sleep and you'll be all right and you won't have a thing to worry about. Peg's all right. She'll

165

come home before you know it and she won't have told anyone about you."

"How do I know that? How do I know what you got up your sleeve?"

"Because I know Peg."

"Listen, you bastard. I know Peg, too. She's a whore. She's nothing but a goddamn whore. Right now she's spreading her legs for some sonofabitch. Right now, you yellow bastard, you lousy pimp."

Nick reached for Mr. Dobbs, who knew it was coming. He knew that the violence in Nick had to be expressed some way. He had hoped for this to happen before Peg came home. Then Peg might be safe. He lifted his shaky hands as Nick lunged at him. Nick grabbed him by his pajama top and ripped it as he hauled Mr. Dobbs out of bed.

"Don't, Ella," said Mr. Dobbs, as he caught a glimpse of his wife's terrified eyes. "Don't make a sound. Not a sound. Don't look."

Mrs. Dobbs put her fist into her mouth and then turned her head away as Nick smashed his fist into Mr. Dobbs' face. Nick began to cry and mutter. He lifted Mr. Dobbs securely by the pajama top and began to slap Mr. Dobbs' wobbling face, back and forth. The knuckles of Nick's hand caught Mr. Dobbs' lips a few times and blood began to stream down from his mouth. Then Nick grew tired. His slaps became weaker. He pushed Mr. Dobbs onto the bed and walked out of the room. He sat down on the couch in the living room and held his head in his hands and shook it wearily back and forth. He heard somebody go to the bathroom. Then he heard the water running for a long while. Then he heard somebody get back into bed. Then he heard Mrs. Dobbs say, "God God God God." And he thought it came from his own throat. Then he heard an automobile stop outside. The motor purred a while before it was shut off.

He jumped to his feet and ran to the window and peered out. There it was, a car outside the house, with the light from the lamp post glinting off it. But inside the car was in darkness. He couldn't see a thing. He couldn't hear a thing. But he knew that Peg was in there. Who was with her? If she had brought somebody with her to gang up on him he would kill them both. He could hardly wait for her to come out. He had a wild desire to rush out and bash the guy she was with over the head and drive away with Peg. His feet couldn't stay still. They scraped the floor as he peered through the window. He wanted to run out and get them. Then, in his mind, he heard the springs of the back seat in the car squeak. He felt as though a fist had rammed against his ribs. He stood there for hours, it seemed, watching, waiting, seeing nothing but wild pictures in his mind and hearing nothing but lewd sounds in his ears, before the door of the car opened and Peg stepped out, alone. She walked slowly up the stairs. The car drove away. He heard the door below open and shut. He heard Peg come up the hallway stairs. He opened the door for her. When she stepped in, he latched the door. He grabbed her purse and the package from her arm. He looked into them and flung them away. He knew that she couldn't have a weapon hidden on her thin dress. He grasped her wrist, dragged her into the living room, and flung her on the couch. He examined her very carefully. Finally, standing tall above her with his legs spread and his hands stretched taut, he said hoarsely:

"Where the hell were you?"

"Out," she said.

"Where?"

"What do you care?"

"Listen, you."

"Leave me alone. I'm tired."

"Damn right you're tired. How many times?"

"Leave me alone, will you, Nick? I don't know what you mean."

"You know what I mean, all right, you slut."

"Shut up. Shut up."

"Why, you—" His stretched hands reached for her.

"Shut up," she said tensely. "Shut up. Shut up."

"I ought to cut your heart out."

"Why? What's the difference? What's it mean to you?"

It happened suddenly to Nick. Maybe it was the way

167

she looked up at him, with her whole throat exposed, with her red hair soft on her shoulders, with her eyes clean and unafraid, with her voice crying. Maybe it was the words: there was a difference, there was a meaning. Maybe it was his urge to kill her. He didn't know. His hands grasped her throat and he raised her to himself without choking her. Her head and hair were flung backward; she was like a rag doll he had lifted, she was so resigned and limp; and all at once he wanted to crush her to him and he wanted her to ease out the violence and the loneliness and the fear in him. He wanted her to help him escape from the man who was himself that pursued him all the time. And when he felt her respond, when he felt her body clinging to him, when he felt her arms holding him, his legs grew lifeless; he fell on the couch with her. He had stopped running. Then he slowly let her go. He wanted to think. He wanted to get a good hold on himself.

"You go for me, Peg. Don't you, Peg?"

"Yes."

"Why?"

"I don't know why."

"But you go for me."

"Yes."

"You'll help me, then."

"I'll help you, Nick."

"We can get away. You and me, we can get away."

"Whenever you say, Nick."

"Where'll we go?"

"Wherever you say."

"We'll go far. We'll go far away."

"Yes."

"But where? We got to know where. We got to know how."

"We'll figure it out."

"Can I trust you, Peg?"

"You must, Nick. You must."

"If I only could."

"You've got to trust me, Nick."

"Jesus, if I only could."

"You've got to, Nick. You'll never escape if you don't.

You'll be a prisoner the rest of your life, if you don't, or you'll be caught."

"But where'll we go? Where is it safe?"

"I told you, Nick. We'll see. We'll figure it out."

"Nothing happened tonight, huh?"

"Nothing."

"I mean, you and the guy in the car."

"Nothing. You've got to trust me, Nick."

"You almost drove me off my nut waiting. I was going to kill you. The next time you do that—"

"I won't."

"Jesus, Peg."

He put his head on her lap and sat that way awhile. Then he became confused. He didn't know what to make of anything. Peg was tricking him. How were they going to get away? Where were they going? When would they stop? She was playing a trick on him. She was trying to make him fall for her. He was going nuts in the house. Maybe she knew that. Maybe she thought she could make him fall for anything. She just wanted to get him out of the house. Then she would toss him up for grabs. She was smart. And supposing they did get away? She would know about him. She could tell on him. He would be no better off. He would have to keep his eyes on her for the rest of his life. Or he would have to kill her. Jesus, what was she trying to do to him? But he wasn't going to let her mix him up any more. He was going to be careful of her. He was going to work things out his own way. If she came into the picture, okay. But he was going to figure things out his own way.

He stood up and walked into the bedroom where Mickey lay sleeping. Now he was going to get some sleep. Now he was going to get over this night and wake up fresh in the morning and be the boss.

Peg stared at the door of the bedroom. She sat on the couch a long while, feeling limp. Her insides had no life to them. She felt as though she had lived a million years and that her insides had become brittle. She did not know when they would break and fall to pieces. She hoped it would be soon. Then she could let the exhaustion that was in her carry her away. She hoped it would be soon.

169

Chapter XVII

AFTER Nick locked the door to his bedroom the house grew very quiet. Each room seemed to mingle into another. Each room, crouched and waiting, seemed to stalk another.

A sigh was heard. Each room seemed to gang up around this sigh. And the house became filled with the sounds of rustling sheets and disturbed beds.

Nick wriggled deeper into his bed. To hell with it, he thought. I got to get some sleep. I got to get some sleep. I got to!

Mickey turned over on his stomach and groaned.

Mr. and Mrs. Dobbs looked at each other in the darkness.

"Do you hear, Ella?" said Mr. Dobbs softly.

"Yes."

"Peg's crying."

"Yes."

"What shall we do?"

"What can we do?" asked Mrs. Dobbs.

Their tension, aching from the helpless vigil, eased into the quiet sobbing.

"Why don't you see what's troubling her?" said Mr. Dobbs.

"We know, don't we?"

"Yes, Ella. But she needs somebody."

"You go to her, Casey."

"No, you go. It's a woman's job. It's a woman's duty."

"I'm afraid, Casey."

"Of Nick? He's locked himself in with Mickey."

"No. Of other things."

"How do you mean, Ella?"

"Of things I might not like to know."

"I don't understand."

Mrs. Dobbs didn't understand, either. Nick had her all mixed up. That afternoon when he had told her that he had had Peg she had felt the greatest pain of her life. It seemed that he had torn Peg from her. Peg seemed strange to her. In her mind they looked at each other and there was no recognition. They were strangers suddenly. She did not understand Peg any more. There was the great chasm, over which she could not leap, between the child and the grown woman. And now, tonight, though she felt that she had lost Peg, she was afraid to face what might have happened in the living room and she was afraid of the talk that had gone on between Nick and Peg.

"Nothing happened in there, in the living room, did it, Ella?" said Mr. Dobbs with great effort.

"Nothing, Casey," she said quickly. "Nothing, nothing. Don't you think about it."

"Then you mean you're afraid of what they were talking about."

"Yes."

"Do you think it's true, Peg's wanting to go away with Nick?"

"You heard, Casey." And after a pause, she said: "I don't want to think."

Mr. Dobbs faced her and pressed his fingers into her shoulders.

"It's impossible," he said.

"I hope so."

"She's trying to get him out of the house. She's willing to die for us. That's it. That's the reason."

"I hope so."

"It couldn't be otherwise. You don't think she would fall in love—tell me, Ella. Tell me."

"I don't think so. She couldn't, Casey. She couldn't. But you heard. What are we to believe?"

171

They stared blankly at each other. Then the sobbing they had heard stopped. The house was once again very quiet, waiting.

"If I could just do something!" he said. "God, if I could just do something."

Mrs. Dobbs drew closer to him.

"All day, Ella, I've beeen racking my mind trying to think of what to do," he said. "But I feel so helpless. You don't know how many times I'd begun walking toward the police. Suddenly I would see a picture of you or Mickey or Peg dead and I would stop, chilled. If we only had someone to turn to. If only somebody could help us. But there is only ourselves. There is only me. And I'm no good. I'm no goddamn good, Ella. Peg sees that. She knows I'm no good. That's why she's doing what she's doing. She knows how it is. I'm no good, Ella. I'm no goddamn good. I'm nothing, Ella. Nothing."

Mrs. Dobbs put her arm about him and drew him close to her, giving him the warmth and security of her body to feel.

"Don't say that, Casey," she said. "You're good. You're the finest man in the world. You're everything. Something will work out."

"Nothing will work out, unless we make it work out. We have nobody to turn to, Ella. Only ourselves. And we're so weak, so damn weak. And if Peg has fallen in love with him—but she couldn't have. She couldn't have. She's trying to help us. I know she is. She's pretending that she's in love and she's trying to help us. Isn't she, Ella?"

"Yes."

"Will you go to her and try to find out? We must know."

"Yes."

"When?"

"Later. She must be sleeping now. Let her sleep."

"But you *will* find out, Ella?"

"Yes. But," she said slowly and with effort, "what if Peg says, yes, she is in love with him?"

Mr. Dobbs stared at her.

Chapter XVIII

THE day came late, gray and threatening with rain. It was a different Sunday than any that the Dobbs family and Nick had ever faced. Ordinarily, the house was strewn with newspapers and the comic sections, which Mickey read on the floor. There was the breakfast ritual on the one morning when the whole family sat down to eat together. There was the elaborate planning of what to do with the day; and except for going to church, they seldom passed the day through together, but it was good to plan it. After church, cleansed, starched, and ennobled, they were ready to relax and linger and go their separate ways, still feeling together along the different paths they walked. But today, separated, doubtful, and distrustful, Mr. and Mrs. Dobbs and Peg lay in their beds after awakening, dreading to get up to face the remainder of the sunless day. As for Nick, Sundays were like any other day. He always dreaded to get up and confront the long hours ahead. He couldn't get comfortable within any day. Nightfall left him uneasy and when he got to bed, finally, he was exhausted but restless. And now, he slept, blended with the gray and threatening day. But Mickey, who eagerly looked forward to each new day as one that held a great promise for him, was alert. He was the first to crawl softly out of bed. This day held the promise of escape for him. If he could get away he could then rescue his mother and father and Peg. Oh, this day had to keep its promise!

He tiptoed to a chair, placed it in front of the door,

stood on it, and tried to pull the lock open. He gave up after a while and stood in front of the window studying the ground below. He was afraid to jump. There was no way of climbing down. He walked quietly to Nick's side and looked for the gun in his clothes. It wasn't there. He saw the key to the lock attached to a string around Nick's neck. He reached for the string and tried to break it. Nick's hands came up and grabbed his wrists. Nick jerked on them and Mickey fell to his knees.

"What are you trying to do, kid?" said Nick.

"Don't," Mickey whimpered. "You're breaking my arms. Don't."

"I said, what are you trying to do, kid?"

"Don't. Ooooh, don't."

"Say you won't try it again."

"I won't."

"You little punk." Nick released Mickey's wrists. He felt under his pillow slip. The gun was still there. "Get back to bed."

"Let's get up and go out," said Mickey.

"Get back to bed."

"I don't want to."

Nick sat up.

"You going to get back to bed?" he said.

Mickey got in but wouldn't lie down.

"You little punk," said Nick.

"When we going to get up?"

"When I say so."

But Nick knew that he wouldn't be able to fall asleep again. His face felt puffed and hot from lack of sleep. He felt like he wanted to kill the kid for waking him. Now he had the whole day ahead of him, a whole day and a night of watching. And the day had already started out bad. He could kill the kid for that.

He watched Mickey punch through the air in the direction of the window. The day had broken its promise to Mickey. He did not know if he could ever trust the beginning of a day again. All right for you, day, said Mickey inwardly. You'll be sorry. You'll see if I ever do anything for you. You'll see. And Nick, looking at Mickey grind his teeth, thought: the kid's going nuts, everybody's going nuts, I'm going nuts. Nick! he called to himself. Hang on! Jesus Christ, Nick. Hang on!

He stood up, took his gun out from under the pillow, put it in his pants pocket, and got dressed.

"Come on, kid," he said. "We'll go to the can and then we'll eat."

With Nick and Mickey up, Mr. and Mrs. Dobbs and Peg got out of their beds and dressed. Soon, everybody was gathered in the kitchen. They sat down awkwardly to their breakfast. They consumed the meal, brooding in distrustful silence. Like Nick, everybody watched and waited suspiciously, afraid for and of each other. Mr. and Mrs. Dobbs felt very uncomfortable in Peg's presence, as though she had betrayed them, as though she were a conspirator against them, as though she were another antagonist to contend with. Mrs. Dobbs sighed occasionally. She glanced at Peg, who rigidly stared into her coffee cup. She yearned to reach for Peg and to come close and to ask about Nick and herself. Her breath seemed to catch and she wanted to but couldn't cry out: Peg! Peg, Peg, Peg, baby! And Mr. Dobbs, aching and crying inwardly, caught up by a force that he thought he had killed for himself in his mind, dared not open his eyes wide. He asked himself: what is happening to us? Why are we so distrustful? Is it that the bad in us, which we have been fighting down so hard all our lives, now has come to the surface? Does it take evil to bring out evil? Will we ever survive this that has already twisted our lives? Will we?

"What's the matter?" said Peg suddenly, her eyes downcast, smudged by the reflection of the coffee. "What's the matter with everybody?"

Nobody, except Nick, who had been observing everybody very carefully all along, looked up or said anything.

"Something's wrong," said Peg. "I never felt this way before. I think you hate me. All of you hate me. You want to kill me, too." She paused, still afraid to look up and face her family. Her voice began to quiver. "It was my fault. All right, I'll admit it was my fault. I made a mistake. But I didn't know. Honest, I didn't know. I'll do anything, but I didn't know, and don't hate me. Please, don't hate me." She felt her voice rise and suddenly stop; then it fell and thumped into herself and her eyes smarted from the salt of her tears. She stood up and walked out of the room.

"Why, you crummy bastards," said Nick, "your heads down like you're praying, afraid to give the kid a break. You cheap, crummy bastards." He stood up and began to walk out of the kitchen. "But don't get me wrong," he said at the doorway. "What goes for you, if anything goes out of line, goes for Peg, too. Don't get me wrong and think I'm going soft. Peg's guts is worth no more to me than yours is. So don't get a funny idea. Just don't."

And after he left, Mickey said: "We're never going to have any fun again."

Mr. and Mrs. Dobbs looked at each other and at Mickey's pout, and for a moment, through the strangeness of what Mickey said, there was a Sunday morning tenderness in them that might have made them smile or laugh softly in another time. But now, Mr. Dobbs cleared his throat and said: "I guess you better take Mickey and Peg to church, Ella."

"And what will you do, Casey?" said Mrs. Dobbs.

"I'll stay with Nick."

"I'm afraid, Casey. I'm afraid for you to do that. You might get wild. You might try to do something crazy, like the other morning. And if something happened to you—Casey, I don't know what I'd do."

"Don't worry, Ella. I'll do nothing to upset Nick. I promise you."

"Perhaps I better stay, though. How am I going to face some of my friends? They might want to know why I wasn't home to them yesterday morning. I won't know what to say, Casey."

"You'll just show them your bandaged finger. You'll just say something. But I want you to go. And I want you to take Peg along. I don't want her around the house with Nick."

"It'll look very strange, all of us not being there to-
176

gether, Casey. It'll look very strange and suspicious. People will think something is wrong between us."

"But you'll go, Ella. Please go."

Peg wanted to stay, while the others went to church, but nobody would listen. Finally, Mr. Dobbs was left alone with Nick in the living room.

"So it's you and me now, huh, Shorty?" said Nick.

"It's you and me," said Mr. Dobbs.

"What'd you get rid of the others for, Shorty? You got something up your sleeve? You think you're going to pull something off?"

Mr. Dobbs didn't answer. He picked up a newspaper very deliberately and sat down on the couch and began to read it.

"What's it say?" asked Nick.

"Nothing you'd be interested in."

"Why not?"

"You're too interested in yourself. Nothing outside yourself makes any difference to you."

"So what? That's how you get along. Screw everybody else."

Mr. Dobbs turned a page.

"Don't it say something about me?" asked Nick.

"Yes."

"What's it say?"

"Read it and see."

"You nuts? Me read the paper and give you a chance to run out or get funny? You nuts?"

"There's a story on you and your partner, Al. But if you want to know what it says you'll have to read it."

"You lousy bastard."

Mr. Dobbs turned another page.

"Ah, what the hell can the paper say?" Nick said. "They're still looking for me, it says. They're going to nab me any minute, it says. Like so much crap, they'll nab me. They don't figure a guy can turn smart. They don't figure they're up against a brain guy, the dopes. Well, they'll never get me. You know that, don't you, Shorty?"

Mr. Dobbs didn't answer.

177

"Sure, you know it," said Nick. "They'll get me over your dead body. That's the only way they'll get me. So you'll never let them get me. You want to live too goddamn much. And if you're tired of living you want your kids and the old lady to keep on living."

"You know everything, don't you, Nick?"

"Goddamn right. But what's the paper say about Al?"

"Nothing."

"Doesn't it say how he is and what's going to happen to him?"

"You know what's going to happen to him."

"Sure, I know. Al's going to burn. But don't it say anything else? About what else he's ratting about?"

"Nothing."

"To hell with you. What's there to know anyhow? Al's going to burn and I'm safe. What the hell else is there for a guy to know?"

"Nothing."

Nick settled down to watching Mr. Dobbs. He couldn't see his face; it was hidden by the newspaper. His eyes began to hurt. The print began to waver. He felt that his eyes were slowly consuming his whole body. He became a little frightened. Nobody was going to get him. But his eyes, the heaviness and the pulled feeling of his head, were getting him. Nothing else. Not even the dead cop. He never even thought about the dead cop. He felt nothing about him. He felt something about Al. But not even Al was going to get him. Nothing was. Not even the old man or the old lady or the kid or Peg. He had them all, right in his hands. They couldn't move. All they could do was squirm. No matter how far they went he had them, right in his hands. But his eyes. He had to put them in his hands. Himself. He had to hold himself, tight. He couldn't let himself get away. Then nobody could get him.

He saw Mr. Dobbs lower the paper so that he could see his face.

"Nick," said Mr. Dobbs. "What goes on in your head?"

"Nothing."

"And what goes on inside of you?"

"Nothing."

178

"You mean you're dead?"

"I mean I got you by the balls."

"What do you do all day? Just watch?"

"What do you think?"

"Isn't it enough to drive you out of your mind?"

"If you think I'm going nuts, you're nuts. You think I will, then you'll get me. You're the guy that's going to go nuts."

"Why don't you relax, Nick?"

"Okay. I'll play you some cards."

"I don't play cards."

"No. You beat your brains out on them boats."

"Yes. They help me relax. Why don't you come down to the basement with me, Nick? I'll give you something to do. I'll let you help me build a boat."

"You're really blowing your top."

"No, I mean it."

"Don't be nuts, Shorty. You know I'm not leaving this house. You know you're not leaving, either. You'll take your shot in the arm later."

"It can't hurt you to take a short walk down the stairs. You won't be seen. You've got a gun, I've got nothing, you'll have me covered. What's there to be afraid of?"

"No. I said: no. And shut up."

"All right." Mr. Dobbs raised the newspaper and hid his face.

Nick dwelt upon the image of going outdoors, even for a moment, from the second floor to the basement. Himself hitting the air, taking a deep breath, busting the unseen bands around his chest, expanding, stretching his legs, his head growing clear and light. Himself walking down the street, not noticing anything, not looking at a thing, never turning around suddenly. Himself with his eyes wide open, not creased and cramped and pulling, and not seeing a thing. Himself lying on the soft warm sand of a beach with the sun dazzling his shut eyes, making diamonds glitter before his closed lids, never having to open them, feeling the sense of life in the power of the sun upon him, then cooling off his eyes in the gently swelling clean green water; then his eyes suddenly loosened from his head and there was no pain and there was all open spaces in his head and his eyes began to float away, but they were still attached to his head, for they suddenly began to tug at his head and, becoming stronger than him, began to pull him out; he reached desperately for the cords from which his eyes extended and yanked them, and they rushed, plop, back into their sockets, and became set, starry, smudged by the wavery newsprint that hid the old man's face.

"Hey, put down the goddamn paper and let's talk," he said.

Mr. Dobbs laid away the newspaper and looked at Nick. He picked up a pipe from an end table, filled it with tobacco, lit it carefully, sucked up smoke and let it curl lazily out of his mouth. He stretched out and sank deep into the couch.

"All right, let's talk," he said. "What do you want to talk about?"

"You'd sure like to be out of this spot, huh?"

"Yes."

"You'd like me to blow out of here, huh?"

Mr. Dobbs drew on his pipe and nodded his head.

"It's no picnic for me, either," said Nick.

"You made the decision to stay. You're free to leave any time."

"Like hell I am."

"What's to keep you here?"

"You."

"You're not my prisoner."

"The hell I'm not. You hit it the first time I told you what the score was. You said I was going to be your prisoner. I laughed. I laughed my insides out. So long as you live, Shorty, I'm your prisoner. How do you like that? . . . Oh, you won't answer that one. But you're a tough guy. I'll tell you. When I knock you off I'll be free. Okay?"

"When are you going to knock me off?"

"When I'm ready. Okay?"

Mr. Dobbs puffed hard at his pipe. His head nodded in the smoke he blew out.

"But I want you to know it ain't my fault," said Nick.

180

"I don't want you to have hard feelings against me. You're a good Joe, maybe. Your missus and your kid and Peg, they're good Joes, too, maybe. Who the hell knows about that? But what's going to happen around here ain't my fault."

"Whose fault is it then?"

"It's the cop's fault. He shouldn't of walked in when me and Al already pulled off the job. It was his goddamn fault." Nick paused, measuring Mr. Dobbs carefuly, then continued: "It's Al's fault, too. He should of got away. Or he should of died when the cop shot him. Then he wouldn't of talked. Then I'd of been in the clear. Then I'd of never met Peg. Then I'd of never met you. Did you ever stop to think about that, Shorty?"

"Many many times."

"So don't you wish there was no goddamn cops in the world and that my pal, Al, had died when the cop shot him?" Nick waited for Mr. Dobbs to answer him. "Why the hell don't you?" he said impatiently. "The cop's dead. Al's going to burn, he's going to be dead, so why the hell shouldn't you wish Al died when the cop shot him? Then I'd be in the clear. I'd never have to look at you. You'd be in the clear. We'd all be in the clear." In measured tones, Nick added: "Listen, you punk, don't you wish that had happened? Don't you wish Al hadn't ratted on me? Don't you wish you never saw me and I was the hell out of here?"

"Yes."

"Okay. But it sure took you a long time to make up your mind."

"I didn't like to justify people dying."

"Well, you'll get a little taste of it pretty soon."

"Why are you talking, Nick? What are you trying to do?"

"Nothing. Just talking. Just telling you the score."

"I know the score."

"Who's on the winning end, Shorty? You or me?"

"You can't win."

"Jesus, you're a tough guy. I could give you a winner right now. I got what it takes. And I could do it with my bare hands. I could rub you out in a minute, Shorty. So where do you get that noise, I can't win?"

"No matter what you do to us, you'll lose in the end. In fact, you're losing now, wanting to talk. Did you ever need to talk before, Nick? You never had to talk before? You got alone fine alone, you said. Why do you need to talk now, Nick? Something bothering you?"

"No."

"Why did you do it, Nick? When you did it, what did you want?"

"I don't know."

"You must have wanted something."

"Sure I wanted something. You think I go around knocking off people, just like that, for nothing?"

"But what did you want?"

"Money. Okay?"

"Well, you've got money now. What did you plan to do with it?"

"Plenty."

"What, for instance?"

"To buy things. To do things."

"Like what?"

"What are you, a dick?"

"No. I'm just wondering what drove you to do what you did."

"Ah, shut up. Cut out the wondering."

"I'm wondering why you don't do now what you wanted to do. You've got the money. You've got what you want."

"I got crap. Just plain crap."

"If you knew what you wanted out of life you wouldn't feel that way. If you made up your mind what you wanted you'd leave us alone and do it. Life isn't long, Nick. It isn't measured in years and days. It's you, right now. What did you want, Nick?"

"What the hell do you want, smart guy?"

"I want to be left alone."

"Just like a jerk. Well, you ain't going to be left alone. And shut up giving me the third degree. Shut the hell up."

Nick stood up and walked toward Mr. Dobbs with his eyes pulling on the insides of his head.

Mr. Dobbs picked up the newspaper and began reading. Nick watched the smoke curl from the pipe. The newsprint seemed to jiggle. He moved backward and sat heavily on an easy chair.

"Do you feel bad about killing the cop?" asked Mr. Dobbs from behind the newspaper.

"No."

"You never think about it?"

"Hell no. What for?"

"How about Al? Do you feel bad about Al?"

"Christ no, the rat."

"Then you feel fine, don't you, Nick?"

"Sure."

"You have no conscience then."

"That's for yellow bastards like you. Besides, who says I killed the cop?"

"Al."

"Sure he said it. Because he killed the cop, not me. If he hadn't of killed the cop he wouldn't of ratted on me. I'd like to see somebody prove I did."

"The police could prove it."

"They'll never get a chance."

"Suppose they catch you?"

"They better not. You better hope they don't. They'll catch me over your dead body. I told you that. There'll be some other dead ducks around, too. And when they get me, they'll never get a chance to prove anything, they'll never get a chance to burn me. I'll die first, shooting."

"You're scared, Nick. What are you scared of?"

"Nothing."

"You scared to die?"

"No. I ain't going to die."

"You scared of the cop you killed, ourselves whom you plan to kill?"

"No. I suppose you ain't scared."

"No. I never harmed anybody. I have nothing to be afraid of."

"Boy, you're a sweet holy sonofabitch. What are you trying to do?"

"I'm trying to get you out of here. Leave, before you crack up. Leave before you harm us."

"Ha, ha," Nick laughed dryly.

"You're cracking up now, Nick. Leave before it's too late. We won't say a word about you. You can go scot free, right now, and you can get away, while you're all there."

"Suppose I left, but I didn't leave alone?"

"It wouldn't do you any good, Nick. You'd be in the same spot. Have pity on us. Have pity on yourself."

"I don't pity nobody. A guy alive or dead don't make any difference to me. They both stink for my dough."

"Have pity on yourself," Mr. Dobbs pleaded.

"Okay. Supposing I do and I go away with Peg?"

The newspaper in Mr. Dobbs' hands began to rattle. Nick's eyes teared up as he tried to stare through the paper to see Mr. Dobbs' face.

"You couldn't, Nick," said Mr. Dobbs.

"The hell I couldn't. All I got to do is snap my fingers and she's off with me."

"Then what? Where would you be? Where would you go? How would you get along? Why should you trust Peg? Would you be any better off than now? Think, Nick. Think it out. Leave now, alone. It's your only chance. Get away alone, Nick. Be alone like you always were. That's the way you get along good. Alone."

"You know," said Nick, "I thought maybe you was whoring your daughter after me, making her give me the come on. Maybe you wasn't, though."

"You're rotten, Nick. Through and through."

"Peg can maybe do things for me. She goes for me. She's a pretty hot number, too. A redhead."

Mr. Dobbs couldn't hold the newspaper in his hands any longer. It fell to the floor, wrinkled, torn at the edges.

"Shut up," he said tensely.

"Redheads are hot, Shorty. You ought to know that. You got a redhead. You want to hear about it?"

184

"Shut up."

"Look who's telling me to shut up. You crummy punk, telling me to shut up. Why don't you do something, you crummy punk?"

Mr. Dobbs quivered inwardly as he glared at Nick. Yes, why didn't he do something? What could he do? There was no way of getting at Nick. If he only had something to offer him. He couldn't offer him money. He couldn't even offer him his life. There was nothing he had that Nick wanted. What else was there for him to do? Words had failed him. Words had boomeranged around Nick and had hurtled back to stick in his chest. His brain had failed him. His body had been beaten. Could he try again with his body? But he had to. He had to make a last attempt. He could rush at Nick. He could try to get his gun. Could he suddenly become fused with a superhuman strength, just for a moment, just to attack Nick and to overpower him? But it was senseless. Nick was too wary. Nick had him caged with his relentless eyes. But he wasn't far from the door. If he rushed for it, perhaps he could get there before Nick could jump to him, perhaps he could escape that way, rush to the church to get his family and run to the police. And even if he didn't get away and he was shot while racing down the stairway, the shot would attract the neighbors and the police might get to the house before his family arrived. He might be killed, or he might be wounded, or he might get away; but his family would be safe, Peg would be able to live. He had to do this. He held himself tensely, waiting, crouching carefully for the moment when Nick might relax. But Nick wasn't relaxed. Nick sat on the edge of his chair, his toes on the floor, ready to spring, as though his thoughts had been perceived. They seemed to circle each other as they sat.

"Don't try anything funny," said Nick.

Mr. Dobbs didn't answer. He kept waiting. Something seemed to sink upon him, become heavy, and pinned him down. He couldn't seem to get loose. He saw himself trying to jump up, but he never got off the couch; Nick sprang upon him and smothered him. And he struggled to

185

yell for help. He strained to yell and yell and yell. But in his mind, Nick rushed over and knocked him senseless before he aroused anybody.

"Don't get funny," Nick warned.

The other way was better, thought Mr. Dobbs. Yelling might fail. He had to try to escape. It might be suicide. But he didn't care.

"Don't get tired of living," said Nick.

The way he felt now he didn't care if he lived or died. He had lost all respect from his family. He saw himself standing small before his wife and children while they nodded their heads in pity. He had failed them. He was a weak and frightened and quivering man. He was finished as a man. What must Peg, who had taken it upon herself in the only way she knew how to get rid of Nick, think of him? And Mickey, what must he think? And Ella, what must she think? If he died in escape and saved them, then he would end his life as a man, strong in their eyes. If he lived on after Nick got away, through Peg, he and his family would never be the same; they would be scarred by the wounds Nick had inflicted; and he would be dead inside while his body moved. He had to try to get away. He would die as a man, with his family secure; or he would get away and live like a man, with Nick gone and his family together.

He moved carefully toward the end of the couch, closer to the door, with Nick's eyes upon him. And then he couldn't bear it any longer. He jumped up and bolted toward the door and started to yell, "Help!" But Nick sprang up and leaped at him and brought him down to the floor and covered his mouth. He tried to bite Nick's hand, which was clamped over his mouth. He tried to tear away the crooked arm that was about his throat. The pressure against his throat became stronger. His squirming legs and pinioned body grew weaker. A jagged bone seemed to stick in his throat. The room began to revolve. It turned black. A million white dots began popping into the whirling black spaces about him. Then he felt himself coughing. It came from far away, almost apart from him. The cough-

186

ing came closer. It began to hurt. It stuck in his throat. And his eyes opened.

He found himself back on the couch. His mouth was gagged and his legs were tied and his hands were bound behind his back. Nick was sitting on the easy chair. He closed his eyes to escape the sight of Nick. He began to cry softly, overwhelmed by his futility. There was no escape. There was only a leer before his shut eyes.

When he opened his eyes, they were wet and he could hardly see Nick but he could make out the leer on Nick's face. He found it hard to breathe. His eyes begged Nick to take the gag out of his mouth. The tears seemed to be drowning him. But Nick paid no attention to him. Nick just looked at him, folding and unfolding his hands.

Chapter XIX

THE sky muddied up outside and sank lower upon the city. But the rain didn't come. First there were the deep rumblings of thunder. That kept up a while, snarling, becoming exhausted, and snarling again. Then came the lightning and the wind and the heavier crashes of thunder. Then a gust of wind embraced the windows and shook them, and left them rattling. And just as the downpour came, Mrs. Dobbs, Peg, and Mickey ran up the stairs.

Nick unlatched the door and let them in. He searched them and, finding nothing, put his gun away. They stopped stomping about and wiping the wetness from their faces; their eyes were riveted to Mr. Dobbs lying on the couch.

"What happened to Mr. Dobbs?" asked Mrs. Dobbs. "What did you do to him, Nick?"

"Nothing," said Nick. "He just got tired of living. I tied him up to keep him alive."

Mrs. Dobbs rushed to her husband. She took the gag out of his mouth. She wanted to know what had happened. But she couldn't wait for an answer. She wanted to know if he had been hurt. He shook his head and swallowed with pain. She wanted to know why he had been so foolish as to try to take his life in his hands. She wanted to know what would happen to her and Mickey and Peg if he died. Why was he so foolish? Why was he such a little boy? She should have known better than to leave him alone with that monster. She began to cry and continued wanting to know many things.

But Mr. Dobbs couldn't talk. He looked at Peg and at Mickey. His mouth was dry and he could hardly swallow. Peg came to her knees beside him and began to untie the knots around his hands and feet. He felt spent. He wanted to get out of the house and be alone. He wanted to get away from his deep humiliation. He hadn't wanted his wife and children to see him this way. He wanted them to think and to believe that despite his inferior strength he still had control over the situation. Now they had seen the last remnant of himself bound up and gagged. He had shown them that they were completely at Nick's mercy. He was nothing, crumpled in cloth and rope. Now they had nobody to turn to. Now Nick could do as he pleased. Nick was no longer a prisoner, as he had thought. Now only they were. And now he wanted to escape more, he felt, than Nick did. But, like Nick, he wondered from what, how, and to where. Was it possible? he asked himself, with his back to everybody as Peg worked on the knots binding him. Was it ever possible to escape from a world of oppression, from the oppression of oneself more so than from the outer world? Was that what he had been doing all his life, trying to escape both himself and the world, only to be caught? But he had faced Nick and himself. He had battled with both. And he had lost. What was there left for him? A dream? A sailboat? A world safe in fantasy? But now, there was the oppression of himself that he must get away from, rather than from Nick.

As soon as he was untied he walked quickly into the kitchen and drank two glasses of water. Then he went down into the basement. He looked at the sailboat he had been making. The hull was long and sleek, with graceful lines. It had been a thing he loved, growing from his heart and out of his careful tender hands. It was to have been for Mickey. It was not the ornate type he had made for Peg, nor was it the sturdy kind he had made for himself. This was like a thoroughbred horse, sleek and shiny and powerful. It was for winning races. It was for victory. It was for winning the Lipton Cup. So it was flawless, with nothing to mar the great victory it was intended to win in the minds of himself and Mickey. He picked up the top-mast and began to sand it carefully. This working with his hands began to calm him. His hands seemed to reach out and present the self of his imagination to him. The promise of this boat began to extend itself. He grew taller and stronger in the sense of its shape. But when he lost the far-gaze of his eyes and looked down to the mast he noticed that Mickey was by his side.

"Hello, son," he said warmly.

"How do you feel, pa?"

"All right, son. All right."

"Ma sent me down to see how you was."

"Tell her I'm fine," said Mr. Dobbs slowly.

"You weren't hurt, were you, pa?"

"No, son. Did you have a good time at church?"

"We saw lots of people. They asked about you, why you wasn't there."

"What was the sermon about?"

"We didn't hear so good."

"Why?"

"We was thinking."

"Of what, son?"

"Ma was scared of you with Nick."

"And you? What were you scared of?"

"I don't know, pa."

Mr. Dobbs scraped the sandpaper hard over the mast.

"Ma and Peg, they didn't even talk like they always do," said Mickey.

"Yes."

"Like they was mad on each other."

"They're not mad, Mickey. Just disturbed."

"I know, pa. But it's funny. Everything is funny."

In the silence that followed, only the sound of the scraping sandpaper and the rain was heard. Mickey took a deep breath and said:

"It's raining out, pa. Raining like anything."

"Yes."

"When's the boat going to be ready, pa?"

"Soon, Mickey. Soon."

190

"Then we'll race it, huh, pa?"

"Then we'll race it."

"Who we going to race it against?"

"Sir Lipton and Vanderbilt."

"And we're going to win, huh?"

"We're going to win."

"And I'm going to be chief mate?"

"Aye, aye, laddie."

"Boy, we'll beat them. We'll beat them like nothing."

"We will that, matey."

The talk stopped again and they stood awkwardly looking away from each other.

"But I wish it was a real boat," said Mickey finally. "A real real boat."

"It is, matey. It is."

"Naw, it's just a toy boat for the lagoon, and you have to chase it and hang on to it by a string and you can't stand on it."

"But if you think hard enough it can be a real boat, son. Just let your imagination open wide and let the big sea rush up. Hear it, son?" His voice got soft and husky and his eyes lighted up. "Hear the sea smashing upon the shore? Hear the surf, the way it sings big and mighty? And you're out there, way out on the rolling sea. The sails are bellied by the wind, going forty miles an hour, sailing along, and the spray is full against your face. We're tacking now, the race is close, and you're hauling the sail, matey. And the sea, matey, the sea is rushing at the boat and it's like great clean music—"

"It's just raining, pa. It's just the rain in the rain pipes making gurgles."

Mickey started walking out of the basement.

"I'll tell ma you're all right, pa," he said.

Mr. Dobbs tried to reach out and hold on to Mickey. But Mickey was gone. Everything was gone. He looked at the boat he was building for Mickey. And that seemed gone. He felt sapped, empty, intensely alone, puttering uselessly within great spaces that he couldn't fill. Now he had nobody to fill up the great spaces of his mind. Now he felt that he had lost his children and his own childhood. He had lost the sense of having someone take his hand to walk out with him into the great fanciful world and to help him shape the beautiful and lovely things somewhere in the world. Now he had nothing. He was a man with empty hands, groping to fill them. And grasping nothing, clutching only emptiness, he felt his hands become cramped. He reached out and grabbed the topmast he had been shaping so delicately, held it tight with both hands and, with one twist, he heard a snap; the topmast was broken. He picked up a chisel and flung it into the hull. Then, with tears moistening his eyes, he pulled the chisel out and ran his fingers quiveringly over the mar in the wood that he could never fix. The chisel slowly slipped out of his hand and clanked to the ground. There was no help for the way he felt.

CHAPTER XX

ONCE again Nick could not fall asleep that night. This that he had always craved so much, this that took him away from himself and the world, this that gave him peace even in troubled dreams, would not overtake him. What agonized him more was the way Mickey could sleep beside him. Mickey seemed to rise and sink, rise and sink, seemed to float away and drift back, float away and drift back. His hands began working; he couldn't hold them still; he stopped himself suddenly from grasping Mickey's throat and choking the sleeping life out of him; he got out of bed. Be still, he said inwardly, squeezing the silent words deep within himself. Jesus, Jesus, Jesus, be still.

He moved about, holding his hands laced tight. He knew that if he didn't get away soon something would snap in him. But how could he get away? he asked himself. Where could he go? Where could he be safe? Where could he sleep? He tried to think very carefully. If he went out of the country, could he get away with it? No, there was no way of getting out; even if he could get by with phony visas and passports; a foreigner was still a foreigner, a suspicious guy, a guy to be watched, there would be too many eyes on him. If he stayed in the city he knew that he wouldn't be able to move about; he would only be holed in another room. If he went out of the city, where could he go without attracting attention; again he would be a foreigner, even in his own country.

Each time he tried to think of a way out he felt himself

up against a wall; he scratched and dug against it; he tried to leap over; but he couldn't get through or over. He wished Al was around. Al would have an angle. Al always had an angle. But if Al had listened to him and had paid attention to his dream this would not have happe~ ˙¹ They could have put off the job for another day: would have got away and they would have been toge̩ and they would have lived like kings. Why hadn't Al paid attention to the warning he had got in his sleep? Why did Al have to be such a smart guy? Now he had nobody, when he needed somebody to help him. The way he was now he couldn't think straight. Tell me, Al, he pleaded. Don't let me stay cockeyed. Tell me what to do, Al. Come on, Al. Be a pal and do me a favor and I'll blow the jail up and get you out but do me a favor and give me an angle. What do you say, Al?

He stood still, listening intently. The sound of Mickey's regular breathing came to him. He started pacing the room again. Supposing, he thought, he opened the door and walked out and ran away. Everybody was asleep. He could do it. But if he did sneak out, they would surely tell the police as soon as they awoke. How far could he get? Then where would he be? But they might be pretending sleep. And as soon as he did get out of the door, they would run for the police and he would be picked up before he could even get a street car ride. No, he couldn't do that. He couldn't leave them behind. He would have to kill them or take them with him. But where was he going to take them? How could he take all of them with him? What would be the use? Would he be any better off in another place? Still, he had to leave. If he stayed another day he would go nuts. How could he get away and make sure the police would not be told about him?

He stopped walking and stared out the window and saw a guy and a girl walk by and suddenly his head felt light and clear.

"Sure," he said aloud. "That's the way."

He punched his fist into his palm. There was only one way to get out and still be safe and keep from going nuts.

He would take Peg with him. He would tell the family that they better see to it that he's not caught, or Peg would be a dead pigeon. They better see to it that nobody gets to know about him and Peg. If the police should find him, he'd tell them, there would be a gun battle. Peg would be killed first, though. That's what he'd tell them. And they had better believe it. Because that's exactly what he was going to do. He would never let himself be caught. If he had to die he would die instantly without knowing what hit him. And that's the way Peg was going to get it, without knowing what hit her. They would know that. They would keep quiet, plenty quiet. That was the angle, then. Peg wanted to go with him anyway. Maybe she meant it. Maybe she did go for him. Maybe she was like some girls he had heard about and had seen in the movies, who went for guys like him and would die for a guy like him. If she was that way, Jesus, if she was! He felt a twinge inside of him. He could hardly contain himself. He started walking to the door to unlock it. He steadied himself. He still had to be careful. If Peg turned into the rat Al did, well, he could fix her all right, he could get along alone, too, he had always got along alone. And what he would do with her later, if he had to, well, that could wait; he'd come to that later. Right now he had to get away, but fast.

He opened the door and walked into the living room where Peg was sleeping. He stood over her and watched her regular breathing. He looked at her face outlined in the darkness. It appeared soft and untroubled. He studied her long hair on the pillow, her arms across her chest, and her body outlined under the sheets. He saw himself as a kid, long ago, beside his mother's bed, lifting the covers and crawling in beside her and feeling the warmth of her body and being able to fall asleep untroubled and safe. He saw himself as a young man, with a woman lying naked on a bed, her face empty, her legs raised, and her hard face moved by stony lips said: "Okay, okay, you looked, now hop on." And he had to run out. But always there was in him the curiosity and the passion and the notion that he had to make himself a man, like the other guys, that made

195

him try. He wondered, as he stood over Peg, whether she would make a man of him and whether she would also keep him safe.

She sighed and opened her eyes. When she saw him she drew the sheet up to her chin and backed away from him.

"I ain't going to hurt you, Peg," he said.

"What's the matter? Can't you sleep?"

"No. I haven't slept since I came here."

"What's the matter?"

"I'm going nuts."

"You brought it on yourself."

"I want you to help me, Peg."

"How?"

"You still want to go away with me?"

"Yes."

"You still go for me?"

"Yes."

"Why?"

"I don't know why. I just do. Believe me, I do. You go for me. Why?"

"I don't know, either. I'm balled up. But can I trust you?"

"You trust me now, don't you?"

"Sure. But now is different. Maybe you're afraid of me."

"If I ever deceive you, Nick, you can do with me what you want."

"You're not afraid, then?"

"No."

"I want to blow out of here and you're coming with me."

"When?"

"Right away. I'll need a car to get away."

"That'll take time."

"It's the only way. We can't take a train or a bus or a plane. Too many people. Too many dicks. Too many many. But in a car we can be alone. Just you and me, Peg. We'll ride the highways. I'll give you a grand and you buy a car tomorrow."

"All right, Nick."

"What else? Yes. We'll need a license. You buy the car in your name and you buy the license in your name."

"That'll take more time, Nick."

"That's all I got is time."

"All right."

"What else will we need?"

"I don't know."

"Can you drive, Peg?"

"No."

"You'll have to learn tomorrow. You'll have to get a driver's license, too. You'll learn and get that tomorrow."

"Yes."

"And maps. Get plenty maps for all over. Then where'll we go, Peg?"

"Somewhere. Far away."

"Where? Where? I got to know where. I got to know where it's safe."

"We'll figure it out, Nick. We'll look at a map and figure it out."

"California, maybe. That's far. That's nice places, too. Jesus, Peg. California."

"Yes."

"Then what'll we do?"

"I don't know. Something."

"I mean, I got to know what I'm going to do, how I'm going to act, how I'm going to live."

"I'll work."

"No you won't. You'll stick with me. You think I'm going to have you go with me and then leave me and then —" He couldn't finish the thought out loud. He was in the middle of the same circle again. Would he have to kill her to be free? But he wasn't going to worry about that now. He would save that for later.

"I'll stick with you, Nick."

"Sure you'll stick with me. I ain't worrying about that. I got ten grand. That's two years. And when I need more for us, I'll get more. Are you willing?"

"I'm willing, Nick."

"We'll get a place where there's nobody around. We'll relax. We'll show up like married. We'll be like married people. But we can't get married legal, Peg."

"No," she said huskily.

"It'd be too risky."

"Yes."

"We'll show them, Peg. We're going to beat the law. We're going to go places. We're going to leave right away, the day after you get the car. Okay?"

"Yes."

"Show you go for me, baby."

Peg sat up and put her arms about him and brought his face toward hers. She kissed him dryly with tight lips. She felt her bones being crushed as he wrapped his arms about her. He let go suddenly, stood up, and walked away. Peg lay heavily on the couch. A slow sob rose within her. She stared at the ceiling and fought down the sob, and she felt that a knife was sticking in her throat.

Chapter XXI

PEG slept restlessly. The alarm rang and she shut it off and went back to sleep. Later she was awakened by her mother.

"What's the matter, Peg, baby?"

"Nothing.'"

"Did you oversleep? Didn't the alarm wake you?"

"I'm not going to work today, mama."

"But why?"

"Nick said he's going away."

"What!"

"I'm going to buy a car for him and he's going away. He told me during the night."

"No," said Mrs. Dobbs, stepping backward. She sat down and leaned limply into a chair. "No. . . . But I knew my prayers would be answered. I knew it, just knew it."

"I'm going with him, mama."

"No, Peg. No!"

"That's the way it is, mama."

"You can't, Peg. You're a child, baby. You don't know what it means. Oh, no, Peg. Don't you see, baby? You can't."

"It's the only way."

"Oh, God no, Peg." Mrs. Dobbs' mouth began to quiver. Peg moved to her side and kneeled down and put her arm about Mrs. Dobbs' shoulders and patted them awkwardly and said: "No, no, please, mama, don't." And

199

Mrs. Dobbs muttered: "Oh, no, Peg. Oh, please, God, no. Oh, no. Oh, God. No."

"It'll be all right, mama. You'll see. Don't worry, mama. I know what I'm doing. It's going to be all right, mama. You'll see. Oh, please, see."

"But don't you see what will happen to you, Peg?"

"Nothing will happen, mama. I'll just go with him and we'll get away and you'll be left alone and we'll all be free again and nothing nothing nothing will happen."

"You can't, Peg. Sooner or later you'll be caught. Sooner or later you'll be killed. You'll have to live with him, too. How will you be able to live with him? And what will happen to us while you're with him? Oh, God, Peg. Don't. Oh, Peg, baby, don't."

"It's the only way," said Peg firmly.

Mr. Dobbs walked into the room.

"What's the only way?" he asked.

"Peg's going away with Nick," Mrs. Dobbs whimpered.

"Peg," he said, his voice catching.

"It's the only way, papa," said Peg. "Don't you see, papa? It's the only way."

Mr. Dobbs cleared his throat. He said as firmly as he could with a fluttery feeling in his throat: "It isn't, Peg. There's nowhere you can go. As soon as you step out of this house, Peg, it means death. He can't force you, Peg. Say you won't go, baby."

"I can't, papa. I've got to go."

"You could refuse," said Mrs. Dobbs. "We could all refuse. What could he do to us? He wouldn't dare kill all of us."

"He would, mama," said Peg. "He would."

"He wouldn't," cried Mrs. Dobbs, then desperately: "Would he, Casey? Would he? Would he?"

"He might," said Mr. Dobbs dryly. The fluttery feeling was gone from his throat.

"Then what's the good of living?" said Mrs. Dobbs. "If he tears us apart and Peg is to be— God, what's the good of living?"

"I can handle him, mama," said Peg. "That's why I

must go with him. I am the only one safe with him. I can handle him. He likes me. He needs me. I know it, mama. That's why I must go with him and make us all safe before something terrible happens. Please, trust me and believe nothing will happen to me because I can handle him."

"Can you, Peg?" said Mr. Dobbs slowly. "Can you handle something that acts blindly? Can you handle what fear makes a person do? Can you handle the crazy battlefield raging inside Nick? Can you handle the violence in him that you know nothing about?"

"It's the only way, papa. It's all of us, or just one of us, or just none of us. I'm not afraid of him. I'm not."

"Better not go, Peg," said Mr. Dobbs. He knew that he was failing. He had already failed. But he tried to assert himself. "Something will work out yet, Peg. Slowly he will crack. He's already cracking. He can't help but destroy himself. We can wait. Wait just a little while, Peg. All of us can come out of this together. You will see. Trust what I say, Peg. Trust me, Peg. Just wait a little while."

"We can't wait," said Peg. "Don't you see? When he cracks, like you say, all of us will be in danger, all of us may be killed. But this way—" she took a deep breath and braced herself—"this is the way it is. This is the way it's going to be. Besides, this is the way I want it. I want Nick to get away. I think he's had a dirty deal. I want him to get away and have a chance to start a good life again. Maybe, with me, he might change, he might become a good person in this world. Maybe he'll love me and he'll not harm me and he'll never harm anybody ever again. I want to give him that chance. I want him to get away. I want to get away with him. That's the way it is."

Mr. and Mrs. Dobbs stared at each other and looked away, their minds trying to force away what Peg had said, shunning but still seeing vaguely the agonizing lives that lay ahead of Peg and themselves.

And as they stood there, unbalanced and bereft, Nick entered the room with Mickey.

"Okay, break it up, break it up," said Nick. "Let's have some food. I got to store up energy. I'm blowing. Did Peg tell you? Me and her is blowing. Let's have some food."

201

Mr. and Mrs. Dobbs walked slowly into the kitchen with Mickey.

"I told them, Nick," said Peg.

"I guess you did, kid. They look like somebody died."

"Don't rub it in, Nick. Just let them alone and let us go peaceably."

"Okay, baby."

"This is the last day, Nick. Make it as easy for them as possible. Please, Nick."

"Sure, baby. Okay. I feel pretty good anyway. I had some sleep finally, after I left you. You're good for me. You're a good sleeping pill. Now I know I'm going to be all right."

"Yes, Nick."

"Boy, you don't know what it is to know you're going to get away, you're going to get out. This is the way I felt once when I was in prison. When I knew I was going to get out I almost couldn't stand it. The last few hours I almost went nuts. Boy, you don't know what it is. I hope you never have to know."

"I hope so, too," said Peg softly.

"But we got to leave soon, baby. Soon. Tomorrow."

"Yes, Nick."

"I don't want no trouble with your folks, Peg. I hope they don't start to get funny. Tell them to shut up. Tell them not to get any funny ideas. Because I know I'm going and I almost can't stand it I want to blow so bad. And nobody's going to stop me and you. Nobody's going to get in our way."

"No."

"Now let's put on the feed bag."

In the kitchen, Nick said to everybody there: "I don't want no trouble. Me and Peg's leaving. We're leaving tomorrow, first thing in the morning. I don't want nobody to know about it. If you give us a chance to get away, Peg will be all right, she'll be alive like you and me. If you don't give us a chance to get away, I want you to know I ain't dying alone. I want you to know I'll never be caught to be fried and I ain't dying alone. That's the score. If you understand it, we'll be all right. You'll be okay and I'll be out of here and me and Peg will be okay. If you think I'm kidding, Peg will come back to you in a coffin, and then you'll know I don't kid."

Mr. Dobbs glanced at Peg and his heart sank as he seemed to see a picture of her as a bony, freckly, shivering kid, long ago. Then heavily, almost without interest, for he knew that there was only one final resting place for Nick, he said: "Where will you go?"

"What you don't know won't hurt you," said Nick.

"I mean, do you yourself know where you're going?"

"Yah."

"Don't irritate Nick, papa," said Peg.

"You can escape right here." Mr. Dobbs wanted to say that there was only one way for Nick to escape: in death. Nick had only to put his pistol against his head, pull the trigger, and find final escape only six feet away from himself. But he added: "Will it be any different somewhere else? Do you think you'll stop going through what you're going through now anywhere else? Why don't you give us a break? Leave Peg here with us."

"Why don't you give me a break?"

"Because we have no choice. But you do have a choice."

"Ah, shut up."

"At least, why don't you continue staying here? You're safe here. Nobody will harm you. Live out your life here, Nick, but don't take Peg with you. Why don't you, Nick?"

"Because here I go nuts. Here I got nothing. Here I got to watch till I think my eyes are going to pop out of my head. Here I got to watch I'm not murdered."

"But if you go out you'll expose yourself. Suppose you do get into another house? You've got to live some place. Won't you have to watch then? Won't you have to be just as careful?"

"It'll be different."

"It'll be worse. You know, at least, you're safe here. Outside, you'll be passing people who have seen pictures of you. Police patrol the highway and they're liable to see you. You don't have a chance to get where you're going. You're wanted, Nick. And they'll get you if you give them a chance. You'll be giving them that chance by leaving here. If you step out of this house, you're doomed, Nick."

"What are you trying to sell, you punk?"

"I am trying to tell you to leave us alone. Don't drag us down with you. You're through, Nick. Finished. You're as dead as a doornail, if you step out of here. Even if we don't say a word, the police will pick up your trail outside. If they do, you say you'll kill Peg. You'll say it was our fault. Leave Peg out of this. Try it alone. Give us a break."

"I can't make it alone. You know that, you wise guy. Shut up."

Peg stepped to Nick's side and held his arm.

"Don't pay any attention, Nick," she said.

"Peg," said Mr. Dobbs, turning to her. "Please, Peg, try to understand what you're going into. Please don't do it for us. None of us are worth it. None of us will be worth anything, if you're gone."

Nick yanked his arm loose from Peg's hands.

"You going to shut up?" he said, glowering at Mr. Dobbs.

"Nick, don't," said Peg. "We're going. Nothing my father says will stop us. Don't do anything to spoil our going away. We'll get away, Nick. You'll be a free man again. Don't pay any attention to my father. Don't spoil this last day."

"Tell him to shut up, or I'll shut him up for good."

"Leave us alone, papa," pleaded Peg. "Will you please, papa, leave us alone?"

Mr. Dobbs looked steadily at Peg for a while. Then his shoulders sagged and he said hoarsely: "If that's the way it is, that's the way it is." He walked out of the house without breakfast.

Chapter XXII

LATER, Nick gave Peg a thousand dollars.

"You know what to do now, kid," he said.

"Yes."

"The car and the licenses."

"Yes."

"And the maps."

She put the money in her purse and Nick went to the door with her.

"You do like I say, kid," said Nick, "and we'll get away and your family will be left alone okay and don't believe what I said before about me bumping you off if the cops try to nab us. I just said that to make them keep their mouths shut. We've got to get away and we'll do it, if you do like I say."

"Don't worry, Nick. I'll do everything right."

"Jesus, I can't wait till we get going."

"Stay away from my mother and Mickey till I get back, Nick. Don't let them irritate you. We're going. Don't forget that. Don't hurt them."

"No. I'll just watch them. What the hell, my eyes can stand up till you get back. Come back with the stuff, kid. Come back fast."

Peg walked out of the house, exhausted, crying, her insides feeling ripped. She did not know if she could maintain the strength to do what she had to do. Her eyes were dull and there seemed to be no life in her limbs when she entered a used car salesroom. Nobody paid any attention to her for quite a time. Finally, a salesman walked over and asked her if he could help her. She said she wanted a car. The salesman screwed up his face and winked at another man in the place. He asked her if she had any particular kind in mind. A good kind, she said. Oh, said the salesman, she wanted nothing but the best, eh? He asked her who she was buying the car for. His eyebrows went up when she said for herself. A person had to be twenty-one, he informed her. She swallowed hard. She was twenty-two. The salesman said you could never tell just looking at a person. But cars cost money, lots of money, he told her as he looked at her clothes critically. She had that, enough money, more than enough, and please please would he sell her a car. The salesman started showing her the automobiles in the showroom, explaining their virtues. She didn't pay much attention to him. She wanted a car that was good and that wouldn't give her any trouble and that would take her as far as California. Oh, she was going to Hollywood, the salesman told her. Yes, she said. Well, then, he would have to give her the best in the house. She didn't know which one to select. Finally, the salesman stopped before a 1940 Plymouth. When they didn't move away from it, after fifteen minutes of talk, Peg said she would buy it. She paid for it in cash and asked the man to give her a driving lesson so that she could drive the car home. The salesman spent two hours with her and taught her how to drive well enough to pass the driver's test.

She drove the car to the front of her house and parked it. Then she took a street car to pick up the city and state licenses and the maps. When she came home at the end of the day, she did not know how she had managed to climb the stairs. She sat down in the living room and, with Nick eagerly listening, told Nick what she had done. Her voice had no body to it. She wanted to cry but couldn't.

"Kid, you done fine," said Nick.

She glanced at him wearily.

"Snap out of it, Peg. This is it."

"Yes."

"We're going to get away now, really get away. We're going to be free, kid. Jesus!"

"Yes."

"All we got to do now is wait, wait just till tomorrow. Jesus, I almost can't stand it."

She saw his eyes light up and his body seemed to dance. "Jesus!" he said.

But in the next few hours Nick reverted back to his weighted, tense, shifty-eyed, consuming self, as they began to wait in the living room for Mr. Dobbs to come home. It was past eight-thirty, an hour later than the usual time Mr. Dobbs came home for supper. Mr. Dobbs had never been late before. Mrs. Dobbs and Peg were more worried than Nick; they sat under watchful and scrutinizing eyes, anxiously wondering what Mr. Dobbs was up to or what had happened to him. Nick's head began to ache, his heart began to pound; something was wrong. There again came the pulled feeling at his eyes. A slow terror began to mount in him.

"Hey, ain't it time the old man's home?" he asked.

"Sometimes he's late," said Peg.

"Why?"

"Maybe an extra edition is out on the streets," Mrs. Dobbs tried to explain.

"What the hell is extra?"

"Don't worry, Nick," said Peg. "He'll be home soon."

"He's up to something, the old man." Nick tried to pick out what was in their minds as he looked at them. "If he's trying to pull anything—"

"He wouldn't do anything," said Peg. "He wouldn't, Nick."

"I don't know. I don't like the way he left. He left the house this morning too easy. He left like it was all over. I didn't like the way he left like he was finished. He knows about us leaving tomorrow. If he gets any funny ideas to stop us—" He rose to his feet. He tried to get beyond the crazy feeling that was mounting in him. He tried to strain out of the halter he felt about his shoulders. "Jesus, if he tries anything funny, just when I'm set to blow. Jesus, if he tries to pull off anything."

He didn't see Peg, Mrs. Dobbs, and Mickey as people

any longer. They were dark shapes whose movements he kept watching as he tried to trample the dark feeling rising in him and as he tried to get back the buoyant sense he had earlier of finally getting away. He was beginning to feel the same way as the night Peg didn't show up until late. He didn't want to lose himself again. He had to get away. He couldn't spoil that. He had to get away with Peg. He had to hold on to himself very firmly. But if the old man was making a last move to stop him, if the old man was telling the police. . . .

He heard a siren. He stood still. He whipped out his gun.

"Don't move," he said. "Don't move."

He watched the dark shapes. They seemed to writhe as he stood still, listening.

"Don't move," he threatened. "Goddamn it, don't move."

The handle of the gun became slippery in his moist hand. He kept grasping it. The siren was a great whirr stretched through his ears. Bang. Bang. Bang. The three of them. For not letting him go. Bang. The old man. For telling. For not letting him go. Then. Bang. Bang. Bang. How many others? And himself? Bang. Jesus, and himself? Bang. No. Oh, Jesus, NO.

"We're not moving, Nick."

The voice came to him as from a distance.

"We're not doing a thing, Nick."

The voice came closer.

"We're still as mice. Oh, Nick, please."

It was a wet, frantic voice. The voice was for him.

"Nothing will happen, Nick. Believe that. We'll get away. You'll see. We'll get away. Put the gun away and we'll get away. Please, Nick, we will."

The sound of the siren became fuzzy, whirled out, faded away. It was still. Very still. He waited a long time. And it was still. The dark shapes took on curves, form. He made out Peg and Mrs. Dobbs and Mickey. But the old man wasn't there. The old man was out doing something. He peeked out the window. The car was there, the hood glinting yellow under the lamppost light. Nothing else. It was quiet.

"Kid," he said to Mickey. "Go see where your old man is."

Mickey glanced at his mother.

"You go and tell your old man to come home quick before he gets any funny ideas and something happens," said Nick. "Now go on to hell out there and bring that old man of yours back and tell him I'll blow the heads off the old lady and Peg if he don't get back here fast."

Mrs. Dobbs nodded her head for Mickey to go. Nick put his gun back into his pocket. His hand was all wet. Mickey walked past Mrs. Dobbs and she whispered quickly: "Don't come back alone, Mickey. Don't come back alone, baby." When he reached the door, Mickey nodded that he understood.

"What'd you say to the kid?" demanded Nick.

"I told him to be sure to find Mr. Dobbs and to bring him home right away," said Mrs. Dobbs.

"You sure?"

"I'm sure."

"You better be sure. The punk better bring the old man home. I'm not kidding about what I'll do. The old man'd better get here fast." He opened the door for Mickey. "Okay, kid. Blow."

He locked the door and came back to the living room. They began to wait for both Mr. Dobbs and Mickey to return.

Mrs. Dobbs and Peg sat on the edge of their chairs. Nick paced the floor. He kept them in his eyes constantly. He had to keep moving. But it was hard. Something was pulling at him. He began to breathe heavily. The pain in the back of his head would not stop. It forced him to keep moving and straining. The terror kept mounting in him. Suddenly, pulling Peg and Mrs. Dobbs with him by his eyes, he took off in flight. And then he got that crazy sensation, as he felt his whole being leaping and running in mad flight, of somebody following him, matching his steps, his whirls, his dodges. And, still pulling Peg and Mrs.

209

Dobbs along by his eyes, his pursuer pounced on his back. And when he jerked his head about he almost screamed from the shock and the torment; he had looked at himself. He tried desperately, still hanging on to Peg and Mrs. Dobbs, to shake off his pursuer. Was he ever going to get away? Was he ever ever ever holy Jesus Christ Almighty going to get away?

And when after an hour, but for Nick a whole lifetime, of running and leaping and dodging and squirming, neither Mr. Dobbs nor Mickey had returned, Nick grabbed Mrs. Dobbs by her dress, hauled her to her feet, raised her to her toes, and said:

"You, Pinky. You go get that punk husband and that punk kid of yours back here. Don't try any funny stuff. I still got Peg here. If you want Peg to live you won't try anything funny. Just because she's going away with me don't mean she don't get her head blown off if I'm caught. Now bring that old man of yours and that kid back here so we can blow. Now beat it and get back here quick. Get back here goddamn quick before something happens."

Mrs. Dobbs hesitated. She looked at Peg and at Nick's contorted face. She didn't want to leave Peg alone with Nick. She was afraid of what Mr. Dobbs might be planning in his desperation. Tears welled out of her eyes. The sight of Peg and Nick became blurred. Her insides felt blotted up by the terror engulfing the house. But Nick wouldn't let her hesitate long. He yanked her to the door.

"Now bring them back in a hurry," he said. "Bring them back before something happens, before I have to knock somebody off. Tell her, Peg." He turned to Peg, still holding on to Mrs. Dobbs' dress. "I don't want nothing to happen to you. But goddamn it, if they try something and they don't show quick. . . . Goddamn it, Peg, tell her to get them. Tell her."

Peg didn't say anything.

"The hell with you, too," he said. He pushed Mrs. Dobbs out of the door and said to her: "Now blow. And bring them back."

He locked the door. Now he was alone with Peg. He

felt trapped. No matter where he turned, he felt something holding him, tugging him. He was afraid to look at Peg. She might change into something else, somebody chasing him, the thing holding him down. He needed her. There was no other way to escape. He didn't want anything to happen to her. He had to keep himself firm, away from her. He had to keep from going wild. Otherwise, she would be finished. He would be finished. Both of them would be finished. He tried to fight down the pain in his head and his mounting terror.

Mickey was at the newsstand, harassing the night man.

"But didn't you see where my pa went?" asked Mickey.

"For the last time, kid. I'm telling you I don't know."

"But he must of went some place."

"Sure he went some place. For Christ sake, where else could he go?"

"But where?"

"Kid. Please. Will you get out of my hair? Will you ask him when he comes home and let me alone?"

"But he didn't come yet. That's why I got to know where he is."

"Ask him when he comes home later."

"But my pa's got to come home now. Something might happen if he don't come home. Somebody might get hurt, maybe killed, if he don't come home now. Jesus, mister, don't you know where he went, which way he went, and didn't you see him go away?"

"Please, kid. You been here over an hour. Go home. Maybe he's home now, your old man. Go home and take a look, and if he ain't there, then come back. Will you, kid? Will you go home and get out of my hair?"

"But I can't go home. My ma said I shouldn't come home without my pa. I can't tell you why. My pa told me not to tell nobody why. But I can't go home. My ma said I shouldn't. So I got to know where my pa is. I got to know, mister."

"Holy Christ!"

When Mrs. Dobbs arrived, the night man sighed.

"Thank God you're here, Mrs. Dobbs," he said. "The kid's been turning me in circles. He's got me dizzier than a top."

"Then you don't know where my husband is, or where he went?"

"What! You, too, on the hunt for him? Jesus, Mrs. Dobbs, I wouldn't of believed it of Casey. I always took him for a sober and steady man, a man who brings home the change every night."

"It's not that."

"Then what? What's wrong? You think something happened to him, he got hurt, waylaid, parlayed, somewayed?"

"I don't know. I wish I knew."

"Should we tell the police and have them look into it?"

"No. No, no."

"But maybe something serious happened. A guy like Casey, he—"

"No." Mrs. Dobbs began to back away from the stand. "Thanks. Thanks very much. I'm sorry we troubled you. Thanks for your concern. Thanks very much. Thanks for your help."

"It's all right," said the man, bewildered.

"Goodnight," she said. "Come on, Mickey. It's all right. Come on, son."

She took Mickey's hand and walked away from the stand quickly. The night man stared after them, then shook his head.

"Where'll we look now, ma?" asked Mickey.

"I wish I knew," said Mrs. Dobbs slowly and weakly.

"So where'll we go now, ma?"

"I wish I knew, son."

Their walk became slower. Mrs. Dobbs held Mickey's hand tightly. They walked slower and slower as they neared their house. Finally, in front of it, they saw the lights from the living room windows. No sound came out from the apartment. It was quiet, very quiet. Nobody was on the street. It looked dead.

Mrs. Dobbs was afraid to enter the house with Mickey. She led Mickey to the back of the house and sat down with him on the porch steps. Her mind kept saying: I can't leave Peg alone with Nick. Something will happen. I can't leave them alone together. But she couldn't get herself to rise.

"Ma," said Mickey. "Will Peg be all right?"

Her eyes found Mickey's face, then went beyond it in sight. She did not know how she was going to live through the night.

Mr. Dobbs, meanwhile, was sitting in a movie house. He had not been able to get himself to go home. He knew that his family would be worried. He knew that Nick might become terrified and that he might hurt or kill someone at home. But he also knew that he had to make one last effort to collect himself and to prevent Nick's escape with Peg. He also was compelled to find some means of establishing himself once again in his household and of keeping the integrity of his family alive. But at home, he was scattered. Once he got home, he knew that whatever means he had of averting Nick's escape would be lost. He tried to think of a way to stop Nick from taking Peg with him until he thought he would go out of his mind. Finally, he was overcome with a great need to relax, for just a little while, then perhaps he might be able to think better, and he went to a movie house. But there he was restless. He disturbed the people about him. Somebody told him to sit still or get out. There was grumbling. The movie wasn't helping him at all. He became frightened of the people surrounding him. And in his fear, he strained his attention to the screen. For a little while he lost himself. He was thrown up into the screen and he started to move among the people there. But a shock of music shook him out of the film's problems. He came back to himself and walked out of the theatre. He did not know how long he walked. His mind wouldn't let him alone. It kept pushing him. It kept working hard, progressing rapidly to a certain point, then it seemed to stop up against a gray wall. He could get no further.

"Hyah, pal."

Mr. Dobbs stopped. He felt very peculiar. He did not know how he had got there and what made him go there.

213

He was off the entrance of the gambling joint around the corner from his newsstand. Big Moe leaned against the building, as usual, with his hands in his pockets and with his face working on a cigar.

"Around kind of late, aren't you, pal?"

Mr. Dobbs stared at Big Moe: the once-firm face that had grown flabby, the strong shoulders that had become beefy, the dull eyes that somehow missed nothing, the weary slouch that hungered for action. He could not frame an answer.

"You see something funny, pal?"

Suddenly, Mr. Dobbs knew why he was there.

"No," he said. "No, Moe."

"Then take the goofy look off your face. You give me the shakes."

"I came here to talk to you, Moe." Mr. Dobbs moved closer to him.

Moe put his hand on Mr. Dobbs' chest and held him from coming closer.

"Okay, okay," he said. "Talk. I'm listening."

"What I told you about the other day, Moe—"

"You're not going to pull that one on me again, are you, pal? I told you once. The guy's in a tough spot. Somebody's going to get hurt."

"You know Robey? Nick Robey?"

"The guy that knocked off the Pier payroll and the cop?"

"Moe, you've got to promise not to tell a soul."

"Okay, okay."

"You've got to promise to help me, Moe."

"Okay, okay, what's the story?"

"Promise by all that you hold holy, Moe, not to tell a soul and to help me."

"Come on, pal. The dice is yours. Shoot."

"That story I told you, it's about Nick Robey and me. This Nick Robey, he's in my house."

"Jesus, pal."

"He's taking my daughter, Peg, with him tomorrow to make his escape good. He's taking her and is going to keep her as a hostage, to make sure we don't talk. If the

214

police catch up with them, he'll kill her. I've got to do something, Moe. I've got to stop him."

"My Christ."

"That's why, no matter what happens, you must keep quiet, Moe."

"So what do you want me to do, pal?"

"Keep quiet and help me."

"My Jesus Christ, pal. I can't go there with a gun. He'll start shooting. That guy ain't like an ordinary gunman. He's a killer, pal. He's scared crazy. Guys like that you don't trust. They're scared crazy, nuts from the word go. What the hell can I do?"

"I don't want you to help me that way, Moe. I want you to give me a gun. I'll do the shooting."

"How? He'll plug you before you get a chance to blink an eye. He won't even let you in the house with a gat."

"Never mind how I'll get him, Moe. Just get me a gun."

"Why don't you forget it, pal? Let him get out with your kid. Something else might work out. This way she might get plugged, too. I hate like hell to be a party to getting you and your kid knocked off. Think on it a little, pal. Forget it."

"I have thought about it, Moe. A lot. Will you get me a gun?" Mr. Dobbs' eyes began to fill with tears. His hands trembled at his sides. "Please, Moe. Will you?"

"My Jesus Christ, okay. When'll I get it back?"

"Tomorrow morning."

"For sure?"

"Please, Moe." Mr. Dobbs laid his quivering hand on Moe's coat sleeve.

"I'll be right out."

Moe went into the gambling joint. In a few minutes he came out of the entrance. He put a gun into Mr. Dobbs' coat pocket and patted it.

"You know how to handle one?" he asked.

"Yes."

"Where'd you learn?"

"In the war. The first one."

"Okay, pal. Here's lead in his guts." Moe raised his thumb to his open mouth.

215

"Thanks."

"And if you don't know how to handle it, pal, I un-latched the safety. All you got to do is pull the trigger. Just point the gun at him and pull the trigger. That's all. Finished. But you pull the trigger first, pal. Be sure you're the first guy to pull that trigger Don't wind up in a tie or second best. Just pull the trigger first."

"I'm grateful, Moe. Thanks." Mr. Dobbs turned away.

"I'll look for you tomorrow, pal. And don't renege on me. And while you're at it, pal, pick a good nag for me at Lincoln Fields for tomorrow."

Mr. Dobbs walked away quickly. He felt the gun in his pocket. It sent a strange quiver through him. He had to steady himself. He had to steel himself. He slowed his rapid strides. He had all night to get to his house. Nick and Peg weren't leaving until morning. He had all the time in the world. He had to be careful, to get done what he had to do. And he had the time. He took a different route homeward than his usual one. He could not afford to be noticed now. He began to stroll. He was out for some night air, if anybody should ask him. He was out for just a walk. He put his hands in his coat pockets so that they might appear to be making the bulge in his pocket instead of the gun. He was just out for a breath of air, if anybody should ask him. But the feel of the gun made his insides tremble.

He knew exactly how he was going to do it. He was going to get into the back of the car and stay hidden until Nick and Peg sat down in the front seat. Then he was going to rise up slowly on his knees, point the gun against the back of Nick's head, and pull the trigger. Or . . . if Nick should decide to open the back door of the car to investigate, he would be ready for him then, too. Even if Nick fired at him, he would still have his gun levelled; he would get in at least one shot. He didn't care if he died, if he could get in that one shot and if he could save Peg and the rest of his family. But he wanted to pull the trigger first. Like Big Moe said. Pull that trigger first.

Soon, he approached the block on which he lived. He saw the car with the shiny new license plates. He walked to the alley of the next street and moved along its garbage heaps until he came to a passageway whose entrance faced his house. He stalked through the passageway and stopped at the opening to the sidewalk. He stood rigid against the brick building, hidden by its dark shadows, and tried to control his quaking heart and jittery legs. He looked at the lighted windows of his house. The shades were drawn. As he kept looking, he noticed one of the shades wrinkled back. A face peered through. Nick's face. Suddenly he became terrified. Nick might try to escape during the night, perhaps at any moment. When the shade settled back in place, he scurried across the street, opened the rear door of the car, crawled in, then shut it soundlessly. He crouched on the floor, facing his house, and began to wait, with his gun drawn.

Inside the house, Peg watched Nick closely. She could hardly breathe. He was pacing about. Occasionally, he groaned. His eyes looked pained, hunted, almost shocked at times.

"No," he muttered once. "Oh Jesus, no."

She sat stiffly on the couch, her hands gripping the cushions.

"This is it," he said.

His eyes never met hers. They seemed turned inward. She felt that she had to get out. She had never seen him this way before. Something was going to happen. Soon. She had to get out. She stood up slowly, breathing deeply, watching him and watching the door. But she didn't get a chance to take a step. He rushed to her quickly and pushed her back onto the couch.

"You stay there," he said, standing above her, his face working hard.

For a moment, she saw herself being dragged through him; she felt her heart flutter and then pound heavily against her throat. Inwardly, she raised her fists and began to beat against the walls of his chest, in which she felt imprisoned, smashing against the chaos and torment that enveloped her. He moved away suddenly; she felt released and thought she would crumple up. But he came back and her heart leaped to her throat again and began to pound there.

"If they don't show in a minute," he said.

"They'll come home, Nick. They'll come home."

"They're after me."

"They're not, Nick. They'll come home soon. Then we'll get away."

"He's running after me. Jesus, I can't get him off. Jesus, he's driving me nuts, I can't get him off of me."

"Nobody's after you, Nick. Nobody."

His forehead strained to bury his eyes. He whirled about and twisted his head; his mouth opened wide and his eyes almost started out of his head and the muscles of his sweating neck bunched up and his whole body became poised for a tremendous leap.

"Nick!" Her whole being clamored against her throat and pulled her to her feet. "We'll get away. You and me, Nick. We'll get away. Oh, Nick. Oh, no, Nick."

He came toward her slowly, his shoulders writhing, the creases around his eyes pressed tight, his teeth biting into his lower lip. Then his eyes opened wide, the fear seemed thrown off, his body moved easily, and instead, a crazy look of ecstasy came over him. He backed her against the couch. She could not move.

Suddenly, frenzied with fear, she reached for him and flung her arms about him and pulled him to herself and smothered his mouth with kisses. He bit her lips and her mouth filled with blood, but she was afraid to let go, smearing his face with her bloody mouth, holding him with all her might, and then they tumbled on the couch. She squirmed and beat against his imprisoning weight as he pulled at her dress and dug his knee between her legs. She felt herself growing taut as he stretched her farther and farther, her back arching higher and higher against him. Her hands dug beneath the cushions of the couch for support, and she came upon the knife she had hidden. With all her strength, she rose against the full impassioned weight of his body and drove the knife into his back. He became limp. She tried to throw him off, but couldn't. She

218

struggled against his dead weight, his face rolling against hers in her violent movements, and when she saw his eyes staring at her she began to scream.

Peg's scream curdled out and struck Mr. Dobbs sharply in the pit of his stomach. The scream lingered, faded, then curdled out again. Suddenly the sound became stifled and was cut short, as though a life had been snuffed out.

Mr. Dobbs rushed out of the car and up the stairs of his house. He fumbled for his keys, found them finally, and opened the door; it caught on the inside latch. He threw his weight against the door a few times and bounced back. He drew out his gun and shot the steel latch apart and rushed into the house.

Mr. Dobbs stopped still. Peg was lying on the couch, her hair strewn, her arm limply extended to the floor, her dress above her hips, and her body covered with blood. On the floor, below her, with his arm reaching for her, his clutching fingers curled taut, his vacuous eyes staring blindly, lay Nick, drenched in a pool of blood, the life still oozing out of him.

Mr. Dobbs walked slowly to the couch. He pulled Peg's dress down over her knees. Then he kneeled beside her and began crying. He found himself unable to utter a word when he saw her lift her arm and turn her back to him. She shriveled up against the couch. He placed his hand tenderly on her back as she gasped and shuddered, digging her heels into the couch cushions, backing, still backing away, and still screaming inwardly.

Mr. Dobbs later felt himself being lifted, carried away, and seated. After a long while he heard a policeman say:

"Can you hear now? Can you talk?"

"Yes," said Mr. Dobbs dully.

"We got you and your family lined up all right, from the neighbors. Who's the dead guy?"

"Robey. Nick Robey."

Mr. Dobbs heard a whistle. Many voices came to his ears. The room was full of people.

"I guess this is the end of the chase for him."

"Yes," said Mr. Dobbs. "My daughter, Peg?"

"She'll be all right. Just shock. A few day's rest and she'll be okay."

"My wife? My son, Mickey?"

"They're okay, too. Just scared. They're downstairs at the neighbors."

"Yes. Thank you."

Mr. Dobbs rose. He felt exhausted, as though he had come off a battlefield. But he could not rest. There was much to be done. There could be no rest for him for a long time. He now had to pick up the scattered remnants of his family and piece them all together.

"You can relax now, Mr. Dobbs."

"Yes," he said.

He walked slowly out of the house and down the stairs.